Code Name Sorrow

V. M. Knox

For Daniel

Also by V. M. Knox

The Clement Wisdom Series:
In Spite of All Terror
If Necessary Alone
Where Death and Danger Go
West Wind Clear

The Neither Despise Nor Fear Series:
Neither Despise Nor Fear

Sydney, Australia
1942

CHAPTER ONE

Tuesday 19th May 1942

Clement stepped from the tram into a bracing morning chill. He pulled his hat down hard and wrapped his scarf around his neck as rain began to fall. Around him, everyone hurried, their heads down, their umbrellas turned to the inclement conditions. Except the recently arrived American servicemen. Groups of them in their naval uniforms congested the city pavements. Despite the widely held fear that the Japanese would invade soon, spirits were high among the servicemen. The recent victory in the Coral Sea was, so Clement thought, the cause. Crossing the road, he increased his stride. Staring at his pounding feet, he pondered the arrival of the US servicemen and what it meant for the war in the Pacific. Their sheer weight of numbers would surely turn the tide for the Allies. He hoped so. Checking his watch, he broke into a slow run. He had ten minutes to be behind his wireless at the Women's Emergency Signalling Corp located at 10 Clarence Street, Sydney.

Of all the skills Clement had learned in this war, wireless operation hadn't been one of them. The lack of that skill had complicated his previous mission and had nearly put the life of a vitally important code breaker in danger. While he had found the lessons difficult, the people at WESC had welcomed him warmly. Not surprisingly, given its name, all were women. From the prodigious founder, Mrs Violet McKenzie, to her staff of two and the fourteen attendees, he was the only male. But today it would be different. The Royal Australian Navy, among others, were now sending serving men to the school, such was its reputation for proficiency. And, after a month of solid work, listening to endless clicks and the musical way Mrs McKenzie and her second in charge, Miss Veronica Evans taught the endless dahs and dots of Morse code, Clement believed he'd mastered the technique.

Today they would begin the more complex Japanese version of morse, Katakana Morse, commonly referred to as Kana. Others, already proficient at standard Morse Code were joining them and he was looking forward to having a few male faces in the class.

Clement pushed open the door to the old former woolshed at number 10, then made his way to the top floor. Veronica Evans was an efficient and attractive young woman with an eye-catching mass of brunette hair drawn back in a loose bun. Tall with a quick, competent manner, she stood before the already assembled group. As Clement entered, she tapped her watch. 'Sorry,' he whispered as he hurried towards the only vacant seat in the room. Removing his overcoat and hat quickly, he sat behind the wireless and reached for the headset. While he was aware of a greater number of people in the room, and that a few were men, he hadn't taken in any of the faces.

'Now that we are now all here,' Veronica began, 'I wish to welcome our newcomers. Especially our new American friend from the *USS Chicago* and some of our own wonderful boys from *HMAS Canberra* and *Westralia*.' There was a small round of applause and beaming smiles from the girls. Veronica continued. 'This morning, we'll begin with a revision of your speed with standard morse code. Then after lunch, a visitor will give us an insight into the Japanese language. It will differ from what you're used to, but you should get the hang of it soon. Just remember that Japanese does not use a Romanised alphabet, so all signals in Kana are syllabic.'

A moan came from someone behind Clement.

'We know morse code, Ma'am. We came here to learn Kana. Can't we just get on with that?'

Veronica Evans's eyes shifted to the American accent seated somewhere behind Clement.

'I am aware of your skills with Morse Code, Mr Veretti, however not everyone in the room may have your level of proficiency. This test is simply for us to know if you are ready to progress to Kana. I'm sure you would be the first to want to know that the wireless operator on your ship could correctly record enemy transmissions. Your life, and indeed many others, may depend upon it.'

The room was silent, and Clement guessed Mr Veretti was feeling suitably chastised.

'Clement!'

Clement heard the crisp whisper. Turning, he saw, seated in the next row and two seats behind him, his former colleague Joe Watkins.

'Headsets on!' Veronica called.

Clement smiled at Joe, then hurriedly pulled the headset over his ears. Joe had been with him on his mission to Singapore four months previously. Although Clement knew Joe had remained in Australia, he hadn't seen the American since February. The clicking began in his ears, and Clement focused on the rapid succession of dahs and dots coming through the headset. It would be two hours before he could talk with Lieutenant Joe Watkins, American Signals Traffic Analyst, formerly from Station CAST in the now Japanese occupied Philippines.

Clement handed his transcripts forward and switched off his wireless.

'We'll have a twenty-minute break now,' Veronica said, gathering the transcripts.

Some girls were already chatting to the newcomers, their green uniformed bodies huddled around the only heater in the room.

Clement stood. 'How good to see you, Joe!' he said and grasped Joe's hand in greeting.

'You too, Clem. It sure is a crazy place to learn Kana. Not at all what I expected. Although, I don't mind seeing beautiful girls every day.'

A tall, young man with a profusion of wavy dark hair joined them. He had a boyish face and a broad grin. His body seemed to sway in perpetual movement, and he chewed something continually.

'Hank Veretti, this is Clement Wisdom,' Joe said.

'Not *the* Clement Wisdom you're always going on about.'

Joe shook his head. 'He's joking. Just ignore him, Clem.'

'We're in the same business for Uncle Sam, Joe and me. Except, I got out of CAST by the skin of my teeth.'

Clement stared at Veretti. 'Perhaps you shouldn't say too much about it, Hank,' Clement said. 'While this place isn't a military institution, it is run on strict military lines. Regardless, *loose lips*, you understand.'

'Loose lips? As long as those lips belong to the delightful Win Hughes, I won't say a word,' Hank said, winking, his stare fixed on Edwina Hughes, the chewing becoming more vigorous.

Clement glanced at the girls huddled around the radiator like birds in a rookery. Edwina Hughes was a beautiful young woman, blonde with a vivacious spirit and an alluring smile. She sat perched on the windowsill, her legs drawn up and her feet on the radiator. In the month Clement had spent at WESC learning Morse Code, he knew Edwina to be a vibrant, yet naively innocent girl. Beside her was Billie Caide, a country lass who was always laughing. The third in the close-knit trio was the most serious of the three, Joan Olivant. Slightly older than the other two, she was also clever and practical.

And, she had the fastest morse code tapping speed in the class. The three young women had joined the group on the same day as Clement, so they had formed a bond of sorts. But while he had learned something about their pre-war lives, he'd been careful not to disclose too much about himself. All anyone there knew was that he was English and could not return home when war was declared. Only Mrs McKenzie knew his true rank and position with the Secret Intelligence Bureau in Melbourne.

In addition to Joe Watkins and Hank Veretti, two other men sat at the back of the classroom. Clement could hear from their accents that both were Australian.

'I'll leave you guys to chat about old times,' Veretti said and sauntered towards the girls.

'Don't mind Hank, Clem. I'm sure he knows what *Loose Lips* means,' Joe added. 'Where are you living?'

'At the barracks in Paddington. You?'

'Same. Victoria Barracks. Only this one is in Sydney. She got around a bit, that queen of yours.'

'Actually, she didn't...' Clement heard the door open, and everyone reluctantly resumed their seats as two women entered the room. The first to enter was Veronica Evans. His gaze shifted to the other woman. Clement stared in amazement. The visitor who had come to introduce them to the vagaries of the Japanese language was Evelyn Howard, code breaker and linguist originally from Bletchley Park in England then the Far East Combined Bureau in Singapore and more latterly of Commander Eric Nave's Secret Intelligence Bureau based at Victoria Barracks in Melbourne.

'Well, I never!' Joe said under his breath.

'You know her?' Hank asked, taking his seat, but Joe didn't reply.

Clement watched her. Evelyn Howard had been full of surprises when he'd met her previously. He knew she spoke Japanese, but after he'd left Melbourne, he'd thought it unlikely their paths would cross again; he to Special Operations and Evelyn to the tiny offices of the Code Breakers. And, as Veronica had not introduced Evelyn Howard by name, he guessed she was still operating in a clandestine capacity.

Clement glanced around the room. All eyes were on Evelyn. Without waiting for any introduction, she grabbed a piece of chalk and began scribbling on the blackboard. The room fell silent, everyone trying hard to memorise the symbols and sequences of dahs and dots they needed to operate Kana Morse. He wasn't even sure Evelyn had seen him in the class, such was the level of her concentration.

Three hours later, Veronica thanked the nameless visitor for coming and escorted her to the door. 'This side of the room is to go downstairs now,' Veronica began, gesturing to his half of the classroom. 'We'll take it in turns to transmit to each other between the floors. Try to remember, syllables not letters.'

Clement followed his half downstairs to the middle floor. His eye searched for Evelyn, but he didn't see her, and he supposed she'd already left. As he passed Mrs McKenzie's office, the woman's secretary, Peggy Seaton, was operating the switchboard beside her desk. Clement could hear her bright voice on the telephone.

'Mr Wisdom!' Peggy called from Mrs McKenzie's office door.

Clement turned.

'A letter for you.'

'Thank you.' Shoving it in his pocket, Clement went to the nearest wirelesses and sat down.

'Teacher's pet!' Hank said, winking, a slow smirk spreading over his chewing lips.

Clement glanced at Joe, then Hank. But while Veretti's manner irritated him, he said nothing. He placed the headset over his ears and turned the frequency dial. While he waited for the transmission to start, he tore open the note. It was from Evelyn.

Couldn't talk earlier. Meet me in Hyde Park near the fountain at half-past five. Clement folded the note and placed it in his pocket.

Three hours later, Clement's head was spinning with the sing-song dahs and dots of Kana Morse. Winding the cables around the headset, he switched off the transmitter, wondering if he was too old to learn new tricks.

'Beer, Clem?' Joe asked. 'Looks like you could use it.'

Clement laughed. 'Maybe tomorrow. Thank you, Joe.'

Off to his right, he could see Hank talking to Win Hughes and Billie Caide.

'He doesn't waste much time, does he?' Joe said.

Clement watched the young man. 'Is he also at Victoria Barracks, Joe?'

'No. He's on the *Chicago*. It's moored in the harbour.'

8

'Is he really in your line of work?' Clement asked.

'No. He's just a radioman.'

Clement nodded. 'Good.'

Joe laughed.

'Well, I must go.' Clement paused, then turned back to Joe. 'I thought you may have learned Kana by now, Joe. Is there another reason you're here?'

'I did. But I haven't used it in a while.'

'And the other reason you're here?' Clement said, knowing Joe hadn't fully answered his question.

'Maybe they just want to make sure I haven't forgotten it. Can't really say.'

Clement smiled and nodded. 'See you tomorrow, Joe.'

'Sure thing, Clem. And don't worry, I haven't told him or anyone about what we did four months ago.'

'Glad to hear it.' Clement paused. 'Perhaps best not to mention to anyone that you know Miss Howard.'

'Sure thing, Sir.'

Clement left the middle floor and took the stairs to the street. Outside, he saw Hank Veretti still talking with Win Hughes and Billie Caide. Joan Olivant had joined them, her large satchel over her arm. Clement thought Hank too forward, but the ladies were laughing and seemed happy to be in his presence.

The afternoon rain had abated, but the wind was still strong and miserably cold. Hurrying, he left Clarence Street and walked across the city to Elizabeth Street. Just after half-past five, he entered Hyde Park. In front of him, the large fountain had been turned off and pigeons pecked the wet paths, hopeful of a scrap of food left there. People scurried past him, most heading for the nearby underground railway station, their working day over. Ahead of him he saw her standing by the fountain, her wispy brown hair contained under a scarf.

'Clement. How good to see you,' Evelyn said, smiling as he approached.

'And you, Miss Howard.'

'I thought we'd got beyond that.'

'Well, I haven't seen you in a while. Are you still based in Melbourne?'

'Yes, but things are changing there now that the Americans have arrived.'

'Do I detect a note of sadness? Or is it frustration?'

She smiled. 'Nothing many escapes you, does it?'

'Do you have time for tea?' Clement asked.

'I'd like that.'

'*David Jones* is still open; despite the rationing, we can still get some there.'

Walking into the adjacent large department store, they took the lift to the dining room on the top floor.

'This is rather grand,' Evelyn said, staring at the long-arched windows and heavy blue brocade curtains. A man in a dinner suit was playing a grand piano and numerous chandeliers sparkled their brilliance over the gathering. A woman in a black dress escorted them to a table.

'How have you been?' Clement asked.

'I'm fine, Clement…'

'But?'

Evelyn smiled, but it lasted only a moment. 'I've been recalled.'

'Ah. I suppose it was to be expected. When do you go?'

'Next week.'

'Of course. You're needed. I'm sure they'll be happy to see you back.'

'Apparently Mr Tiltman isn't happy I didn't return sooner. But we've done some valuable work here in the meantime. And I'll be sorry to leave Eric. He's undervalued now. Shall I play mother?' Evelyn said, reaching for the teapot.

He waited while she poured the tea. Clement visualised Commander Eric Nave, an unassuming man of immense intellect. Nave had introduced Clement to the seemingly unsolvable Japanese Naval Code known as JN25. But it was a subject that couldn't be discussed in public. 'Do you know which way your ship will go?'

'East, I believe. To Canada.'

Clement nodded. But the truth was, whichever way the ship sailed, both the Indian and the Pacific Oceans were fraught with danger.

'I have two more lessons to give to your group at Clarence Street, then it's back to Melbourne and pack my things.'

They finished the tea. Taking the lift to the ground floor, he shook Evelyn's hand. 'Maybe best if we don't acknowledge each other tomorrow. Just causes unnecessary gossip.'

'I saw Joe seated behind you.'

'He won't say anything. Can I walk you back to your accommodation?'

'That's kind, but I'm staying at a guest house in Glebe. I'll get the tram. It's not far. But thank you for the offer. It was good to see you again, albeit briefly. Goodbye, Clement.'

Clement reached for her hand again. 'Goodbye, Evelyn. Safe onward journey and may God be with you.'

He watched her walk away until she disappeared into the crowds. He felt a strange sense of sadness; that mix of parting from a trusted friend and the likelihood of never seeing them again. Securing his hat, he crossed Hyde Park, then caught a tram to Victoria Barracks in Paddington. Staring at the raindrops trickling down the tram windows, he thought about Evelyn Howard. She possessed a self-assurance he very much admired. In his mind, he pictured her quick gait and confident stride. He'd said many times before that no one would replace his beloved late wife, Mary. And no one would. He liked Evelyn, but he didn't believe he loved her. She had shown immense courage in Singapore and that had created a bond between them. But did that bond extend beyond the current time? And only the Lord knew if both of them would survive. For now, they each had a job to do. He closed his eyes and reflected on her code breaking skills. She'd said they made progress with the work. But now petty resentments were causing problems. Clement rubbed his forehead, pondering the stupidity of human behaviour. It was such vital work. Thousands of lives would be lost if rivalries were allowed to forestall deciphering the Japanese codes. Surely, whoever was in charge now wouldn't permit it, especially with the Japanese so close.

As the tram moved along Oxford Street, his eye lingered on the shop windows now taped and covered in brown paper in anticipation of Japanese bombing raids. He thought of the attack on Darwin in February he'd learned about from Commander Long before leaving Melbourne. It had only been because of his *Most Secret* security clearance that he was kept informed of the enemy's advances. The full scale of the shelling on Darwin had, however, been kept secret from the public. Although, the local inhabitants knew only too well what had happened there. They had, by all accounts, been taken by surprise, as had the shipping moored in Darwin Harbour. But Clement knew from experience that frequently intelligence was disregarded and that not only cost valuable time, it also cost lives. Several hundred lives, in fact, had been lost and a great many ships sunk. He'd been there himself in January, leading a team of men to Singapore. He thought about his former sergeant, Tom Archer and the sniper, Mick Savage whose fates he didn't know. Clement's gaze returned to the pavements and the pedestrians hurrying along the street. Many, just like in London, wore military attire. He felt the heavy pall descend. Was it only a matter of time before the Japanese trained their guns on Sydney?

CHAPTER TWO

Wednesday 20th May 1942

Clement smiled at Joe as he hurriedly took his seat for another day of dahs and dots. Settling himself, he unwound the cable around the headset and connected it to the wireless. Reaching for the pen and notepad, he sat ready. But nine o'clock came and went and the normally punctual Veronica Evans had not appeared.

As each minute passed, the general chatter in the room increased. Ten minutes later, she walked into the classroom and the group fell silent. Gone was the quick step and lively, eagle-eyed stare. Her face was pale, and she clasped a handkerchief. Clement saw the young woman draw herself up as though summoning courage.

'I have some dreadful news,' Veronica said, dabbing her nose. 'Mrs McKenzie is with the police now.' Veronica paused, then drew in a long breath. 'Win, that is, Edwina Hughes was found dead last night. She was murdered.'

Nobody moved or spoke. Billie Caide burst into tears, her sobbing audible. Clement glanced around the room. Beside Joe, Hank Veretti's chair was unoccupied. Clement held Joe's gaze, then nodded towards Veretti's empty chair, but Joe just shrugged.

'The police wish to talk with everyone individually. Please stay here and you will be called when wanted,' Veronica said, then left the room.

Clement saw Joan Olivant leave her seat to comfort Billie. He turned to Joe. 'Where's Veretti?

'No idea.'

'Did you see him last night?'

'No. He was pretty keen to spend time with…' Joe paused, his mouth twisting to one side.

'Yes. My thoughts precisely, Joe. I saw him outside on the footpath as we left last night, talking to Win, Billie and Joan.'

'Maybe he's just slept in. Or maybe he…'

'The police will look after it, Joe. As tragic as this is, we have to learn this Kana Morse Code. Lives depend upon it. And the police will find Veretti. Best for us to inform them about what we know, then let them get on with their job.'

'You're probably right, Clem.'

A constable appeared in the classroom doorway. 'Miss Caide and Miss Olivant, please.'

All eyes watched the two young women leave the room. A chair scraping on the timber floor behind him made Clement turn. One of the new Australian recruits walked towards him.

'Hello. I'm John Connor.'

Connor, Clement guessed, to be in his late thirties. He was extraordinarily good-looking, tall and slender, with large blue eyes and a thick head of light brown hair.

'How do you do, John,' Clement said, standing to shake Connor's hand. 'Clement Wisdom and this is Joe Watkins.'

'You from the same ship?' Connor asked.

'Something like that,' Clement said.

'Did you know this girl? The one who's been killed?' John asked.

Joe shook his head.

'A little,' Clement said.

'Do you think her death is connected with what we're doing?'

Clement frowned. 'May I ask why you would think that?'

'Well, what we do is for the war effort, isn't it? I mean, once we know this Kana Morse, we can understand the enemy's traffic.'

Clement stared at the young man. To imagine the Japanese signalled each other unencrypted was beyond credulity. 'Miss Evans said you were from the *Canberra*?'

'Yes, that's right. Joined last week. I'm a radio operator.'

The other new recruit wandered towards them. 'G'day. Jim Lockhart,' the young man said, holding out his hand.

Clement shook it. 'You also on the *Canberra*?'

'*Westralia*. But I'm also a wireless operator.'

'You two know each other?' Joe asked.

'No. Just met yesterday. It's all so…different,' Connor said.

'What did you do before enlisting, John?' Clement asked.

'Journalist,' Connor answered.

'The Herald?' Clement asked.

'No. Just a country-town rag.'

'And you, Jim?' Clement asked.

'I was apprenticed to an electrician. Just finished my time. Never thought I'd end up here, though.'

'What do you think happened to this girl?' Connor asked.

'I think there's no use speculating about anything at this stage. I'm sure the police will have it under control.'

'Of course, you're right,' John smiled.

The door opened. 'Mr Wisdom?'

Clement turned. 'Here.' Leaving Joe with Connor and Lockhart, he followed the police constable to the lower floor. As he passed Mrs McKenzie's office, he saw Peggy Seaton, Mrs McKenzie's secretary, sitting at her desk, sobbing. Veronica Evans was attempting to console the girl.

Off to one side, he saw two policemen talking to Billie and Joan. Joan looked up at Clement as he passed. He could see her eyes held the shock and grief everyone was feeling. Standing in the middle of the room was a man wearing a three-piece suit with a fob watch chain in his waistcoat. There was an air of authority about him, and Clement guessed he was the senior police officer on the case. The man turned as Clement approached. 'Major Wisdom?'

Clement felt his eyes widen. Ranks were not used at WESC. And for a good reason. While everyone there had a job to do for the war effort, some were more secret than others. 'I am,' Clement said, keeping his voice low.

'I'm Inspector Lowe.' The inspector drew Clement aside. 'In view of the manner of Miss Hughes's death, I required Mrs McKenzie to make all her records available to us. I spoke to the head of Naval Intelligence in Melbourne, a Commander Rupert Long first thing this morning. He's informed me who you work for.'

'That is highly confidential information, Inspector.'

'Why don't we go for a walk outside?' Lowe turned to the young sergeant still talking to Joan. 'Preston?'

'Sir.'

'I want a thorough job; names, addresses and I want to know where every one of them was last night. And no one is to leave. I'll be back in fifteen minutes.'

'Of course, Sir.'

Clement and Inspector Lowe went downstairs and stepped out onto the street. Across from them, Clement could see the small park opposite had been cordoned. He'd seen the park before many times, but he'd never been into it. He'd assumed it to be a private park for local residents only, bordered as it was on three sides by houses and enclosed behind a black iron railing. 'Is that where she was found?'

Lowe nodded. 'Can you tell me if Miss Hughes was close to anyone, and by that, I mean a man?'

'I know very little about her private life, Inspector. She said her family lived on the northern side of the harbour. Mosman, I believe.'

'When was the last time you saw her?'

'Last night, in fact. On leaving, just after five o'clock. She was with her two close friends, Billie Caide and Joan Olivant, the two young women your constable and sergeant are speaking to now. They were talking with a man from our group.'

'His name?'

'Hank Veretti. He's American and only joined the WESC yesterday.'

'He inside?'

Clement shook his head. 'No. I understand he's from the *USS Chicago*.'

'Was his absence expected today?'

'You would have to ask Mrs McKenzie about that.'

'Anyone else in there know this Veretti?' Lowe inclined his head towards the building.

'It's possible. Another American in the group, Joe Watkins. I know Joe from a previous time we spent together. I would very much doubt if he had anything to do with Miss Hughes's death.'

'Was this Joe Watkins with you last night?'

'No. But I spent two months in close quarters with him earlier this year. From my assessment, he's not a killer.'

'Doesn't rule him out.'

'May I make an observation, Inspector?'

'Yes.'

'Not all murders are committed by men.'

'True. But it would be unusual for a woman to commit rape.'

Clement took a step back, the action involuntary. He closed his eyes, his heart sinking. In his mind, he recalled the pretty young face of Edwina Hughes. Innocent. Naïve. Guileless. He'd seen a lot in two world wars, but this was a wicked crime.

Lowe went on. 'It seems to me that this was just a case of wrong place, wrong time for Edwina Hughes. We'll contact the family. And we'll locate this, Hank Veretti. Unless he has a watertight alibi, he's our man.'

'May I ask how she was killed?' Clement asked.

'Her throat was cut, and there's a stab wound to her chest.'

Clement swallowed hard. 'Did she defend herself?'

'That's the odd thing. There are no defensive wounds of any kind. She must have submitted completely. Fear, I suppose. Where are you billeted, Major Wisdom?'

'Victoria Barracks in Oxford Street.'

'I know where it is. If we need to speak again, I'll contact you.'

Inspector Lowe left Clement standing by the park and returned to the Women's Emergency Signalling Corps.

Clement stared into the park. His heart was heavy. Senseless death. What could possibly have happened? Wasn't there enough evil in the world? And, with Hank's non-appearance, the young American was quickly becoming Inspector Lowe's prime suspect. Clement felt the frown crease his forehead. Things were rarely that simple. But where was Veretti? And why had Edwina Hughes submitted without some attempt to defend herself? Clement cast his gaze over the walls of the two houses on either side of the park. No windows faced into the garden. And the house behind couldn't be seen from the front gate to the park. At night, the place was completely secluded. Was the whereabouts of her death just opportunistic? Something about the choice of location troubled Clement. Crossing the road, he returned to the front door of WESC. From the corner of his eye, he saw Evelyn walking along the footpath towards him.

He waited by the entrance.

'Are you alright, Clement? You look like you've seen a ghost.'

'Come with me, Evelyn,' Clement whispered, and led her along the street away from the building. He told her about Edwina Hughes. 'Inspector Lowe is treating it as a rape gone wrong.'

'But you don't think so?'

Clement shook his head. 'Apparently, there are no defensive wounds. Her throat was cut, and the knife then plunged into her chest. That method of killing is a learned technique, one used by a special type of soldier. Or an assassin.'

'You think she was deliberately targeted?'

'I don't know what to think.'

'Does this Inspector Lowe suspect Joe?'

'I think he suspects everyone. Everyone male, that is.'

Evelyn stared at the park opposite, then ran her hand over her mouth, the action seemingly unconscious. 'Is it possible the rape was post-mortem?'

CHAPTER THREE

Wednesday 20th May 1942

Clement's mind was reeling. Bad enough that Edwina had suffered the indecency of such an assault, then killed, but if it were the reverse, her death and the manner of the attack took on a completely different meaning. The door opened behind them. Several of Clement's classmates stepped outside. He could see they were wearing their black blazers and carrying handbags as though leaving for the day. Clement pushed open the door to WESC and together he and Evelyn went upstairs to Mrs McKenzie's office.

Veronica Evans was still seated beside the distraught Peggy Seaton when they walked in. Clement glanced at the darkened inner office.

'Has Mrs McKenzie left, Miss Evans?' Clement asked.

Veronica stood. 'She's upstairs checking that all the windows are locked. The class has been cancelled for today. The police said that once everybody was interviewed, they could go home. But everyone is expected back tomorrow.' Her gaze shifted to Evelyn. 'Can you come back tomorrow, Miss...er?'

'Yes. I can do that.'

'I'll escort you out, Miss,' Veronica said.

'That's alright, Miss Evans. I can show this lady out.'

'Thank you, Mr Wisdom.'

'I just need to collect my hat and coat,' Clement said. He left Evelyn and went to the upper floor. Mrs McKenzie was just locking the classroom door. 'Could I retrieve my belongings before you lock up?'

'Of course, Mr Wisdom.'

Clement went straight to his seat and gathered his coat and hat while Mrs McKenzie waited by the door. He put on his overcoat but held his hat. 'Did you know Hank Veretti wouldn't be here today, Mrs McKenzie?'

'I did not. I take a dim view of non-attendance.'

'Another question, if I may. But perhaps best in your office.'

'If you think it's necessary,' Violet McKenzie said then preceded him down the stairs. From the corner of his eye, he saw Joe leaving the gentleman's lavatory. 'Could I have a quick word, Joe?'

'Sure. What can I do for you?'

'Could you ask around about Veretti? Discreetly, of course.'

'Sure. I'll see you back at the barracks tonight.'

Clement nodded, then left Joe and returned to the middle floor to Mrs McKenzie's office. Veronica and Evelyn were still there, but the secretary, Peggy, had gone. Mrs McKenzie unlocked her private office door and switched on the light. She sat behind her desk. 'Miss Evans, would you look after our guest while I have a word with Mr Wisdom?'

'Of course, Mrs McKenzie.'

'That won't be necessary. In fact, this involves Miss Howard,' Clement said. 'Both Joe Watkins and Evelyn Howard are known to me. It has occurred to Miss Howard and me that Edwina's death may not be as straightforward as Inspector Lowe is inclined to believe. I would like to see the files you keep on the men and women currently attending the school?'

Mrs McKenzie's eyes widened. 'They are confidential, Mr Wisdom.'

'You know who Miss Howard and I work for, so you also know our security clearance levels.'

The woman paused, her gaze shifting from Clement to Evelyn. 'I suppose in view of your positions, it would be alright. Do you think Edwina's death is connected to what we do here?'

'It cannot be ruled out,' Clement said.

Violet pursed her lips. 'Very well.' She stood and walked to the outer office. 'Where is Peggy, Veronica?'

'I sent her home, Mrs McKenzie. She was in such a state. I've never seen her so rattled.'

'Miss Evans, could you get all the personnel files for our current class?'

Veronica frowned. 'That is most irregular, Mrs McKenzie.'

'Perhaps, but I have deemed it necessary.'

Veronica walked to a locked filing cabinet and, taking

a key from her pocket, unlocked it, then placed a bundle of files on the desk.

'How long will you be?' Mrs McKenzie asked, checking her watch.

'If you need to go home, Mrs McKenzie, I can stay and see that the files are properly returned to the cabinet when Mr Wisdom and Miss Howard have finished,' Veronica said.

'Thank you, Veronica. I'd be grateful,' Mrs McKenzie said, pulling on her gloves, and gathering her coat, hat and handbag, left the office.

For twenty minutes, Clement and Evelyn sat at the secretary's desk and compiled a list of addresses. The two of interest to Clement were Billie and Joan, Win's closest friends, who, other than the murderer, were possibly the last to see her alive. Clement noted that Billie Caide lived at an uncle's home in Paddington, a poor area in the city's inner east. Joan Olivant lived in a guest house in the more affluent suburb of Cremorne. The last four files belonged to the new men in the group: Joe, Hank Veretti, John Connor, and Jim Lockhart. Joe, Clement already knew, was at Victoria Barracks. Veretti lived onboard the *USS Chicago* while John Connor and Jim Lockhart were on a ship used as a temporary barracks for sailors and tied up alongside Garden Island Naval Dockyard in Sydney Harbour, the *HMAS Kuttabul*.

They handed the files back to Veronica.

'I hope you'll be discreet with this information, Mr Wisdom,' Veronica said, placing the dossiers into the filing cabinet and locking it.

'Have no fear, Miss Evans. It is safe with us. May I ask Miss Evans where you live?'

'You think I am a suspect?'

'It's just routine, Veronica,' Evelyn said.

'I live in Glebe, in Gottenham Street.'

Clement noted her address.

'And Miss Seaton?'

'Newtown. Her file will have the exact address.' Veronica pulled an employee file from the cabinet and Clement added her address to his notebook.

'Thank you,' Clement said, passing the remaining files to Veronica.

Clement watched Veronica lock the cabinets, then go to another filing cabinet in Mrs McKenzie's office. Pulling it open, she withdrew a small black cash box, then put the filing cabinet keys into the box. Both the cash box key and the filing cabinet key she attached to a chatelaine, then pushed it into her pocket.

'What makes you suspicious about Edwina's death?' Veronica said.

Clement stood. 'No reason, at this stage.'

'If you believed that, you wouldn't have asked to see the files.'

'It may be nothing to worry about, Veronica,' Evelyn said. 'Just taking extra precautions. Just in case it isn't a straightforward police matter.'

'What would be worth worrying about?'

Clement observed Veronica. 'First, we eliminate the obvious, then go looking for the obscure. But it's always wise to collect information early.'

'You've done this before?'

'I've worked with the police in England before, yes.' Clement placed his notebook into his coat pocket, then reached for his hat and coat. 'By the way, Miss Evans, who has access to that filing cabinet in Mrs McKenzie's office other than yourself?'

'Only Mrs McKenzie.'

'And her secretary?'

'Well, of course. But she doesn't have her own keys.' Veronica said, tapping her pocket. 'And the box is left in that top drawer overnight?' Clement asked.

'Yes, but as you saw, the cabinet is locked, as well as the office door. And only Mrs McKenzie and I have entry keys to the office and the building.'

'Well, good night, Miss Evans. And thank you.'

'Major Wisdom.'

'Just Mr,' Clement replied, his eye going to the lock on the office door. Like the key to the top drawer of the filing cabinet, the door lock was a simple barrel lock.

They descended to the street. Clement glanced at the entry door lock as they stepped outside. Veronica locked the door, but Clement could see it was another barrel lock. For an experienced hand, it would take only a few seconds to pick. The simple fact was that none of the locks at WESC presented any challenge for a professional intruder.

'Will you be alright to get home, Evelyn?' he asked.

'Of course. You going to see Inspector Lowe now?' Evelyn asked.

'You're a mind reader, too?'

28

Evelyn laughed. 'Perhaps I'm just getting to know your methods. I can come with you, if you'd like?'

'Thank you. Two heads are always better than one.'

They walked back along Clarence Street. Their footsteps fell into a rhythm as they walked together. 'We should take a tram, Evelyn. The Central Police Station is too far from here to walk. Besides, I'd like to get there before Inspector Lowe leaves for the day.'

'You seem to know your way about Clement.'

'I lived in Sydney for five months last year. I know the city moderately well and some of the suburbs to the west but nothing beyond that, I'm afraid.'

Walking to Pitt Street, they rode a tram downtown. Thirty minutes later, they walked along the narrow Central Avenue to the main entrance of the Sydney Central Police Station. Located directly behind Sydney's Central Courthouse, it was a large, architecturally plain four-story building. Clement pushed open the door.

'Could I see Inspector Lowe, please? It is urgent,' Clement asked the duty sergeant. 'It's Sergeant Preston, isn't it?'

'Yes, Sir. Oh, yes. It's Mr Wisdom. Remember something else, Sir? I'll see if the inspector is in.' Preston lifted the telephone receiver and held a brief conversation. 'You can go up, Sir, Madam. Second floor on the right.'

Clement and Evelyn took the stairs to the second floor. Outside Lowe's office, Clement could see the man's secretary typing. Her hands slowed over the keys. 'Major Wisdom?'

'Yes.'

'Please go in.'

Lowe stood as Clement and Evelyn entered the room. It was a wood panelled office of medium size and other than a portrait of King George in a Royal Navy uniform which hung above Lowe's desk; it was rather austere. Two plain wooden chairs were before Lowe's desk.

'You've thought of something to add to your statement, Major?' Lowe resumed his seat.

'Not quite,' Clement said.

'May I introduce Miss Evelyn Howard? She works for the same people I do. We have a question, if we may?'

'Well?'

'Did the rape happen postmortem?' Evelyn asked.

Lowe leaned back in his chair, the leather squeaking as he did so. 'Why would you think that?'

'It makes a difference to the motive, surely, Inspector?' Clement said.

Lowe paused, then rubbed his chin. 'I'll ask the pathologist to do some extra testing in the morning.'

'Time is important for this test, Inspector. If the pathologist is still here, perhaps he could do it now?' Evelyn urged.

Lowe eyed Evelyn but didn't comment. He reached for the telephone receiver and dialled a three-digit number. 'Is Doctor McCowage still there?' Lowe waited a minute or two, then hung up. 'Still here, apparently. I am aware of the nature of your involvement with the Intelligence community, Major, Madam, but I cannot have either of you interfering with my investigation.'

'Of course. Are you aware of what happens at number 10 Clarence Street, Inspector?'

'I am now. What's prompting your thinking?' Lowe asked.

'If the murder was not a random act of evil, but a warning or an assassination that was disguised as a crime of passion, there could be a security breach at the WESC. The security of this city, and possibly the nation, could be in jeopardy.'

Lowe's chair creaked again. 'What makes you think that?'

'The method used to murder Miss Hughes is a very specific way of killing, Inspector. And one learned in highly specialised branches of the military. Do you have the knife?'

'No.'

'Can I see her?'

Lowe sniffed. 'If you think it will help.'

Inspector Lowe telephoned the mortuary again and asked to have the body of Edwina Hughes ready for viewing. 'No, he's not a relative, but I have agreed to it, so if you could, Doctor,' Lowe demanded. From his tone, it was clearly not a request. Clement eyed the inspector as he spoke to the pathologist. Lowe was a large man with big hands and a furrowed face and a voice to match. He looked at Clement. 'It's a confronting sight if you've not seen a mutilated body before.'

'I was in the last war in France, Inspector. I've seen my fair share of horrific injury.'

'As you wish.' Lowe's large palms slapped his desk as he stood. 'But I think Miss Howard should remain here. I'll ask my secretary to see if we still have some tea.'

'Do you mind, Evelyn?' Clement asked.

'Not at all. I'd be grateful for the tea.'

Clement followed Lowe out and along the corridor to a lift at the far end of the building. It was old, with a wire cage and two doors to close before pulling the lever to the lower ground floor.

Lowe stepped from the lift and turned right. Off to Clement's left was a long corridor. Numerous doors led off this hall and Clement could see they were made of metal, the sort used for cells. To his right was another long corridor, at the end of which were some double doors. The word *Mortuary* was painted on it in large red letters.

Lowe's footsteps echoed on the hard floor. 'You said in your statement that you saw Miss Hughes with two other women talking with the American, Hank Veretti,' Lowe said.

'That's right.'

'Did you see those women leave Clarence Street?'

'No.'

'So, you don't know if she was alone with him?'

'Correct. Billie Caide and Joan Olivant were with them the last time I saw Edwina. I don't know where they went after that.'

Lowe stopped short of the mortuary doors. 'And where did you go after your class yesterday?'

'I walked to Hyde Park to meet Miss Howard away from the WESC building.'

'And why would that be?' Lowe asked, pushing the door wide.

'Miss Howard has a highly secret role, Inspector. Even her name is restricted. She wasn't introduced to the class and neither she nor I made it obvious we knew each other.'

'What does she do there?'

'She teaches some Japanese and its syllabic pronunciation. It is important, Inspector, that her name and what she does remain secret.'

'Anyone there, other than you, know Miss Howard and what she does?'

'Yes. The American I mentioned earlier, Joe Watkins.'

Lowe held the door open for Clement, then allowed it to swing to behind him. It was the second police mortuary Clement had seen. The first had been in Cambridge in England at the beginning of the previous year. But while this morgue was larger, the smell was identical, the unmistakable pungent aroma of formaldehyde. Before him, lined up in the centre of the space, were five long, shallow, white porcelain tables that resembled long, thin basins. Each held a body, and each corpse was covered by a long white sheet, except the last, a young man with a gaping cut to his abdomen. The pathologist looked up as they entered.

'I wish to register my stern disapproval, Inspector! This is no place for visitors!' the pathologist shouted; his scalpel held in his gloved, blood-soaked fingers.

'He's not a visitor, George. He's with the Security Service.'

'I don't want him fainting on my floor,' the pathologist said.

'Unlikely! He was in the last war.'

'Be it on your own head then, Henry.'

Going to the table on the right, Lowe whipped back the sheet. Clement looked down at the naked body of Edwina Hughes. Even though she was dead, he felt embarrassed, and he wanted to look away. While it was true, he'd seen hundreds of dead men, he'd never seen the corpse of a naked young woman. He focused on the dark purple bruising surrounding the deep gash across her neck. He bent down so that he could see the cut. It was large and ugly and extended from high under her left ear to just beyond the chin on her right side. In the centre of her chest was a small penetrating wound, less than an inch in length.

The pathologist walked over and stood beside Clement. 'Not a pretty sight.'

'Indeed,' Clement added. 'Killer was right-handed.'

'Yes. You knew her?'

'A little.' Clement stared at the wounds. 'She was attacked from behind, then the knife put into her chest.'

'That's right.'

'Would I be correct in saying that the knife was double-bladed?'

'You would.'

'Was it the same weapon used in both injuries?'

'That would be a fair assumption.'

34

'How far did the knife penetrate in the chest wound?'

'About six inches.'

Lowe stepped forward. 'Do you know what sort of weapon was used, Major?'

'It's possibly a Special Forces weapon.' Clement held the gaze of both the inspector and the pathologist. 'Was the rape postmortem, Doctor...'

'McCowage. It's possible. The semen sample taken had high levels of phosphate acid. In a deceased victim, the sperm can last for days. But it is possible the sexual act was consensual.'

The little Clement knew about Edwina Hughes, he thought that unlikely. 'Do you have the clothes, Inspector?'

'Yes, but a report has already been made about them. I examined them myself. Only the underpants were torn. The dress and her other undergarments are intact, although covered in blood.'

'Could I see them?' Clement asked.

McCowage nodded to the mortuary attendant and within minutes the man returned with a large bag then carefully placed each item on a nearby trolley. The green dress and black blazer, the uniform of the WESC, were heavily blood stained as were the undergarments. Clement stared at each item in turn. Although the blood stains were extensive, only the underpants were torn.

'And there are no defensive wounds?' Clement asked.

'None,' McCowage said. 'And nothing under her fingernails. Nothing, in fact, to say she resisted at all. It was either consensual or postmortem.'

'What's your thinking on that, George?' Lowe asked.

'If the underpants hadn't been torn, I'd say consensual. The evidence of her clothes suggests otherwise. But I'm a mere doctor, not concerned with assumptions. That's your department, Henry.'

'Are there any other wounds, Doctor? Any head injury? Or bruising to her arms?' Clement asked.

Doctor McCowage faced Clement. 'There is bruising to the upper part of her chest. Probably caused by the assailant's arm pinning her to him before he took a knife to her throat. But no other injuries have been noted.'

'And the lividity is consistent with where she was found?'

'Now you're getting technical, Major.' McCowage paused. 'In view of your suspicions about the timing of the rape, I'm inclined to think it unlikely. It is possible the rape took place in the park, but not, I think, the murder. The lividity is quite diverse. It's unusual.' McCowage gripped Edwina's shoulder and hip and rolled her body on its side. 'There is some here, to her upper shoulders and lower back, as would be expected if the body was prone for some time. But note, none to the calves or heels. So, she wasn't lying on her back for long.' He lifted one of her legs. 'There is also blanched flesh under the knees. There is a similar pattern on her upper left side. This occurs from pressure that restricts blood flow. It's possible she was carried some little distance. Note the wrists and ankles. Both have heavy and quite delineated bruising, suggesting her feet and hands were tied. This,

36

of course, could suggest the sexual act was not consensual. Although not always.'

'Inspector, when you first saw her in the park, were her feet and hands bound?' Clement asked.

'Just the hands.'

'You've taken samples of debris from her clothing?' Clement asked.

'Of course. But I'm still awaiting the test results,' McCowage said.

Clement sighed. 'It's possible the killer lured Miss Hughes to her death by feigning a romantic interest. With his arm around her shoulders, she may have believed he was intending to kiss or hug her. She would have been completely defenceless. Thank you, Doctor, Inspector, for allowing me to see her.'

'Seen enough, then Wisdom?' Lowe asked.

'For now.'

Clement and Henry Lowe returned to his office. 'Thank you again, Inspector. I wonder if you would keep me informed about developments and the results of the tests.'

'If you wish.' Lowe paused, then reached for his fob watch. 'I have to go now. Miss Hughes's parents are due any minute. They're here to formally identify her. It's the part I dread the most.'

'Very sad. I won't keep you.'

Evelyn joined Clement, and together they took the stairs to the ground floor. 'I'll tell you about it as we walk,' Clement said.

'You saw her clothing?'

'I did.' Clement told her about the clothes and the pattern of lividity.

'Was she still wearing her shoes? And what about her handbag?'

'Sorry?'

'Her shoes and...'

'Yes, I heard you. I didn't see either of those items. Neither did Lowe mention them.' Returning to the Police station, they hurried back up the stairs to Lowe's office. Seated in front of Lowe's secretary were two people Clement surmised were Edwina's parents. Lowe's door was open as Clement approached. He went straight in. Lowe was still seated at his desk, sorting papers. Clement closed the door to the outer office. 'Was she wearing shoes, Inspector? Are her shoes with the other clothes?'

'And what about her handbag?' Evelyn said, joining Clement. 'She'd left WESC for the day. She would've had her handbag.'

CHAPTER FOUR

Wednesday 20th May 1942

In view of Edwina's parents being there, Clement and Evelyn waited in Lowe's office until the identification had taken place and Edwina's parents had left.

'It's the part I hate the most,' Lowe said, returning to his office. 'Now we can check the shoes and handbag. Frankly, I don't remember them, but they must be there somewhere.'

They followed Lowe back to the lower ground floor and the mortuary at the rear of the building. Ahead Clement could see McCowage locking the doors.

'Hold on, George. Did you see any shoes or a handbag with Miss Hughes's possessions?'

McCowage grunted, then unlocked the door. Stepping inside, Lowe, Clement and Evelyn walked towards the scrubbed autopsy tables and waited while McCowage retrieved the bag containing Edwina Hughes's belongings. He laid the blood encrusted clothes out on a trolley.

But there were no shoes or handbag amongst her possessions.

No one spoke for a few minutes.

'Now, what would he have done with those?' Lowe said, almost to himself. 'What would she carry in her handbag?' Lowe added, turning to face Evelyn.

'Depending on size, of course. Lipstick, a powder compact, handkerchief, her purse. Perhaps an address book or diary...'

Evelyn and Clement exchanged glances.

'I hardly think the motive for killing and sexually assaulting Miss Hughes was theft of a powder compact and lipstick,' Lowe said. 'The killer may have taken her purse, but it's more likely he threw the rest into some nearby bushes.'

Clement wasn't so sure. Murder due to theft of lipstick and handkerchiefs was improbable, but address books and diaries were another matter. 'May I ask if you have found Hank Veretti?'

'We have not. If he's guilty, he'll have gone bush. I've already issued a description of him to all police stations statewide.'

Clement wasn't sure what *going bush* meant be he guessed that if Veretti was the killer, he would be on the run and Australia was a vast country.

'Will you both be at the WESC tomorrow?' Lowe asked.

'Yes. Although, I am supposed to be going back to England next week,' Evelyn added.

'Not until I have our murderer, Miss Howard,' Lowe said, pulling his fob from this waistcoat and checking the time. 'I'll not keep you further tonight, Doctor.'

'Mrs McCowage will be grateful, thank you, Henry.' McCowage withdrew his keys again, and they left the mortuary.

Clement wasn't too sure Inspector Lowe could stop Evelyn from leaving. If Commander Long wanted something, the local police would have to comply. Thanking Lowe, they left the police station.

'May I ask you a personal question, Evelyn?'

'Of course.'

'What do you keep in your handbag?'

'Nothing much. A purse, handkerchief, a hairbrush, a pen, and a notebook. But before you think I'm a security risk, all my scribblings are encrypted so the casual observer or would-be thief couldn't read them.'

'Could she have been carrying something secret?' But Clement was thinking aloud.

'Then she was more than a naïve girl learning Morse Code. If the killer kept her handbag, it's more likely she had an address book. But then he'd keep the address book and throw away the bag. What else could she have? Unless WESC is a front for covert activities? Could she have been working for the Secret Intelligence Bureau?'

'I'll ask Commander Long when next I speak to him.' Clement paused. 'Is your name on their files?'

'I suppose it's possible. Mrs McKenzie wrote to Commander Newman in Melbourne about the school. It was Commander Newman who sent me.'

'Is he at Victoria Barracks in Melbourne too?'

She nodded. 'Jack is in charge of Naval Signals and communications there.'

Clement blew a long sigh into the air. 'So, the names and locations of some of the most important men and women in the Secret Intelligence Bureau could be compromised.'

'It's possible.'

Clement looked around at the closed shops and offices with their brown paper coverings. It was well after sunset now, the brief twilight gone, and a chilly wind was blowing along Pitt Street. 'There's nothing more to be done until tomorrow. But I would like to speak with Billie Caide and Joan Olivant. Can you get yourself home from here?'

Evelyn smiled. 'Of course I can. I'll get the tram on George Street. I'll be fine.'

'Thank you, Evelyn. See you tomorrow.' He watched her walk away, then headed back towards Hyde Park. 'Billie Caide or Joan Olivant first?' he muttered to himself. Billie lived on the city side of the harbour and close to Victoria Barracks, so he could talk to her later. Joan was in Cremorne and that was a ferry ride of about twenty minutes. Hurrying, he walked along Elizabeth Street until he saw a tram that would take him to Circular Quay.

Clement alighted near Custom's House, opposite the ferry terminal. Not too far away, the loud clanging sound of police sirens drew his attention. He waited. Two police vehicles with their police lights flashing drew up further down George Street. He saw Lowe alight from one vehicle, then disappear into a nearby alley. A few minutes later Lowe returned to George Street and stood on the footpath under a streetlight, issuing orders to a small group of constables assembled around him. Clement crossed the road and walked towards the group.

Lowe looked up as Clement approached. 'Thought you'd be at the barracks by now?'

'Has something further happened?' Clement asked.

'There's always something happening here. It's a rough area, especially after dark.'

'So, nothing to do with Miss Hughes's death?'

'Can't rule that out,' Lowe said, switching off his torch. 'A report came in moments after you left the station. It's possible I've just seen our murder site in the alley there.' Lowe pointed to a narrow gap between two buildings. 'There's blood all over the walls and pavement.'

'Who reported it?'

'A local woman on her way home. Slipped in it, apparently. I've got my lads doing a house-to-house search now. Not that I expect that to reveal anything useful. As I said, this is a rough area and police constables are not warmly welcomed. The interesting thing about this, Wisdom, is that there isn't a body there. And from the amount of blood, if they're alive, they can't have gone far.'

CHAPTER FIVE

Wednesday 20ᵗʰ May 1942

Clement waited until Inspector Lowe got back into the police car and drove away. He strode towards the ferry terminal and bought a return ticket for Cremorne Point.

Fifteen minutes later, he boarded the small, double-ended passenger ferry and sat inside at the rear. Clement watched the turbulent waters as the ferry pulled away from the wharf. The harbour, usually so ordered had transformed into a congested array of shipping. Navigational lights, to indicate where each ship was, glowed everywhere. Clement wasn't even sure when it happened. In the two weeks since the Coral Sea victory, Sydney Harbour had become a dockyard. Channel Patrol boats were tied up in the adjacent Farm Cove and moored around the inner harbour were so many ships that the ferry had to weave its way between the small island fortress known as Fort Denison and the numerous battle ships in port. His gaze fell on the enormous American ship *USS Chicago* and beyond it, the *USS Perkins*. Beyond them, in Athol Bight was the *Westralia* while *HMAS Canberra* lay nearby. And all were displaying lights. Moreover, they were highlighted by the searing light from the nearby Garden Island Naval Base where the construction of new docks went on day and night.

Twenty minutes later, he felt the vessel slow, then the roar of the reverse thrust as the ferry drew alongside Cremorne Wharf. The crewman lifted the gangplank into place and Clement descended to the jetty along with two other men.

'Excuse me,' Clement said to one of them. 'Could you direct me to Musgrave Street?'

'That's Musgrave,' the man pointed. 'It's a long street, though, mostly uphill.'

An icy wind blew across the harbour and Clement hurried away from the wharf and up the steep street, checking the numbers as he passed the houses. It took him a while to realise that some homes were accessed via a lane that ran parallel to the main thoroughfare. Halfway along one such lane was a narrow walking path that led to the street behind. The guest house sat at the corner of the lane and the path. Chiselled into the stone fence was the name *Waverley House*. It was a two-storey, dark brick home with lead-light windows, arched doorways, and a tiled, high-pitched roof with several chimneys. A steep flight of stone steps led up to the front veranda. Surrounding the house was a garden of matures trees and thick hedges. Upstairs, and visible from behind the drawn curtains, several lights were on. Clement climbed the steps and rang the front doorbell.

A woman with bright red hair, matching lipstick and thick facial make-up stood at the door. She was dressed in a long, multi-coloured cocktail dress with a fox fur draped over her shoulders. 'Yes?' she said, her gaze fixed on Clement.

'How do you do, Madam? Does Miss Joan Olivant live here?'

'Who wants to know?' the woman said.

'A friend.'

A thin, pale-faced adolescent joined the woman. 'You know Joan, but does she know you?'

'Yes, she does. I would like to see if she is alright. She received some bad news today.'

'You'd better come in then,' the woman said. 'But you cannot go to her room. Nigel, go knock on Miss Olivant's door, would you? Tell her there is a man to see her. And tell her this sort of behaviour will not be tolerated in future. Gentlemen friends call in the daytime. Unexpected after-dark callers are not gentlemen.'

Clement ignored the rebuff. He stood in the cold front hall for several minutes, enduring the silent disapproval of the landlady and, presumably, her pallid offspring.

'Mr Wisdom, has something else happened?' Joan said from the top of the stairs.

Clement eyed the hovering landlady. 'Is there somewhere I can talk to Miss Olivant privately?'

'Very well. In there,' the woman pointed to a door on the left of the foyer. To Clement's right he could see a drawing room. The fireplace was lit there, and a gramophone was playing operatic music. He could also hear several men's voices.

Joan opened the door to the room on the left and switched on a light. The room was cold and uninviting and filled with indoor ferns.

'What is it, Mr Wisdom? Has something further happened?'

'I wanted to see if you were alright in view of today's news.'

Joan hung her head. 'Terrible. She was such a vivacious girl. And pretty. But I'm sure you didn't come all this way at night just to check on my welfare.'

Clement cleared his throat. 'May I ask you some questions about the last time you saw Edwina?'

'Are you a policeman, Mr Wisdom?'

'No. But I am concerned about what's happened. I'm also concerned about you and Billie.'

'You think we are in some sort of danger?'

'The killer, whoever they may be, may be targeting young women. I have no wish to frighten you, but anything you can remember, no matter how small, could be useful. You may recall that I saw you with Billie and Win, standing on the footpath talking to the American, Hank Veretti. Can I ask you where you all went after that?'

'As I told Sergeant Preston, we walked together to George Street, where Billie left us. She lives in Paddington, so took the tram across town. I went with Win and Hank another block, but I left them on Pitt Street. Then I walked to the ferry terminal.'

'Did they say where they were going?'

'Hank asked if we wanted a drink. I said no, but Win said she'd go with him.'

'Do you know where they intended to go?' Clement asked.

'Win said they could go to the *Australia Hotel*. That's in Castlereagh Street. It's really grand.'

'And you saw them walk in that direction?'

'Yes. But, as I said, I left them then to catch my ferry. I'm sorry I can't be more helpful. If I'd stayed with them, perhaps Win would still be alive.'

'You can't blame yourself, Miss Olivant,' Clement said.

'Do you think Hank killed her?' Joan asked.

'That's for the police to decide,' Clement said. He paused. 'Is there anything you thought out of the ordinary about last night?'

Clement saw Joan's back stiffen.

'I didn't say this to Sergeant Preston because I didn't want it to reflect badly on Win, but I thought Hank touched her too much. Even ran his hands over her shoulders and neck when he helped her with her coat. It was pretty obvious that he fancied her. It was also obvious he didn't want me along.'

'You didn't approve?' Clement asked.

'No, I did not. Too familiar by half. I saw her eyes. She didn't like it either. I don't really know why she went with him. Perhaps she just wanted to go to *The Australia*. He just didn't seem her type.'

'Who would you say was her type?' Clement probed.

'A gentleman. And a gentleman doesn't have his hands all over you. There wasn't any respect. Well, that's what I thought.'

'Did you know Win before WESC?'

'No.'

'And Hank? Have you ever met him before?' Clement asked.

'Hardly! Not my type at all! Besides, how could I? He's American and the *Chicago* only docked a week or so ago.'

'Of course, sorry. I didn't mean to offend.' Clement checked his watch. He didn't want to miss the last return ferry. 'Well, thank you, Joan. Sorry to disturb you so late. I hope my coming hasn't made things difficult for you with your landlady. Try to get a good night's rest and I'll see you tomorrow.'

'If it wasn't you, Mr Wisdom, I wouldn't have spoken to you at all.' She walked with him to the front door. 'Good night. Thank you for your concern and coming out all this way.'

Clement left the guest house and walked back towards the wharf. It was a dark night, and the moonlight was scant but the lights from Garden Island were like a homing beacon and almost directly due south across the harbour from Cremorne Point. Huddling into his overcoat, he hurried towards the wharf. On the night air, he could hear the sound of the approaching ferry's engine.

He was the only passenger on the return ferry. He sat inside as it pulled away from the jetty. Staring at the ships, his mind processed what he'd learned from Joan about

Hank Veretti. From what he'd seen of the young American, he was inclined to agree with her assessment. Perhaps that was unjust. He hardly knew the young man. And Joan's description was still only one person's observation. Even though it was late, he wanted to hear Billie's opinion of Veretti.

It was nearly ten o'clock when Clement knocked at the door to the terrace house in Greens Road, Paddington. The house was set back behind a black iron railing and the window to the front room had been half covered with brown paper. It resembled a chess board of small light and dark squares. Opposite was the high western side wall of Victoria Barracks. Given the hour, he considered the proximity of Billie's residence to the military establishment a blessing. A minute later, a man opened the door.

'I'm so sorry to disturb you at this hour, but could I speak with Billie Caide please? It is important.'

'And you are?' the man said.

'Clement Wisdom. I'm helping Inspector Lowe with enquiries. I'm sure Billie will have told you about today's sad events.'

'Yes, she did. Bad business. I'll see if she's still up. Wait here.'

Clement stepped inside the narrow terrace house and the man closed the door. Billie must have heard his voice because she appeared at the top of the stairs, dressed in a dressing gown.

'Mr Wisdom? Have they found out who...' Billie paused, tears streaming from her red eyes.

'Not yet, Billie. Could I ask you about the last time you saw Win?'

'If you think it will help,' Billie said, descending the stairs. 'We can sit in the front room. Alright with you, Uncle John?' Billie asked.

The man nodded, then left them, disappearing down the narrow hall.

Opening the door, she led Clement into a freezing sitting room where he asked the same questions he'd put to Joan.

'I left them in George Street, Win, Joan and the American sailor.'

'How did they seem?'

'Alright. They said they were going to the *Australia Hotel*. It's quite expensive, but I suppose Hank has plenty of money. They all seem to.'

'How would you say Hank was towards Win? Did he show any signs that he liked her?'

'He grinned a lot. Called her *sugar*.'

'Were they close, holding hands, that sort of thing?'

'No. He was a real gentleman. Walked on the outside of the footpath, too, I remember.'

'But otherwise, kept his hands to himself?' Clement asked.

'Oh, he wasn't like that. He was a bit cheeky I suppose, but nothing Win wasn't comfortable with.'

'Well, I'm sorry to disturb you so late. If you remember anything else, just let me know. Even the smallest thing could be important.' Clement stood. 'Thank you, Billie. Try to get a good night's rest.'

'She wanted to go. She was excited about it. It's very swish.'

'Have you been there, Billie?' Clement asked.

'Me! Oh no!' she said, rolling her eyes. 'My family couldn't afford that!'

'Well. Thank you again, Billie. See you tomorrow.'

Clement closed the gate to the street. Standing on the footpath, he looked up and down the road. Every house looked much the same to him. And even at this hour, some children played on the street. It reminded him of photographs he'd seen of impoverished back-to-back housing in the northern cities of England. He thought it grim. The high perimeter stone fence of Victoria Barracks was adjacent to Greens Road, but inside the walled military establishment, it was another world. Clement entered the rear of the barracks just after eleven, his mind on the differing assessments of Hank Veretti's character.

CHAPTER SIX

Thursday 21st May 1942

Clement flipped the rain from his coat as he opened the door to 10 Clarence Street and climbed the stairs to the middle floor. Through the glass partition he could see Mrs McKenzie's secretary, Peggy Seaton. The girl's head was bent, buried behind a mountain of paperwork. Leaning on the doorpost to the office, he put his head around the door. 'How are you, Miss Seaton?'

Peggy looked up, her expression somewhat startled. 'I'm alright.'

Clement glanced at Mrs McKenzie, who sat at her desk in the inner office. He nodded to the woman.

'Oh! Mr Wisdom!' Mrs McKenzie called.

Clement stopped, returning to the office doorway.

'I have a message for you from Inspector Lowe. He asked if you would come to his office after class today. He says you know where that is.'

'Thank you, Mrs McKenzie.' Clement turned to go, but the woman joined him then preceded him up the stairs. He seized the opportunity to speak privately. 'How do you verify your records?'

The woman stopped short. 'What an extraordinary question! We do not vet our students, Mr Wisdom. Our students come to us either from the military or as private citizens. They attend for tuition and because they wish to be of service to our country.'

'So, you don't verify the information they give you?'

'I've never questioned the truth of it.'

'Who has access to your records, Mrs McKenzie?'

'No one other than me and Miss Evans.'

'Not Miss Seaton?'

'She has access only to the administration filing cabinets. Secret or confidential correspondence is kept in my personal filing cabinet and that is locked every night by either Miss Evans or myself.'

'Would you know if that correspondence has been tampered with in any way?'

'Never and impossible.'

'Are the student files ever left out?'

'They are never left unattended. Other than the day you and Miss H collected all the addresses, the files are never removed or seen by others. There is no security breach here.'

'Could your telephone conversations be overheard?'

'I suppose that could be possible. But I never give out the details of anyone who comes here to a stranger over the telephone, which also means that those details couldn't be overheard.'

Clement nodded. 'I see. Thank you.' Leaving her at the middle floor, he climbed the stairs to the upper floor and entered the classroom for another day of Kana Morse. Despite what Mrs McKenzie said, Clement knew from experience that liars rarely tell the truth. Something was going on there. With or without Mrs McKenzie's knowledge.

Entering the classroom, he saw Joe in his usual seat. 'Any news of Veretti, Joe?'

'Nothing.'

Clement sat down and reached for the headset, the action almost involuntary. Clement knew that with every passing day, Veretti's continued disappearance implicated him as Edwina's killer.

Clement closed his notebook and hung the headset on the transmitter. His head was rattling with the sounds of dahs and dots, and he needed fresh air, but he wanted to talk with Joe to learn exactly if he'd learned anything about the missing American sailor. But, as soon as the lunch break was announced, he saw Joe leave the room. Clement stood and hurried after him, but his former colleague had hurried down the stairs and left the building. Clement stood on the footpath. He could see Joe striding along Clarence Street heading down to Circular Quay. Whatever Joe was doing in the lunch break, Clement hoped it concerned Veretti.

Standing there, he breathed in the cold air. The sky was still overcast but at least the rain had stopped and despite the chill, it felt refreshing after the stale air in the heated classroom. Close to him he saw a police car pull up. Lowe got out.

'Got a minute?' Lowe asked.

Clement nodded. 'I got your message. What couldn't wait?' He suddenly thought of the American. 'Have you found Veretti?'

'No. But I have some news about the blood in the alley. All Edwina Hughes's blood. Looks like she was killed in the alley and carried to a waiting vehicle, then taken to the park. And you were right about the rape. Definitely postmortem.' Lowe paused. 'You may also be right about national security.'

Clement blenched. 'What makes you say that?'

Lowe pointed at the police car parked. 'Miss Howard was attacked last night on her way home.'

'What! Is she alright?' Clement asked.

'She suffered a dislocated shoulder. But she's a strong woman. Insisted on coming in here today.'

Clement left Lowe standing on the footpath and went to open the police car door. Evelyn's arm was in a sling.

'Are you alright?'

'I'll be fine. He may not be,' she said, getting out of the car. Lowering her head, she whispered, 'I'll tell you about it later.'

'I'll leave you here, Miss Howard. And if you can remember anything about your assailant, just call me,' Lowe said and, climbing back into the police car, drove away.

'Are you sure you're able to teach today?' Clement asked.

'Of course! It's my shoulder, not my head.'

'Glad to hear it!'

Evelyn smiled.

Holding the door, they went upstairs to Mrs McKenzie's office. Clement checked his watch. The lunch break was almost over, and Joe hadn't returned. Entering the classroom, Clement took his seat. A minute later, Joe came running into the classroom. His face was flushed as though he'd been running. Clement glanced at Joe, but there was no opportunity to talk now.

'Headsets on!' Veronica called.

Placing the headset over his ears, Clement tried to concentrate, forcing himself to focus on the long and short clicks as his hand scribbled down the syllables. Between transmissions, he glanced around the room. He saw Billie and Joan. They hadn't spoken to him today, and he guessed they had compared notes. As soon as the afternoon tea break was announced, he went to join them by the heater.

'How are you both?'

'What's going on, Mr Wisdom? Do you know?' Billie said.

'I wish I did, Miss Caide.' He glanced at Joan. 'Have either of you remembered anything further?'

Joan stared at him. 'I suppose you think one of us is lying. Just because I didn't like Hank doesn't mean I know anything about what's happened to him.'

'Has something happened to him?' Clement asked.

Joan raised an eyebrow, the expression sceptical. 'How would I know? All I know is what everyone knows.

He's nowhere to be seen. Very suspicious if you ask me. And you seem to be more involved than a casual by-stander.'

'Do you have any thoughts on the subject?' Clement asked Billie, evading Joan's comment.

Billie shook her head, the tears welling up in her eyes.

Joan put her arm around Billie. 'The last time I saw either of them was in Pitt Street, and they were both alive and well then.'

'I'm sorry if I gave you the impression that I suspected you, Joan. I'm just trying to help Inspector Lowe and to see that both of you are safe. What happened to Edwina was appalling. And I thought you may feel more com-fortable talking to me than the police.'

'That's alright, Mr Wisdom,' Billie cut in. 'He's just trying to help, Joan.'

Veronica Evans re-entered the room, followed by Evelyn. The general chatter ceased as everyone resumed their seats. 'Our visitor will be going over what you learned yesterday, then for the last two hours of today, we'll divide into two groups and transmit to other each between the floors. We'll be sending messages quickly and transmitting them on two frequencies in both stand-ard Morse Code and Kana. You must find both frequencies and decide which is standard Morse and which is Kana, then transcribe both. When you're fin-ished, hand both transcripts to me. And don't worry if you are having trouble distinguishing the codes. Nearly everyone does. This is a complicated assessment and mistakes at this stage are common. I'll now hand you over to our guest.'

Evelyn faced the class, a stick of chalk in her hand. 'Japanese nouns do not take a plural form. Unlike English, the idea of plurality is conveyed in the sentence's context and is frequently achieved by adding a number. This is called a counter. For example, the word *ships* in Japanese would be expressed as three ship or several ship.'

Clement listened as Evelyn continued with the lesson, but his gaze was on the sling holding her left arm. Why had she been assaulted? Was it a random attack or was it connected to Win's murder? What had Edwina Hughes learned or seen that resulted in her death? Clement frowned. Was she even the intended victim? And where was Veretti?

Veronica stood before the class. 'If you have any questions, please see me separately. Otherwise you can now divide into groups and start transmitting.'

Clement watched Evelyn leave the room, but there were still two hours of transmissions to endure before he could ask her more about last night's attack. And he wanted to know what Joe had learned at lunchtime.

Clement reached for his headset as half the class left for the lower floor. While he waited for the signals to begin, he glanced around the room. Joe was behind him, his head set over his ears and his breathing slightly less laboured. The two Australians, Connor and Lockhart were ready, their pencils poised. The remaining girls in the room sat ready. But something plagued Clement. He felt it, like an icy finger tapping his shoulder. He'd sensed that sinister grip before, in Scotland. Frowning, he lowered his head and tried to concentrate.

As the clicking started, Veronica approached his desk and dropped a note onto the table in front of him. He guessed it was from Evelyn. Finishing the transmission, he removed his headset and made his way to the gentlemen's lavatory. Inside the cubicle, he tore open the envelope. It was typed and from Veronica. It said that she wished to speak to him privately and would he come to Mrs McKenzie's office at the end of the day? Pushing the crumpled note into his pocket, he returned to his desk. He wanted to ask Evelyn about the events of last night. And to see Joe. Veronica's note was an unwanted distraction.

A few minutes before five, he heard the last message for the day. Scribbling the Kana syllables, he tore the page off the pad and left it in the tray for collection. As he put his chair up on the desk, he saw Joe was just finishing. He waited outside the classroom. 'Any news, Joe?'

'Tell you tonight at the barracks.'

Clement nodded, then made his way past the ladies' cloak room on the middle floor and went to Mrs McKenzie's office. Veronica and Evelyn were both there. He knocked and entered.

'Won't you sit down, Mr Wisdom,' Veronica said. 'Miss Howard and I were on the same bus last night.'

'Miss Evans also lives in Glebe, Clement, near to where I am currently billeted. She witnessed the whole thing.'

'What happened, exactly?' Clement asked.

'He grabbed me from behind so it's possible he followed me from the bus. It's a short walk from the bus stop to the house in Glebe Point Road, where I'm living. And despite my shoulder, he came off second best. Although, he was no lightweight.' Clement had always wondered if Evelyn had been trained for other secret duties, but when her ability with codes and cyphers had been discovered, her wartime service had followed a different path.

'And Miss Evans's part in this?' Clement asked.

'I got off the bus at the same stop because I wanted to do some shopping before going home. That was when I saw him cross the road. He was waiting for her.'

Evelyn shifted in her seat. 'I'm not sure that is correct, Veronica. He could have been waiting for anyone who was alone. Perhaps I was just in the wrong place at the wrong time.'

'I saw him! He came out of the bus shelter on the opposite side of the road and went straight towards you. He'd been sitting there waiting for you, I'm sure of it. As soon as I realised this, I hurried back to see if Miss Howard was unharmed.'

'It could have been a random attack, Clement.'

'Well, I don't think so!' Veronica persisted.

'What did you do, Miss Evans?' Clement asked.

'I called out, naturally. I saw him grab her from behind. Then somehow, she swung around, twisting his arm until he fell sideways. He ran off after that.'

'My shoulder was dislocated, so I couldn't hold him down.'

'Did you see where he went?'

Veronica shook her head. 'I was concerned for Miss Howard. In view of Edwina's murder, I wanted to know she was alright.'

'Of course.' Clement paused. 'Did you see his face?' he asked Evelyn.

'No. Too sudden, and it was dark. But I thought from his gait, he was an older man. Not elderly but not young.'

'Did he speak or say anything?'

'No.'

'What does Inspector Lowe say?'

'After I saw a local doctor last night, I telephoned Central Police Station. Inspector Lowe had gone for the day, but the policeman on duty said it most likely was opportunistic. Trying to grab my handbag, he thought.'

Clement saw Veronica's lips purse.

'Does Inspector Lowe think this also?' Clement asked.

'Not sure. Perhaps,' Evelyn said.

'I suppose he's got enough to do with a murder and the disappearance of Hank Veretti, so he's not interested in a woman getting attacked,' Veronica added.

Clement glanced at Veronica. 'Miss Evans, could you do something for me?'

'And what would that be?'

'Can you place a telephone call to Victoria Barracks, Melbourne? I need to speak to Commander Rupert Long there.' Clement scribbled the number on a page from his notebook and, tearing it off, handed it to Veronica.

'Sit at Mrs McKenzie's desk. I'll place the call.'

Veronica went into the outer office and sat at Peggy's desk next to the switchboard.

'Are you sure you're alright, Evelyn?' Clement whispered.

'Yes. It's painful, but I'll live. What do you make of it all?'

'Has it occurred to you that your initials and Edwina Hughes's are the same?'

'You think I was the intended victim?'

'Truthfully, I don't know, but it should be considered. Who here knows your name and actual involvement with the Secret Intelligence Bureau?'

'Just Mrs McKenzie and Veronica.'

'With you incapacitated now, I need more eyes on the ground. And I need trustworthy people not known to anyone here.'

The telephone beside him rang, and he picked up the receiver. He heard Veronica's voice say, 'Go ahead, please.'

Clement kept his eye on Veronica to see if she listened to the conversation. But she placed the headset over the switch board hook and left the office.

Clement lifted the receiver. 'Commander Long, please.'

A minute later, he heard the voice. 'Long here!'

'Commander, it's Major Wisdom speaking. We have a problem that may need your attention.' Clement told Long about the events of the past few days. 'Would you also know if Edwina Hughes worked for SIB?'

'You think they are targeting our people?'

'In view of the attack on Evelyn, it's possible.'

'I can tell you Miss Hughes does not work for me. But Miss Howard's safety is paramount. What do you need?' Long asked.

'I'd like some extra people around please, Commander. People I know and trust. But unknown to anyone here. Can you get Sergeant Archer and Private Savage here as soon as possible?'

The conversation lasted only minutes. Clement knew Long was a busy man, but would make the arrangements. Long, and his extraordinary secretary, Miss Copeland, could move people like chess pieces. Clement checked his watch as Veronica Evans re-entered the office.

'I can get myself back to my billet, Clement. No need to worry about me if you have more pressing things to do,' Evelyn said.

'Can you accompany Miss Howard home, Miss Evans?'

'Of course. I'll lock up upstairs and get my things,' Veronica said, leaving them in Mrs McKenzie's office.

'Please be careful, Evelyn. How many more classes to you have here?'

'Because of the delays, I still have two.'

'Then I think you should move from your current lodgings.' Clement thought for a moment. 'There's a boarding house in Cremorne where Joan Olivant lodges. The landlady there may have a spare room for you for a few days. And Joan could accompany you on the ferry each morning.'

'I'll ask her tomorrow,' Evelyn said.

Veronica returned and together they left the building, Veronica locking the front door to the street.

Clement left them in York Street to walk across town where he could catch a tram to Victoria Barracks. He felt mentally drained. Kana Morse was difficult, and he had to force himself to concentrate. 'You're getting too old for all this, Clement Wisdom,' he muttered to himself. The high wall of Victoria Barracks came into view. Pulling the cord for the tram to stop, he alighted opposite the main gate into the barracks, then crossed the road and reached for his pass.

'What about that drink?' A voice behind him said.

Clement turned. It was Joe. 'Did you learn anything?'

Clement told Joe about his visits to Joan and Billie.

'Well, that is interesting,' Joe said. 'Almost like they're talking about two different people.'

'What took you away at lunchtime?'

They walked through the gate together, heading for the officers' quarters.

'I learned Veretti was given shore leave to attend the course. Which means unless someone checks, nobody onboard the *Chicago* would question where he is.' Joe stopped, then cast his eyes around them before continuing. 'But here's something else interesting, Clem. He was awarded a Purple Heart for bravery when they all left CAST. You don't get those for chasing girls. Apparently, it was quite a feat. They got away from Corregidor Island by submarine in the middle of the night. Veretti was the last man on board. He was fighting a rear-guard action alone so they could get away. Then at the last minute, the

Japs paused their advance, allowing Veretti to escape.'

Clement stared at his shoes. Shoes. And a handbag. He screwed his eyes tight. He needed sleep and time to think and pray. 'Thank you, Joe.'

'Does it make a difference?'

'I don't know. But it adds a lot to Veretti's character, don't you think?'

'It seems Joan was the one who got his character assessment wrong. Sleep well, Clem. See you in the morning.'

'Good night, Joe. And thank you.' Clement walked away, then stopped. 'Joe!' he called.

Watkins turned.

Clement walked towards him. 'You said something to me the other day about the reason you're attending this course. You said you couldn't talk about it. In view of what's recently happened, could you elaborate on that a little?'

Joe smiled. 'I'm not supposed to say, of course. And if it wasn't you asking, I wouldn't, but Veretti is under suspicion for his actions in the Philippines.'

'And you're here to monitor him?'

Joe nodded. 'And to brush up on my Kana.'

'Didn't they give him a Purple Heart?'

'Yes, and maybe.'

'Meaning?'

'It's possible Veretti had help to escape CAST. Maybe the Japs wanted him to board that submarine.'

CHAPTER SEVEN

Thursday 21st May 1942

'Talk to me, Joe,' Clement said, glancing around to check that no one was near enough to overhear them.

'I was asked to keep an eye on Veretti. By the Head of FRUMEL no less. A guy called Rudi Fabian.'

'FRUMEL?'

'The Fleet Radio Unit Melbourne. FRUMEL for short.'

'And this Rudi Fabian is in charge?'

'Yeah! And guards his show like a rottweiler.'

'What's their role?'

'Signals intelligence and code breaking. Made up from the guys from CAST in the Philippines and some Aussie guys. But Rudi likes to keep most things to himself. *What's yours is mine and what's mine's my own*, would be his mantra.'

'What about the others there?'

'Rudi is paranoid about security. Thinks the Aussies are too laid back about it. And, from what I've seen, he could be right. Just look around, Clem. People are meant to observe the blackout at night. Draw the curtains, that sort of thing. But lights are on everywhere. He and Commander Nave have a fractious relationship.'

Clement thought back on what Evelyn had said about Eric Nave being sidelined. 'You were at CAST too, as I recall, Joe. Did you ever meet Veretti in Manila?'

'There were several hundred guys working at CAST. Can't know everyone. Especially if you don't work in the same department.

'Would Fabian recognise Veretti?'

'Unlikely. Besides, Rudi's a lieutenant. Veretti's a lowly radioman. They rarely mix.'

'Why is Fabian suspicious of Veretti?'

'Who knows? Maybe he thought it unlikely such a guy would or could mount a rear-guard action. So maybe he suspects Veretti is a fraud when it comes to earning Purple Hearts. Or maybe he's just jealous because he doesn't have one. Perhaps you should ask Commander Long to have a chat with him.'

'Who do you report your findings to, Joe?'

'Directly to Fabian by secure line telephone here.' Joe paused. 'He asked about you too.'

'Me!'

'Wanted to know if you're the real deal.'

'What did you tell him?'

'That you are the most decent, brave and honest man I've ever met.'

Clement pondered Fabian's suspicions and what was motivating them? 'Do you think there is a security breach at WESC?'

'Beginning to look like it.'

'If they're that suspicious of Veretti, why did they give him shore leave to attend the course?'

'Good question.'

Clement sighed, then looked out at the evening sky. 'Is it possible the US Navy is holding Veretti?'

'Maybe. But why? If they had something on Veretti, then yes, he'd be locked up, not sent on shore leave for a month. Maybe they just want to give him enough rope, as the saying goes.'

Clement nodded. The truth was, he didn't know why Veretti had disappeared. It all pointed to him being Edwina's killer and, as Lowe had said, gone bush. 'Could you find out if Veretti is being held on board the *Chicago*?'

'I'll try.'

'Do you know anyone on the *Chicago*?'

'No. But I have made some inquiries. And almost got my head chewed off!'

'Really! What happened?'

'After you asked me to find out about him, I went to Garden Island after class yesterday and asked to be taken out to the *Chicago*. Not easily arranged. Cost me a packet. I met the captain, Captain Howard Bode. From what I saw, it isn't a happy ship. And I know why; the captain isn't liked. Put it this way, he didn't take kindly to a lowly lieutenant asking questions about his crew. Between you and me, Clem, he's an arrogant son of a ...well, you know.'

'But did you learn anything about Veretti from anyone while there?'

'Couldn't get near any of Veretti's ship mates to ask about him. Bode ordered me off his ship. It'll be in my report to FRUMEL.'

'Thank you for trying, Joe. Perhaps your Lieutenant Fabian would have better luck.'

'I think you're giving Veretti's disappearance greater importance than Fabian.'

A bad feeling was forming in Clement's stomach, and he was beginning to get a headache. He pondered the attack on Evelyn. Had that been purely opportunistic? Was Veretti the intended victim? If so, how had Edwina become involved? Clement rubbed his head. And why had Joan Olivant's assessment of Veretti been so different to Billie Caide's? Having Evelyn living at the same boarding house as Joan suddenly seemed like a good idea.

Thanking Joe again for the information, Clement sauntered back to his room, his mind alive and his head now pounding. Joe's comments about security troubled him, and not just at WESC. Were the authorities in Sydney taking the threat of invasion seriously enough? He thought about the senior Allied Officer, Rear-Admiral Gerard Muirhead-Gould, Naval Officer in Command of Sydney Harbour. Clement had never met the Rear-Admiral, but rumour was that he was unpopular and had a short temper. And from what Joe had said, Bode was no different. Apparently, Muir-head Gould enjoyed entertaining the upper echelons in his palatial harbourside home adjacent to the naval dockyards at Garden Island. Despite the genuine attempts to protect Sydney, from the installation of gun emplacements, anti-aircraft batteries and search lights to the patrol boats and indicator loops set up in and out of the harbour, lights blazed at night all over the city, and no one, least of all Muirhead-Gould did much about it. Clement reflected on all the shipping he'd seen on Sydney Harbour. Given the array of ships moored in the harbour, Clement thought such apathy foolishness. Vessels still showed lights and ferries coursed the waterways as though the war was a figment of someone's imagination.

CHAPTER EIGHT

Friday 22nd May 1942

Colonel Ravenscroft, the Commanding Officer at Victoria Barracks had made a room available to Clement for briefings and had also arranged for a secure line telephone to be installed there. At nine o'clock, Clement rang WESC and told Peggy that he would not be in. He then took a taxi to the airport. As the car approached, he saw the low hangar-like buildings hadn't changed since he'd seen them six months previously. Only then it had been summer, and the afternoon thunderstorms were a welcome respite to the heat. He stepped from the taxi as a gust of wind blew in across the wide tarmac. Paying the fare, he pulled his overcoat tight around him and hurried into the building. Through a large glass window, he watched the aeroplane land. Not ten minutes later, it taxied towards the front of the terminal, the noise of the engines screaming towards him. Three men waited near a gate, then as the plane stopped and the propellors slowed, they moved towards it, ready to secure the rotating blades and manoeuvre a flight of steps into position for the passengers to descend.

When Clement saw them, he couldn't help but smile. Sergeant Archer and Private Savage, dressed in the wide-legged shorts and rolled-up shirtsleeves worn in the far northern climes, came running down the stairs and across the tarmac, heading directly towards the open door into the terminal. As they entered the building, Clement walked towards them.

Archer was the first to spot him in the small crowd. 'Clem! Could have knocked me down with a feather when we got the call to pack our kits and get to Sydney. I said to Mick, I bet Clem's behind this.'

'And he was right!' Mick said, his face breaking into a broad grin.

Clement shook hands with both men. 'Good to see you both. Do you have some warmer clothing?'

'I got the last coat from the stores in Brisbane. It's a bit too big, but it doesn't matter,' Archer said. 'What do you want us to do, Clem?'

'We'll discuss it at the barracks, Tom. Do you have any luggage?'

'Mick, can you grab the packs?' Tom asked.

Mick sauntered towards the luggage trolley and removed two green army packs and a long canvas bag that Clement thought most likely held a rifle. He led them outside and hailed a taxi.

'You've been in Brisbane, Tom? I thought you were in Darwin?'

73

'Darwin! What a shambles! When you've got time, I'll tell you about the biggest cock-up you've ever seen. Bloody disgusting. Lucky for me and Mick they wanted signals operators in Brisbane, so we went by ship with some evacuees. Women and kids mostly.'

'I thought Mick was a sniper?'

'Yeah. Well. We're a team. Besides, I've taught him enough to get by.'

Clement beckoned a waiting taxi parked higher up the street. 'Have you ever been to Sydney before?'

'Nope. Brisbane's bad enough. But Sydney! All those roofs I saw from the plane window! Too many people for my liking. And too damn cold!' Tom said, rubbing his tanned arms.

The taxi drew up beside them and Mick lifted their packs into the boot, then they climbed in. 'I've been here before. But not since I was a kid. You may remember, I grew up on the south coast of New South Wales.'

'Yes, I do recall that, Mick.'

'I saw the Harbour Bridge from the plane window. They were building it when I was last here,' Mick said.

'It's been open for a while. Ten years, in fact,' Clement told them.

'I don't remember much about the place. Except the enormous face of Luna Park with its wide-open mouth. All those teeth. Scarred me to half to death just to walk under it. My brothers called me a sissy.'

'There is a saying, Mick, that *sticks and stones may break my bones, but names will never hurt me*. I don't think that is true. Humiliation from a trusted source lasts a lifetime,' Clement added.

The taxi turned into Oxford Street and pulled up outside the main gate of Victoria Barracks. Paying the fare, Clement showed his pass to the guard on duty. Skirting the parade ground, Clement saw the police car parked adjacent to the briefing room and guessed Lowe had already arrived. He could see Sergeant Preston seated behind the steering wheel, patiently waiting.

Clement pointed to the black door ahead of them. 'The C.O. in charge here has allocated this room for our use. There are two familiar faces inside,' Clement said to Tom and Mick as he opened the door.

'Struth! The gang's all here!' Tom said. Sitting around a long table were Joe Watkins, Evelyn Howard, and Inspector Lowe. Tom beamed his toothy grin and shook hands with Joe and Evelyn. 'Is Major Lyon joining us, too?'

'No. He's away at present, Tom,' Clement said. 'This is Inspector Henry Lowe of Sydney Central Police. Inspector, this is Sergeant Tom Archer and Private Mick Savage. If you'll all take a seat, we'll get started.' Clement gave them a brief appraisal of events to date for Tom and Mick's benefit. 'What I am envisaging at this stage is surveillance,' Clement said, unrolling a map on the table. 'Tom, you and Mick will not be in uniform, so you'll need to get some extra clothing. I've arranged with Colonel Ravenscroft, for us to have Welrod pistols and Fairbairn Sykes knives. These are special issue and must be concealed on your person at all times.'

Lowe leaned forward. 'As Clement knows, I'm not too happy about this, but it seems Commander Long outranks me in these matters.'

Clement continued. 'As you'll be wearing civilian clothes and carrying weapons, you'll need to be especially careful not to alarm the public. The Fairbairn Sykes knife scabbard should be worn on your lower left leg, concealed under trousers. The Welrod holster is worn around the chest, the barrel and grip of the gun should be assembled, and you should carry at least three rounds of ammunition in a coat pocket.' Clement leaned forward and grasped a stack of large envelopes on the table. 'Inside are maps of Sydney,' Clement said, handing them out. 'You should keep these on you until he know your way about. Please be alert. While this is currently a surveillance mission, the people you will be following could be extremely dangerous.'

'Any suspicions, Clem?' Tom asked.

'I don't think this was a straightforward murder, if any murder can be so called. While Miss Howard is acutely aware of the dangers, it is possible Miss Edwina Hughes, the deceased, died because her initials are the same as Evelyn's and it may be a case of mistaken identity.'

'You reckon it's that simple?' Tom said.

Clement glanced at him. 'While I agree, it seems perhaps a bit too obvious or indeed, far-fetched, I have encountered already in this war where a person's initials were of the utmost importance. If Evelyn is the intended victim, the killer will strike again. This killer may have no connection to her. Maybe he, or she, has been hired for the purpose. But I'm almost certain there is a connection to someone at the Women's Emergency Signalling Corps. And they are supplying information. We need to follow three people and note who they meet. They are Mrs McKenzie, the principal and founder of the college, her secretary, Miss Peggy Seaton, and the second-in-charge at the college, Miss Veronica Evans. Only these three women have regular access to classified information at the school. I propose we follow these women Monday evening after they finish work for the day. If you look at the maps, you'll notice I've marked the locations of the three women's residences.'

Everyone opened their envelope as Clement went on. 'Tom and Mick, you both should spend the rest of today and tomorrow visiting these locations and making yourself familiar with the area, noting bus stops, ferry stops if they have them, local shops, even churches. Joe, if you would do the same tomorrow. But be careful, they must not see you. You must all be as familiar with these locations as any local. Do not, however, make contact. Or be so close they could recognise you or be able to describe you. Should any of them become suspicious and telephone the police, Inspector Lowe has briefed his men accordingly. Tom, you will follow the secretary, Peggy Seaton, Joe, you follow Mrs McKenzie, and Mick will follow Miss Evans. I will follow Evelyn in case there is another attempt on her life.' Clement shifted his gaze to Archer and Savage. 'I will meet you both in Clarence Street inside St Phillip's Church at noon on Monday, where I'll give you a description of what each is wearing so you can identify them on leaving the Clarence Street building. However, we should all meet back here tomorrow tonight at seven, unless otherwise instructed, to go over everything that's been learned about your allocated area and any unforeseen problems. Any questions?'

'Seems straightforward, Clem,' Tom said. 'Where do we get these knives and pistols?'

'I have them here, Tom,' Clement said. From under the table, he withdrew a long pack and, opening it, handed out the weapons.

Evelyn stood to leave. 'If I'm moving, Clement, I should probably try to get a room at this boarding house in Cremorne this afternoon. I'll ask Joan about it today at WESC. Do you remember the address and the woman's name?'

'She didn't introduce herself. But Joan will know. I remember the address, though.' Clement scribbled it on a piece of paper. 'Please be careful, Evelyn. Until we know if you are a target, you shouldn't be anywhere in public on your own.'

Joe stood. 'I should get back to WESC. If we're all absent, it could look suspicious.'

'Thank you, Joe. I'll try to get back to WESC this afternoon too. If I don't, I'll see you tomorrow night, here for the briefing.'

Lowe stood and joined Clement by the door. 'Sergeant Preston can drive Miss Howard and Lieutenant Watkins to Clarence Street now. It'll save time. Then he can take Miss Howard to Glebe when she's finished at

WESC. It may be best if he also takes her to Cremorne. That way, we'll know she's arrived there safely.'

'That's most kind, Inspector. Thank you,' Evelyn said.

Evelyn checked her watch. 'We should go, Joe. Should I attend tomorrow evening's meeting, Clement?'

'No need. Just settle into the guest house, and I'll see you on Monday at WESC. Be careful, Evelyn. Any problems call me here at the barracks or Inspector Lowe, if it's urgent.'

Escorting Evelyn and Joe to the waiting police car, Clement then returned to the briefing room. As he walked in, Lowe was standing, gazing at a large map of Sydney Harbour spread out on the table. 'Something troubling you, Henry?'

'There are quite a few ships in the harbour currently,' Lowe said, still staring at the map. 'Most are around Garden Island and in the inner harbour east of the Harbour Bridge. The *Chicago* is right in the centre,' Lowe said, pointing out the locations where ships were moored.

Lowe picked up a pencil and drew some of the other ships in port onto the map. The quantity of shipping there was worrying. Tom and Mick joined them at the table. Clement recalled the map he'd seen in Commanders Long's war-room in Victoria Barracks, Melbourne a few months previously. That map had been of Darwin Harbour. There, back in February, so many ships; Australian, British, and American had been either tied up at the wharves or at anchor in the harbour. Thousands of tons of shipping had been lost and hundreds of military personnel and civilians had died in the Japanese aerial attacks that day. He glanced at Tom. While he couldn't be sure, he guessed Tom was also thinking about Darwin. In his mind, Clement heard Tom's uncensored assessment of the Japanese raids that had continued on the northern city. If mayhem had been the result in the small frontier city, then such a raid on Sydney could be catastrophic.

'I'll leave you now, Clement. I still have an American sailor to find,' Lowe said.

'Any progress there?' Clement asked.

Lowe shook his head. 'I'll call you if I do.' Lowe paused. 'I'm gathering you don't need me tomorrow night?'

Clement thought for a moment. 'Perhaps only come if you've learned something new.'

Lowe went to the door. 'I'll catch a cab from here. I'm trusting you to run this operation of yours to the letter of the law. No alarming the public with those weapons you each carry.'

'We'll be careful,' Clement said. Closing the door behind Lowe, Clement went and stood beside the long table, studying the map. With the amount of shipping in port he knew about, and the additional ships Lowe had drawn onto the map, he felt the alarm bell. He glanced at Tom and Mick. Both seemed absorbed in handling the knives and pistols. Clement went to the telephone on the end of the table and dialled the memorised secure line number. A woman's voice he recognised answered the line. 'Miss Copeland, is he in? It's Clement Wisdom speaking.'

'He is Major. Hold the line, please.'

Seconds passed. 'Long here.'

Clement heard the authoritative voice at the other end of the line. He liked Rupert Long. The man was charismatic in all the right ways. He had invaluable knowledge and a winning ability to get things done, no matter the hurdles. But, perhaps more importantly, he had ready access to the newly created American Naval Intelligence.

'Have you heard anything from FRUMEL about an impending Japanese raid on Sydney, Commander?' Clement asked.

A few seconds passed before Long spoke again. 'What's you evidence for such an eventuality, Wisdom?'

'There's an inordinate amount of shipping in Sydney currently, the *USS Chicago* and *Perkins*, *HMAS Canberra* and *Whyalla*, and the *Westralia*, as well as eight or nine smaller craft and a Dutch submarine among others. And that's not counting about ten anti-submarine vessels. It's just all a bit reminiscent of Darwin, Commander. And perhaps Pearl Harbor.'

There was silence at the end of the line for a few seconds. 'Hello? Hello?' Clement said.

'Yes, I'm here, Major. Tell me how you know about FRUMEL?'

CHAPTER NINE

Friday 22nd May 1942

Clement sat on the veranda, overlooking the parade ground reflecting on his conversation with Long. He'd tried not to implicate Joe, saying he'd heard on the grape-vine about the Americans from CAST establishing their own facility in Melbourne. But he felt sure Long wasn't convinced and hoped it wouldn't reflect badly on Joe, or himself. In fact, he hoped now that Long knew the Americans suspected Veretti, the net for the missing sailor would be spread more widely. Glancing at his watch, he wondered if he should attend the afternoon classes at WESC. Standing, he left the veranda and went to collect his overcoat from the briefing room.

As he walked in, the telephone on the table in the corner rang. He reached for the receiver.

'Clement?'

'Speaking.'

'Good. You're still there. Lowe here. I'm sending a police car to pick you up. I'll explain when you get here.'

The line went dead. Pulling on his overcoat, Clement locked the door and walked towards the main gate. Across the road, he saw Tom and Mick returning to the barracks. Each was wearing a newly acquired coat and carrying a large bag of second-hand clothing.

'We were lucky to get these,' Tom said, raising the bag. 'Apparently clothing is being rationed. You going somewhere, Clem?' Tom asked.

'Yes. Lowe telephoned. It sounded urgent.'

'Should we come?'

Clement thought for a minute. 'No. Better you stick to the plan.'

Clement pulled the collar of his coat up around his neck and walked out onto Oxford Street to wait for the police car. Twenty minutes later, he saw it pull into the barracks. Hurrying, he climbed in. A constable was behind the wheel.

'Afternoon, Sir.'

'Do you know why Inspector Lowe wants me, Constable?'

'Best he explains. Suffice to say, there's been a development.'

'Right.'

Clement stared through the window as the car sped through the city streets. It wasn't far, but the area around the Central Police Station was always congested with people. Clement glanced at the imposing stone façade of the Central Court building; an edifice designed to intimidate. The car turned right, then left into Central Avenue, and finally into a car park at the side of the building.

The constable switched off the engine. 'I'm to take you to the interview rooms on the first floor. If you'll follow me?' Clement stepped from the car and closed the door, then followed the young constable up a flight of back stairs. Along the central corridor were several doors, but unlike the cells downstairs, these doors each had a glass panel and were not locked from the outside. Clement could see several anxious faces sitting in those rooms as he passed. The constable then opened a door on his left, and Clement stepped inside.

Seated with Inspector Lowe was a man wearing a clergyman's collar and a very dishevelled man dressed in a frayed coat with a rope tied around his waist. His dark hair was tangled, and he had a beard of many days' growth. His dirty fingers protruded from a pair of threadbare mittens and the distinctive aroma of methylated spirits hung in the air. Clement glanced at Lowe then the minister.

'Take a seat, Clement. This is Reverend Murray of St Stephen's Newtown.'

Clement sat in the only unoccupied chair in the room.

'And this is Bert Smith,' Lowe said. 'Tell this man what you told me, Bert.'

'I saw them. Four of them. All in coats and hats, so I couldn't see their faces. Two dug a deep hole in the old part of the cemetery. I thought it was an odd time for the gravediggers to be going about their work. Then they went to a car parked beside the church. I saw them take a body from the boot and carry it into the graveyard. I knew then something wasn't right. There was no coffin, and the body wasn't wrapped. He was a tall man.'

'Could you see what he was wearing?' Clement asked.

'Trousers and a shirt, I think. I couldn't be sure.'

'Then what happened?'

'They put him in the grave, then the one standing at the side threw something into it. Then they filled it in. They left after that.'

'Did they all leave in the car?' Clement asked.

'Three did. One walked away. I lay as still as I could until dawn. Then I went to look at it. They'd even put grass and leaves over the dirt. After that, I went to knock on the reverend's door. I don't think he believed me at first. But after I showed him the fresh grave, he did. Then he rang the police.'

'What Bert says is true,' Murray said.

'And you saw all this?' Clement asked.

Smith nodded. 'There's a large tomb with a ship's bow on it near the path. I hid behind that.'

'Did you follow them?' Lowe asked.

'No! I didn't want to end up in that hole, too.'

'Do you regularly sleep in the graveyard?' Clement asked.

'Most nights.'

'Could these people know this or learn this from anyone?'

'Perhaps. I put a couple of planks of wood on the ground near the wall. It's warmer there. No one's found me so far.'

'Is it safe there for you?' Clement asked with genuine concern and looking at Murray.

'Not always. But you'd have to know I was there. That lot didn't.'

'And you were there when you saw these men?' Lowe asked.

'I heard the car on the gravel. It woke me. So, I went to see what they were doing. Like I told you.'

'Where in the graveyard is it?' Lowe asked.

'At the back, in the old section, near the tall red gum.'

'Then these men left?' Clement asked.

'Did I say they were all men?'

'There were women there too?' Clement asked.

'One was. The one that walked away.'

'Did you see her face?'

'No. As I said, they all wore coats and hats. But I knew it was a woman. Shorter than the others, and she wore perfume. When you live in the streets, you don't smell perfume much.'

'Did you overhear anything they said?'

'One man was in charge. He got impatient with the gravediggers. Told them to hurry up.'

'Did he have an accent? Like me? Or perhaps American?' Clement asked.

Bert shook his head. 'No. I don't think he was foreign.'

Clement looked across at Reverend Murray. 'Is there not somewhere this man can go at night? A hostel or something?'

'Yes, but Bert doesn't like them. Values his freedom. Isn't that right, Bert?'

'I don't want any closed doors. Rather be on my own.'

Clement held the man's gaze. 'Would you say it was common knowledge that you sleep in the graveyard?'

'It would be among the other homeless.'

Clement turned to Lowe. 'Henry. Could you find somewhere safe and pleasant for Bert to live away from St Stephen's graveyard for the time being?'

'We'll get him scrubbed up. The Salvation Army can take care of him. Or maybe you could be useful around here with a mop and bucket,' Lowe said.

Clement saw Bert's eyes widen. While life on the streets was undoubtedly harsh, perhaps a job with the police wasn't Bert's idea of a pleasant life.

'It is for your safety, Mr Smith,' Clement said. 'I feel certain that the Salvation Army will find you suitable lodgings. Besides which, I'm sure, a bed in the men's hostel is preferable to planks of timber for a bed during the coming winter months. Pneumonia isn't pleasant and could be deadly,' Clement added, the sound of his late wife Mary's hacking cough echoing in his memory.

'Neither is having your throat cut if anyone tells them they may have been seen,' Lowe added.

'Thank you for your information, Bert. Best you stay away from St Stephen's and Newtown for the time being,' Clement said.

'We may want to question him further, Reverend. Could you stay with him while we ask the Salvos to take him in?' Lowe asked.

'Of course.'

'Thank you for your recollections, Bert,' Clement added.

Lowe escorted Bert and Reverend Murray out. Through the door, Clement saw Sergeant Preston waiting to take them back downstairs.

'Nothing untoward in Cremorne, Sergeant?' Clement called through the door.

'Miss Howard is safe, Sir, in her new lodgings.'

'Thank you.' Clement turned to Lowe. 'Do you think Smith will abscond?'

'It's possible. I wouldn't want our star witness to disappear.'

'When will you leave for St Stephen's?'

'Are you free to come along, Clement? You can also identify the body, I'm assuming, if it is Veretti.'

The car pulled into Church Street, then drove through St Stephen's large ironwork gate into the churchyard. Clement and Lowe stepped from the police vehicle. While the busy high street of Newtown bustled with shoppers and traffic, St Stephen's church occupied a secluded position about a hundred yards from the main thoroughfare and down a narrow side street. It was an old church, and Clement considered large for its parish. Built of stone with stained-glass windows, it felt familiar to him. Yet it also had an impoverished ambiance. Large weeds grew beside dilapidated graves. Mature trees sat randomly amidst the decaying headstones, their roots uplifting the stone monuments until they toppled over, lying forlorn on the ground, their occupants' names long since obliterated by weather and time.

Clement walked along the wide gravel path towards the double front doors to the church at the southern end. He tried the handle, but it was locked. He felt the sudden sadness the war had forced on churches of all denominations. Used as dead letter drops, the churches in England were required to be locked when a service was not in progress. He didn't know if that routinely applied to churches in Australia. Standing on the steps, he surveyed the area. The graveyard was large, surrounding the church on three sides, to the east, south and west. From the size and nature of some headstones, Clement knew the church had been there a long time. To his right and left, he could see a long stone wall of about eight feet in height bordering the site and further down the twisting gravel path, the graveyard extended into an unkempt thicket of tall trees and long grass. His eye searched for the ship tombstone Bert Smith had told them about. A moment later, he saw the stone prow. It was carved into the front of a mausoleum, and a person crouching beside it at night or in the day would not be visible to anyone walking along the path or at the far end of the graveyard.

'Bert said the grave was beside a tall red gum. That must be it,' Lowe said, pointing.

They walked towards the tree, the wind in the trees and their footsteps the only sound. Clement studied both sides of the overgrown path as the foliage thickened. It was an isolated place, the eerie solitude juxtaposed with the bustle of the nearby high street.

'Where better to hide a body!' Lowe muttered.

'Indeed.'

Picking their way between the derelict monuments, they found a low mound of recently disturbed earth. As Bert had said, the diggers had attempted to conceal their work by placing grass and leaves over the site. Several footprints were visible in the replaced earth where feet had tampered down the dirt. The footprints led back to the gravel path. But beside the ancient gravesites, it all looked recent.

Lowe reached for his fob watch. 'They'll be here any minute.'

'Will Reverend Murray be attending?'

'I asked him not to, actually Clement. He'd have to record the exhumation in his reports to the Bishop and I'd sooner the fewer people who know about this, the better.'

Clement walked back along the path. A van drove into the yard and Clement signalled to the driver to bring the vehicle closer to the burial site. Switching off the engine, three men wearing overalls and carrying shovels approached them. With the earth so loosely packed, the exhumation did not take long. The men lifted the body from the site and laid him on the ground.

Clement walked over and stood beside the corpse. It was a confronting sight, but he recognised the dark wavy hair immediately. The face had suffered repeated blows and a gaping cut across the man's neck showed the method of his death. Clement stared at the naval uniform. It was dirty and stained from the damp soil and dried blood. And from the amount of blood on his clothing, Clement surmised McCowage would find a stab wound to the heart. He looked again at the young man's face, remembering Veretti's exuberance and cheeky manner, then cast his eye along Veretti's torso. He'd been a tall man, but lying on the ground he seemed smaller.

Clement looked up and surveyed the surrounding area. Neither the arrival of the ambulance nor the exhumation had drawn any local attention. Was this unusual? Perhaps not just Bert used the graveyard as a place of refuge, and over the years the locals were used to seeing the homeless taken away in bags only to be brought back later in coffins. Clement looked at the high walls surrounding St Stehpen's. Despite the number of homes packed into the crammed streets surrounding the church, there was no direct line of sight into this part of the graveyard from any of the neighbouring dwellings.

'Henry, I could ask my sergeant, Tom Archer, to keep a watch on the graveyard tonight. If a local is complicit, they may inform the guilty of today's events and they may return. Best I'm here also, just in case there are a few too many for Tom to engage.'

'Of course, Clement. Not a bad idea. I'll have some of my lads in Newtown on standby as well, just in case. What about Miss Howard?'

'She should be safe enough now in her new lodgings.' Clement paused. 'But to be sure, could one of your men check on her this evening?'

'Of course. I'll have Preston knock at the door. He can say a neighbour has reported an intruder in the vicinity. That should satisfy any curiosity from the owner.'

Off to Clement's right, the ambulance men lifted the body of Hank Veretti onto a stretcher, then carried him into the rear of the ambulance.

'Take the body to the police mortuary and ask Doctor McCowage to start the postmortem as a matter of urgency,' Lowe instructed. Closing the rear doors, the men climbed back into the ambulance, and it slowly drove away.

Lowe returned to the gravesite. 'Fill in this hole properly, Constable. And make sure the grass is replaced. If the killer returns, I don't want him knowing we've removed the body. I especially don't want the press learning about it until we know more about the circumstances of his death.'

'And not even then,' Clement added. 'Once the Americans request his body, you'll lose any evidence his corpse could provide.'

'Don't I know it, Clement. Mum's the word all around.'

'Will Doctor McCowage be able to do the postmortem today?'

'I hope so. I want as much time with Mr Veretti as I can.'

'Would you mind if I attended?'

'Not at all, Clement,' Lowe said. Lowe gazed around the churchyard, his hands in the coat pockets, his gaze slowly coursing over the old, silent church and its grave-yard. 'Gives me the heebie-jeebies, this place.' The Inspector sniffed the air. 'There's something fishy going on here and no mistake.'

'Sir!'

Lowe turned around.

'This was in the grave, Sir.'

The constable handed Lowe a soil-encrusted hessian sack.

Pulling the draw strings apart, Lowe reached into the pouch and withdrew a small black handbag.

'The shoes?' Clement asked.

Lowe shook his head. 'Just the handbag.'

'I suppose Joan or Billie can identify it as Edwina's.'

Lowe opened the clasp and looked inside. 'No address book here. Or a diary. Just a compact and handkerchief.'

'May I?' Clement asked. Opening the bag wide, his hand reached into the side folds. He felt something hard, like a card, and pulled it out. It was a drinks coaster. Turning it over, he read the words, *The Australia Hotel.*

CHAPTER TEN

Friday 22nd May 1942

Clement stepped from the taxi at the gate to Victoria Barracks. He went straight to the officer on duty for the day to leave a message for Joe Watkins, Tom and Mick to join him in the briefing room at eight o'clock that evening. Then, feeling hungry, he went to the Mess.

Just before eight, he walked back to the briefing room and turned on the light. With his feet propped on a chair, he sat facing the wall and closed his eyes, reflecting on what he'd learned from Bert Smith and the visit to St Stephens. By having a few quiet minutes to contemplate the past few days' events, he hoped to separate facts from assumptions. Tonight, however, no matter which way he thought about it, he could find neither clarity nor motive. A few minutes later, Tom and Mick walked in, followed by Joe.

'Something wrong, Clem?' Tom asked.

'A development you should know about. Please sit down,' Clement said, swinging his feet down. Facing them, he told them about Bert Smith and the exhumation.

'And it was this American, Hank Veretti?' Tom asked.

'He's been rather badly beaten, but it would appear so. Anything to tell me?'

Joe leaned forward in the seat. 'Nothing unusual happened at WESC this afternoon. Although Joan asked where you were.'

'What did you tell her?'

'I said I didn't know. But most likely you were helping the police.'

Clement nodded. 'Did you go to Cremorne?'

'Yeh. I took the evening ferry with the commuters. It's an affluent suburb. And all just as you said. I located the guest house and checked out the lane beside it. It's just a foot path that leads to the street behind. All rather overgrown. There's a garage at the rear.'

'Is it in use?' Clement asked.

'I'd say so. The double doors swing outwards and there are scratch makes on the concrete drive. There's also a small door and a window at the side, and the windows are covered in brown paper.'

'Did you see anyone there?'

'No. But I could hear music.'

'And Mrs McKenzie's?'

'Further up the street and on the other side of the road. Overlooks the water. It's quite steep. There's a pathway to a central front door. From the look of it, I'd say it's an apartment building.'

'Did you have a look around the property?'

'No. I could see an old woman sitting at an upstairs window. I figured if I lingered around too much she might want to know what I was doing and call the local police. She may even tell Mrs McKenzie that an American was asking questions about the place.'

Clement nodded. 'Probably best. And Mick? How did you fare?'

'Glebe's quite palatial in parts, although not where Miss Evans lives,' Mick added. 'There are some big terrace houses nearby and a few boarding houses and a pretty big church further up the hill. There're also a lot of shops on the main road; it's called Glebe Point Road. Miss Evans's house is a two-storey terrace, built almost onto the street and no garden. There's a rear lane and from what I could see when I looked over the fence, not a blade of grass anywhere. Pretty grim, if you ask me.'

'And you, Tom?'

'Newtown! What a rabbit warren! It has a long main street with plenty of pubs and shops and narrow streets leading off it. Working man's domain would be my assumption. But I can add something to what you learned today, Clem,' Tom said. 'Miss Seaton lives in a tiny wooden house in Horden Street. Except for a small front veranda, it's built straight onto the road.' Tom shook his head. 'Don't know how anyone can live like that. All jammed packed into the place like sardines. And. Guess what's around the corner?'

'St Stephen's?'

'You guessed it!'

'I've asked Inspector Lowe to have one of his people check on Miss Howard tonight, so that you and I, Tom, can watch goings on at St Stephen's and at Miss Seaton's. I think it unlikely, whoever these people are, that they will attempt to investigate the gravesite in broad daylight. But tonight, it could be a different matter.'

'I'll go now, if you like,' Tom said.

Clement glanced at the clock on the wall. Half past eight.

'Good idea, Tom. I'll join you there as soon as the postmortem on Veretti is over. But be careful. Watch and follow only. And if it looks like they even suspect you're there, get out as fast as you can.'

'Will do.' Archer checked his weapons, then left.

'What about us, Clem?' Joe asked. 'Should we watch Mrs McKenzie and Miss Evans's places tonight too?'

Clement thought for a moment. In view of what he'd learned from Bert Smith, it sounded like a good idea. 'If there's any activity, watch only. Do not intercept. Get a description of anyone you see them meet and try to get the registration number of any vehicles in use. If there is no activity and you are sure each of these ladies has retired for the night, return here.'

'Are you expecting anything in particular to happen?' Joe asked.

'No. Not really, Joe. There are too many unknowns. For now, it's wait and watch.

Joe pulled on his heavy overcoat and he and Mick left, closing the door behind them.

Clement stood and, locking the door behind him, walked out to Oxford Street. He took a cab to the Central Police Station. The city at night shone, the wet pavements glistening in the reflection from the streetlights. Nightclubs were still open, and people streamed along the footpaths. 'So much for the blackout,' Clement muttered. Servicemen from all nations sauntered arm-in-arm with local girls. Sydney was evidently seen as a safe city, far from the war and the jungles of the South Pacific.

Lowe met him in the foyer at the police station just after nine o'clock and together they took the lift to the lower ground floor. Lowe pushed open the doors to the mortuary. McCowage stood over the deceased body of Hank Veretti, a clipboard in his grasp.

'I owe you one, George,' Lowe said.

'My wife was none too pleased about it, Henry. Friday nights at the pictures are sacrosanct. You can make your apologies to her.'

'Any similarities with the attack on Miss Hughes?' Clement asked, approaching the body on the autopsy table.

'Same method, same killer, in my book. And before you ask, Major, a double-edged blade was used with precise wounds to the throat and chest. But there is something different from our other murder victim, Miss Hughes. Other than the obvious, of course. Someone else, in my opinion, had a go at him. And I don't mean the repeated blows to the head and face. There are three smaller stab wounds to the chest. Done by a small, serrated kitchen knife, would be my guess.'

Clement stared at the body of Hank Veretti.

'And,' McCowage went on, 'these smaller stab wounds were done postmortem.'

'What?' Clement asked, staring at Veretti's corpse.

'So, you'll be looking for one killer and one angry person with a grievance,' McCowage added.

'Would you say that the same force was used in all stab wounds?' Clement asked.

'You want to know if a woman could have done it? Quite possibly. The double-bladed stab wounds definitely inflicted the fatal blows. The serrated knife wounds are random. Is it a case of *hell hath no fury* as Mr Congreve once wrote?' McCowage said. 'The phrase is often attributed to Shakespeare but in fact...'

'George! His clothes? Where are the clothes?' Lowe asked.

'Over there already laid out for you,' McCowage replied, returning to his work.

Clement walked with Lowe towards the table and scrutinised each garment. The trousers, while showing signs of wear and stained from soil, were in good condition. But they appeared to be saturated with an oily substance. 'Have you tested what this is?' Clement asked.

'Machine oil. And there are some fungal spores as well.'

Clement's gaze slowly moved along each leg. But how the engine oil or fungal spores had got onto Veretti's trousers was puzzling. Next to the trousers was a white cotton short-sleeved shirt. It had a large amount of dried blood on the front. Next was a collared shirt, also blue but paler in colour to the trousers. Blood stains covered the entire front of the shirt most profoundly around the collar and descended the front of the garment as though the victim had been either standing or sitting at the time of the attack. Beside this was a short coat. It had wide lapels, was double-breasted and had no epaulettes. Clement had seen such uniforms worn by US enlisted naval personnel. There were no markings or rating insignia on any of the clothing. Neither was there a cap. Clement's eye settled on the belt and shoes. The shoes also had a large amount of blood on the uppers especially around the laces. This had turned a deep reddish black. The belt lay beside the shoes. It, too, was stained. 'Mind if I touch the belt?'

'Go ahead. I've already taken samples from that item,' McCowage said.

Clement picked it up and unwound the long leather strap. The buckle was encrusted with dried dark blood and near to the holes was a deep indentation where the buckle had resided for years. Two holes further along was another mark although perhaps more recent and considerably less well defined. 'In your opinion, Doctor, would you say our victim had lost or gained weight lately?'

'Why do you ask Clement?' Lowe said. Clement handed him the belt. Lowe ran his finger along the leather. 'I see what you mean. Could be he lost weight.

The *Chicago* was at sea and in battle recently. Perhaps he skipped a few meals.'

McCowage joined them. 'It may interest you gentlemen to know his stomach contents showed a meagre meal of very thin porridge or gruel. Slim rations indeed for a serving man, given that the US Navy, I hear, feed their crews rather well, even in wartime.'

A door opened and the mortuary assistant entered and handed a clipboard to McCowage.

McCowage eye ran down the page. 'Ah. Blood test results.'

'Well?' Lowe asked.

McCowage flipped through the pages. 'Interesting. While some of the blood on Mr Veretti is a match for Miss Hughes, I can guarantee there wasn't a drop of his blood on her clothing. But then, that's not surprising.'

'Why do you say that, Doctor?' Clement asked.

'Oh! Didn't I say? Mr Veretti died at least twelve hours before Miss Hughes.'

CHAPTER ELEVEN

Saturday 23rd May 1942

All Clement could think about was how Miss Hughes's blood got onto Hank Veretti's clothing, if McCowage was correct about the timings. And how was it that Veretti had fungal spores and engine oil stains on his trousers? Where had he been? From the veranda near his room in the officers' quarters at Victoria Barracks, Clement stared into the dull morning sky. His body yearned for sleep, but the night's surveillance with Tom at St Stephen's had yielded nothing but frozen feet and an aching back. He'd given Tom and Mick the morning off to rest, but he couldn't allow himself the same luxury. Joe, he suspected would still be asleep. Clement closed his eyes, the intermittent weak morning sunshine on his face. The complexity was confusing. Instinct told him that whatever was happening involved more than one person and that WESC was involved.

'Mind if I join you?'

Clement opened his eyes and turned to see Joe standing behind him. 'Of course, Joe. Sorry, I was miles away.'

'Yes. I saw that, Sir,' Joe said, pulling up a chair to sit beside Clement.

'Joe, could you do something for me?'

'Name it.'

Clement smiled. There was a quiet confidence about Joe Watkins that Clement very much liked.

'Monday night, once you're sure Mrs McKenzie is at home for the night, could you check again on the guest house in Cremorne?

'Any particular reason?'

'Nothing specific.'

'But?'

Clement sighed. 'I can't shake the feeling that Evelyn could be in danger.'

'I know it seems a bit too coincidental that this guest house and Mrs McKenzie's home are in the same street, they aren't anywhere near each other, you know, Clem. Maybe Mrs McKenzie recommended it to Miss Olivant because she knows it's there.'

'Could she know the owner?' Clement said, but his question was rhetorical, and Joe seemed to know that. Clement thought back to the colourful proprietress. Given the woman's exuberant manner and attire and Mrs McKenzie's rather simpler tastes, he thought it unlikely the women had ever met much less knew each other. 'Had you met Hank before joining WESC?'

'No. But we talked briefly before class on our first day at WESC. That was when he told me he'd been at CAST.'

103

'Would you know if the US Navy as requested his body?'

Joe shook his head. 'But I'm not the one to ask, Sir. Inspector Lowe should have had a request by now. You could just call the mortuary to see if he's been collected.'

'Yes. I'll do that. Thank you, Joe.' Clement stood, a frown creasing his forehead. A nagging thought was swirling around his mind.

'Anything I can help with?' Joe asked.

'That's good of you, Joe and thank you for asking. There's just something I want to check.' Clement hurried off to the briefing room where he could use the telephone without being overheard. He dialled the police station number.

'Would Inspector Lowe be in today?' Clement asked.

'Not today, sir.'

'Would Sergeant Preston be in?'

'I'll put you through.'

A moment later Clement heard Preston's voice on the line. 'Major Wisdom here, Sergeant. Would you know if the US Navy has requested the release of Hank Veretti's body?'

'I'll check with the mortuary attendant, if you'll hold the line, Major.'

Clement waited. Minutes passed before he heard Preston's voice again. 'He's still with us, Sir. And no request has been forthcoming. I can, however, inform you that Inspector Lowe has placed a call to the captain of the *Chicago*. I don't yet know the outcome of that conversation, Sir.'

Thanking Preston, Clement hung up. He knew from Lowe that Edwina Hughes's grief-stricken parents had officially identified her, but what of the American? Clement knew Lowe wanted to keep Veretti's death from the Americans a little while longer, but that decision had inevitably delayed Veretti's official identification. Clement frowned, his mind racing. He reached for the telephone again and re-dialled the number for the police station.

'Sergeant Preston, one more thing, if you please. No one is to remove the body of Hank Veretti under any circumstances. Do you understand? No one. Not Captain Bode or anyone from the US Navy. Not even General MacArthur. Should you receive such a request, or in fact, if anyone comes to collect Mr Veretti, keep them there, then call me. Lock them up if you have to.'

'Not sure I can do that, Sir.'

'Well, keep them busy, then. We don't want this corpse disappearing.'

Clement hung up. He wasn't certain he'd learn anything new, but he wanted to see the corpse again. Pulling his overcoat on, he left Victoria Barracks. He was almost running as he hailed a taxi on Oxford Street. Something disturbed him about the body of Hank Veretti.

Twenty minutes later, he paid the fare and opened the door to the police station in Central Avenue.

Sergeant Preston was at the reception counter. 'No one's come for him, Sir.'

'Could I see the body again, Sergeant?'

'Of course, Sir. I'll telephone the mortuary attendant and let them know you're coming down. You remember where it is?'

Clement nodded and took the lift to the lower ground floor. Pushing the mortuary door wide, he waited while the attendant went to retrieve the body of Hank Veretti then position it under one of the overhead lights.

Clement pulled back the sheet. He stared at the fatal wounds, the stab wounds to the neck and chest. Precise and completely unemotional. The handiwork of an expert. But the other wounds told a different story. That they had been inflicted postmortem showed utter contempt. Even hatred. Clement pulled the shroud off the corpse and slowly allowed his gaze to course over the torso. 'Could you retrieve the man's clothes for me again?'

'Certainly, Sir. I'll get them for you.'

Clement waited only a few minutes before the man returned. The attendant arranged the blood encrusted clothes on a nearby trolley, then left the room.

Clement stared at each item, paying careful attention to the shoes. The soles were worn, but pressed into the leather soles was the black substance he'd seen on the belt and in the shoelaces. He believed it was congealed blood. But there was a copious amount. Had the man been standing in it? Was it even his blood? 'Are you there?' Clement shouted.

The attendant re-emerged.

'Do you know if the soles of these shoes have been tested for blood or any other substance?'

'I'll check the report, Sir.' A minute later Clement heard the sounds of a filing cabinet being opened, then the returning heavy footsteps of the attendant.

'Dr McCowage states that the boots, although in reasonable condition, had significant amounts of blood in the seams of both shoes. This blood was tested, and it belongs to the victim. There was also particulate matter along the edges of the soles. Fragments of mould and fungal spores were detected. Also traces of engine oil. The trousers also have similar traces of oil and fungal growth, especially the seat of the trousers, indicating that the man may have been sitting on a damp surface.'

'Thank you,' Clement said. The attendant disappeared again. While Clement knew about the engine oil and fungus, he didn't understand where Veretti could have been for long enough that his clothes had collected such material? Clement reached for the shroud again, then tossing it high, flung it over the body, making sure Veretti's naked frame was properly covered. He held the sheet in both hands ready to cover the man's face, but the disfigured face of Hank Veretti held his gaze. Clement stared at that face. In his mind he tried to visualise Veretti as he had been, the chewing lips, the wavy black hair he'd seen that first day at WESC. But Veretti's face was too misshapen and disfigured from a fractured jaw and repeated blows to the head. Folding the sheet back, Clement bent down to study the wounds. He gently touched the cold flesh. It was then he saw a small, oval-shaped brown mark, like a thumb print, under the man's chin. Despite knowing the corpse had been washed, he gently rubbed at it. It was a large, well-defined mole. Clement stared at it. He called again to the attendant. 'Do you have a photograph of this on file?' Clement pointed to the mole.

'Yes, Sir. Photographs are always taken in such cases.'

'Could I have a copy?'

'I'd have to check it with Inspector Lowe.'

'Of course. As soon as you can, please.'

Thanking the mortuary attendant, he left the building and caught a tram on Elizabeth Street for Circular Quay. Alighting near the ferry terminal, he strode across Circular Quay towards George Street to find Mill Lane. From what Inspector Lowe had said about the area, Clement had expected there to be more people about. But all seemed quiet on the waterfront. Perhaps it was the hour or the day. The wharves, usually so busy with men and cargo through the week, now lay silent. He turned his gaze to the harbour beyond and the collection of grey painted ships anchored there. Only small pleasure craft and the little ferries that took people across the harbour disturbed the waters. Keeping his eyes peeled for Mill Lane, he strode past the local police station, then asked a woman who stood loitering outside one of the public houses for directions. Not five minutes later, he saw the narrow opening between the buildings. About halfway along it was a flight of steps that presumably led to the street above. Walking along it, he slowed, his eyes scanning the cobblestones for oil or mould. A pungent aroma filled his nostrils, a mix of urine, vomit, and years of grime and rats. At the foot of the steps was an alcove. Clement stared at the little door secreted there. Was it here that Edwina Hughes had drawn her last breath?

And what of Hank Veretti? Despite the filth in the alley, Clement saw no evidence of mould or any oil slick.

At noon, he wandered back to George Street skirting Circular Quay. Across the harbour, his gaze lingered over the ships at anchor. The large *USS Chicago* lay in the middle of the harbour, several other ships nearby. Above him, he heard the roar of a single aeroplane. It flew in low from the east, coming almost directly down the harbour towards the Harbour Bridge. Clement stood and watched it bank over Circular Quay, then fly over the city. Shielding his eyes, he squinted into the sky. It continued to fly further south across the city, and Clement surmised it was heading for the airport at Mascot. In the glare of midday, the aeroplane looked white, and although he couldn't be certain; it appeared not to be showing any markings. Looking around, he checked to see if anyone had raised any alarms about the aeroplane's presence, but nothing stirred, and no sirens sounded.

As Clement walked towards the tram stop, he glanced up at the building that housed the Combined Defence Headquarters situated adjacent to Circular Quay. Surely the people on duty there would have both seen and heard the aeroplane and raised the alarm, if its existence was anything to worry about.

Taking a seat on the tram, Clement pondered what he'd learned about Veretti. He wanted to know if Lowe had spoken to Bode. He also hoped Lowe had had more luck than Joe with the irascible Captain of the *Chicago*.

At seven, Clement walked into the briefing room. Tom and Mick sat to one side. Next to them were Joe, Henry Lowe, and Evelyn. He glanced around the faces. While he was intrigued to see Lowe, it surprised him to see Evelyn.

'Preston called me to say you'd been back to see Veretti again? Any reason for that?' Lowe asked.

'Yes. But first, as you are here, I'm guessing you have something to tell us.'

Lowe nodded and taped a large brown envelope on the table. 'The photograph of Veretti you asked for. And a couple of things to tell you. Preston called on Miss Caide and Miss Olivant. Both have identified the handbag as belonging to Miss Hughes. I've also been in touch with Rear Admiral Muirhead-Gould, the Senior Allied Officer here. He'll contact Captain Bode on the *Chicago*. Said he'd be back in touch as soon as they'd spoken. I'm guessing it could be Monday before I learn anything.'

'Have you contacted the US Military Police about Veretti's death?' Clement asked.

'Not yet. I want to hear what Bode has to say first.'

'And you, Tom?'

'Mick wanted to go the Luna Park. So, I thought I'd look into that church, St Phillips where we're meeting on Monday. After that, I walked along Clarence Street to that park opposite your signals school.'

'And?'

'Found a shoe. It was under a bush there.' Tom reached into his pack and withdrew a black leather, low-heeled woman's shoe.

'Just the one?' Clement asked.

Tom nodded. 'Could belong to anyone.'

Clement reached for the shoe to examine it. But its discovery, if it was Edwina's, only confirmed what they already knew; that Edwina had been in the park. That there was only one shoe didn't alter that fact. The other could have been lost when the killer carried her there. Or be under a nearby bush, as Lowe had initially said. Or it may not be Edwina's at all. 'And you, Joe?'

'I took the ferry with Mick to Luna Park. Then, we decided to go to Cremorne Point again.'

'Why?'

'Just wanted to see that guest house in the evening. You seemed quite anxious about it earlier,' Joe said.

'Did you learn anything?'

'Didn't want to get too close in case we were seen, but the house lights were ablaze everywhere. She must have a house full of paying guests. And we heard music,' Joe added.

'She's an opera buff, Clement,' Evelyn cut in. 'Warbling sopranos mostly. It's played day and night. And she has the gramophone turned up quite loud, so it's difficult to think at times. She likes to perform for the older men who live there. They seem to like it and frequently join in. But I had to get away. Said I wanted to see the harbour bridge at night. Should buy me a few hours. What about you, Clement?'

Clement told them about seeing Veretti's body again, and about the mole and the mould and traces of oil on his clothing.

Lowe leaned back in his seat. 'I put that down to the general filth of Mill Lane. Can't imagine there are too many house-proud women living there cleaning their front doorsteps. Well, if you're finished with me, I'll leave you. And I'll let you know what I learn from Bode as soon as I hear something.'

'By the way, Henry. Did you notice an aeroplane fly over the city earlier today?'

'I heard it.' Lowe stood and pulled his overcoat on. He leaned in close to Clement's ear. 'There's a top-secret Radar Unit in Sydney, Clement. They're practicing using it and tracking aircraft. My guess is it was another practice flight to test out their latest toy.'

Clement nodded.

The other men stood to leave, and Clement followed them to the door as they left. Evelyn remained standing beside the table, staring at the map.

'I heard that flight too, Clement. You saw it?'

'Yes.'

'Perhaps you should check on it with Commander Long tomorrow.'

'If you think it is necessary, I will.'

Evelyn smiled.

He walked with her to the door. 'How are you getting on at the guest house?'

'Well enough. It's alright. Except for the music. I quite enjoyed it to begin with, but it goes endlessly. Especially *Madam Butterfly*. It's Mrs Pendleton's favourite. Do you know the plot of that opera?'

'Not really my thing, Evelyn.'

'It's about a young Japanese woman who marries an American sailor and had a child. Only he's already married. So, she kills herself.'

'Cheerful.'

'They never are. Well, I better get back. Hopefully she'll be playing *The Merry Widow* tonight.'

Clement laughed. 'Will you get a taxi?'

'Perhaps best at this hour.'

'You will be careful.'

'I'll be fine, Clement.'

'You have the Welrod?'

'I do. And a knife.'

'Really?' Clement paused. 'I realise this may be a loaded question, Evelyn, but can you use them?'

'It is. And I can.'

'One day, I may ask you about that.'

'One day, I may tell you.' She smiled.

Clement returned the grin. 'You haven't mentioned Joan. How is she?'

'Haven't seen her. I hear from our landlady that Joan has a suitor. John Connor, no less.'

CHAPTER TWELVE

Sunday 24th May 1942

Clement rose early. For an hour, he read his Bible. It was something he'd once done daily. When life was predictable. Before the war. Before his involvement with the Secret Intelligence Service in England and the Secret Intelligence Bureau in Melbourne. Closing his eyes, he thought about all that had happened since joining WESC. He tried to sort everything into chronological order, but order was something missing from the events of the past week.

Dressing, he went to the Mess for some breakfast and ate a hearty meal. An hour later, he walked to the briefing room and closing the door, sat by the telephone and dialled the secure line for Commander Long's office, hoping that someone would be there.

A young woman with a brisk voice put him through.

'Commander Long's office.'

It was a voice Clement knew. 'Miss Copeland? I'm a little surprised you're in this morning.'

'Major Wisdom. Sadly, the Japanese do not respect Sunday as we do.'

'Can you get a message to Commander Long for me, please?'

'You've just caught him, if you'd like to speak with him.'

A few clicks sounded in Clement' ear before he heard the authoritative voice.

'Long speaking.'

'Good morning, Commander. I'm just checking that you and others there are aware of an aeroplane that flew over Sydney yesterday at midday. It appeared white to me, but it wasn't showing any markings.' Clement paused. He didn't wish to implicate Lowe in any security breach, so he withheld what he knew about the Radar installation in Sydney. Besides, Long would already know about it.

'I'll look into it. Any news about the American?'

Clement told Long what he knew. 'Are you aware the Americans suspect Veretti, and that Joe Watkins was asked to monitor him while at WESC?'

'On whose orders?'

'A lieutenant called Rudy Fabian.'

There was silence at the end of the line for a few seconds. 'I'll look into that, too,' Long said. 'And Clement, you learn anything that even hints of sabotage or collusion with our enemy, call me directly, do you understand?'

Again Clement paused. There was something in Long's voice that implied he was already suspicious about something.

'Can you add anything to what I've told you, Commander that could be relevant to what's happening here?'

There was a long silence before Long spoke. 'Your suspicions about Japanese activities may be correct. Although, it's beyond audacious if it was the Japanese who flew over Sydney yesterday in broad daylight. But I will tell you this: a Russian merchant ship was attacked by a Japanese submarine about ten days ago. It was just off the coast of Newcastle. Two torpedoes were fired at it. Both missed. However, the submarine then surfaced and attacked the ship again, this time with deck guns.'

'Really? And exposed itself by surfacing!' Clement said, aghast.

'Hard to believe but that is what happened.'

'Is it still in the vicinity?'

'Hopefully not. Muir-Head Gould has ordered an air and sea search for it, but so far nothing.'

'Do you have confidence that everything that can be done is being done in Sydney?' Clement ventured.

'I'll ignore the implications of that remark, Wisdom. Sydney is not unprotected, you know. The sonar indicator loops under the entrance to the harbour and within it should inform us of any movement. And we are alert to any possible aerial activity in the vicinity. It is unlikely at this stage anyway that Japanese bombers could reach Sydney. The distance from Sydney to the Japanese-occupied islands is too great.'

Clement hung up. He sat at the table, his gaze on the map, but his mind was on the likelihood of a Japanese invasion. He thought about the defences around Sydney he knew about. Barbed wire festooned the city's beaches and boom nets had been installed in strategic places in the harbour to guard the ships in port. The practice air raid sirens and search light drills were a frequent event that everyone knew about.

His gaze settled again on the map and the ships there. What if the submarine's presence had more to do with attacking the ships? What Long had said about a Japanese submarine patrolling off the coast set alarms clanging. Surely, Muirhead-Gould would have everyone on high alert for an attack? Could a single Japanese submarine enter Sydney Harbour undetected? While it was a magnificent waterway, it was relatively narrow and big ships had to manoeuvre carefully, especially when the port was so congested with ships. His mind went to Scapa Flow in the Orkney Islands north of Scotland and the attack on the Royal Oak in 1939 that he'd read about in preparation for his trip to Caithness in February '41. That ship had been at anchor there and had been sunk by a single German U-boat. Over eight hundred men had died. Surely Muirhead-Gould would suspect such a possibility, given that he was in Scapa Flow at the time.

A knock on the door broke Clement's concentration.

Tom came in and closed the door behind him. 'Thought I'd find you here, Clem. Would you like me to watch the graveyard tonight?'

Clement thought for a moment. 'Thank you, Tom. Given that it's Sunday, I think it is unlikely they will return to the graveyard today or tonight. Reverend Murray will be conducting services. Too many people around. Too much chance of being seen. Tomorrow night, however, it may be a different story.'

CHAPTER THIRTEEN

Monday 25th May 1942

Clement took the Oxford Street tram into the city, then a second tram to Clarence Street for another day of dahs and dots. The morning was spent listening to Evelyn's vast knowledge of Japanese and how it applied to Kana Morse. But they'd been careful not to make any eye contact.

At exactly noon, Clement handed his transcripts to Veronica and left the classroom, taking the stairs to the middle floor. He stuck his head around the door to the office and glanced at the principal's inner domain. Mrs McKenzie was not there.

'Mrs McKenzie not in this morning, Miss Seaton?'

'She will be Mr Wisdom. She had some things to do this morning.'

Clement smiled. 'How are you faring, Miss Seaton?'

'I'll be alright,' Peggy said.

But Clement could see her anxiety. The young woman's once bright voice now seemed on edge. 'It's been quite a shock for us all.'

'Did you want to see Mrs McKenzie?'

'I can see her later,' Clement added. He noted Peggy's apparel and the coats and hats on the stand in the corner. He knew Veronica always wore a green overcoat and hat, and as Mrs McKenzie was yet to arrive at the school, he reasoned that the other coat and hat belonged to Peggy. 'I mustn't keep you,' he said, smiling. Clement hurried down the stairs to the door to the street and strode away. He went straight to St Phillip's. As he walked down the short path to the front door of the church, he noted the state of the small garden around it. It looked neat and well attended. In his mind's eye, he saw St Stephen's and its rambling graveyard. St Phillip's didn't have a burial ground that he could see, but it was a complete contrast to the Newtown church. He reached for the door handle and turned it. It was unlocked.

Entering the quiet, dark nave, he sat on a pew towards the back. A woman was dusting the pews when he knelt to pray. He breathed in the quiet solitude, his mind, for the first time in a long while, was quiet. Perhaps it was the familiarity of being in a church, but he closed his eyes and allowed the refreshing quietness to filter through his soul.

A loud click broke into his brief tranquillity. He turned and saw Tom and Mick enter the church. Both men pulled their hats from their heads. Standing, he went to join them. With the woman still there, they left the church and stood in the porch outside.

'What are they wearing?' Tom whispered.

'Mick, Veronica Evans is wearing a pleated, tweed grey skirt with a pink blouse. She'll also be wearing a green overcoat and matching green hat. Do you know what a tweed looks like?' Clement checked.

'Yeah. My mother used to wear it.'

'And the secretary?' Tom asked.

'She's wearing a blue skirt with a white blouse. Her hat and coat are also blue. Be careful, both of you. I'll see you in Newtown tonight, Tom.'

Leaving them, Clement hurried back to WESC for the afternoon session. As he passed the office door, he saw Mrs McKenzie seated at her desk, giving instructions to Peggy.

At five, he and Joe left the building. Joe crossed the road and stood near a bus stop. Clement walked in the opposite direction. Stooping, he pretended to tie his shoelace. Turning his head, he saw Evelyn and Veronica leave the WESC building. They stood on the pavement for a few seconds talking, then Evelyn walked away, heading east towards Circular Quay. Joan had joined her. Veronica continued along Clarence Street towards the tram stop. Clement scrutinised the surrounding people. He couldn't see Mick or Tom, but he knew they'd be there somewhere, watching. Standing at the corner, he glanced back along Clarence Street. Joe was still at the bus stop. Several minutes passed, but he saw no sign of either Mrs McKenzie or Peggy Seaton.

A minute later, a police car drove along the street and pulled up near WESC. Clement saw Henry Lowe alight.

Clement left the corner and hurried back. As he approached, Lowe opened the rear door of the car. 'We've got a witness! Get in!'

'How did you find him or her?'

'Him. I had Preston go to *The Australia* this morning. He made some preliminary enquiries.

'And the body is still in the mortuary?'

'Yes. And I've heard from Muirhead-Gould. I was left in no doubt he thought I was wasting his valuable time. Captain Bode confirmed Veretti was given shore leave to attend the course at WESC. He was living temporarily on the *Kuttabul* moored at Garden Island Dockyard, apparently. Got the distinct impression they have no idea Veretti is dead.'

Clement remembered the ship's name. He also remembered that Connor and Lockhart had said they were also living onboard the *Kuttabul*. He made a mental note to ask them about Veretti. 'So that's why the Americans haven't asked about him. As far as they are concerned Veretti is alive and well. Did you tell them he's dead?'

'Not yet. But I can't leave it much longer. Wouldn't be right.'

'And, for the record, he should be officially identified.'

'You think he isn't Veretti?' Lowe asked. 'I thought you'd met him?'

'I did. But it should be done by the Americans, even if only for the records.' Clement drew in a long breath. Puzzles. Once he'd loved them. When they were made of wood. Now they usually ended in betrayal and death. 'Who's the witness?'

'Barman at *The Australia* remembered her green uniform. Apparently, he asked to see her identity, believing she was underage.'

Lowe drove the short distance to *The Australia*, pulling up in Castlereagh Street outside the main entrance to the glamorous hotel. It was a grand edifice, with elegant stairs and formal columns, and was, so Lowe told Clement, the most expensive and stylish hotel in Sydney.

'I hear it even has a dining room for servants. That actress, Sarah Bernhardt, has a suite here,' Lowe said, as they climbed the steps and approached the front door. A man in a long coat and cap stepped forward and opened the door for them.

Entering, Clement took in the lavish décor of a hotel that could easily have been in the West End of London. It was impressive and clearly only frequented by the well-heeled, inquisitive foreigner or by locals out for a special occasion. They walked towards the hotel reception desk.

Lowe showed his inspector's warrant card. 'I need to speak with Brian Harrison. I understand he works here.'

'He does, Inspector.' The man came from behind the desk and led Clement and Lowe towards a long room at the side of the entry foyer. It was even more ornate than the entrance, with large windows, heavy draped curtains, mirrors, and chandeliers. Lounges and cushioned chairs lined the room. At one end was a grand piano where a pianist was playing a song Vera Lynn had made famous.

A mature-aged man in a white jacket was at the bar.

'This is Inspector Lowe of Sydney Central Police, Mr Harrison. Give him any assistance he requires. I must return to the front desk now, Inspector.'

'Thank you,' Lowe said as the man left.

Lowe turned to face the barman. 'Were you here Thursday evening between five and six o'clock?'

'Yes. I work every day, Monday to Saturday from three till midnight, Inspector,' Harrison said.

'And you remember a young woman coming in here with an American serviceman in naval uniform?'

'We get many American servicemen in here these days, Inspector. While I don't remember the American well enough to describe him to you, I do remember the young woman.'

'But she was with an American serviceman?' Lowe urged.

'Yes, I believe so.'

Clement stepped forward. 'He is about six feet tall with wavy, dark hair and chews gum almost perpetually.'

'Oh, yes! That I remember. I thought it most undignified. I do recall now that he was with the young woman in the green uniform.' Harrison gazed into the large lounge in front of him. 'They sat there,' he pointed. 'Another lady joined them.'

'Another? Can you remember what that person was wearing?' Clement asked, hoping he'd say a green dress with a black blazer.

'A cocktail dress. Pink. With pink satin shoes. Most elegant. In fact, I wondered why she'd joined them.'

'Why do you say that?' Clement asked.

'Well, she was sophisticated. Worldly. I couldn't see any similarities between any of them. Poles apart, I would have said.'

'And this woman in pink? Did she arrive with them?' Lowe asked.

'No. She joined them and sat with them for a while. Ordered champagne that the American paid for, then they all left together. I do recall they didn't drink that much. And they weren't here for very long either. I'd say about twenty minutes. I threw out more than half a bottle. Wasteful, especially in these times of rationing. Where they went after that, I couldn't say.'

'What time would this have been?' Lowe asked.

'Hard to say but before dinner. Somewhere between five and six, would be my guess.'

'Thinking back on how they were with each other, Mr Harrison, and in your opinion, would you say the woman in the cocktail dress knew one or both of them? Or did you get the impression they'd just met?' Clement asked.

'Well now, I can't be sure, of course, but if I had to say, I got the impression she knew them.'

'What makes you say that Mr Harrison?' Clement said.

'The woman was quite friendly towards them. Then the two ladies left the bar. I presumed to go to the ladies' powder room, for they returned a few minutes later. They seemed quite amicable with each other. They chatted and had some more champagne, then they left not long after that.'

'Would you know if this other woman was a hotel guest?' Lowe asked.

The barman shook his head. 'As she didn't pay or sign for the champagne, I couldn't say, Sir.'

'Was this other woman younger or older than the young woman in the green dress?'

'She was mature. A woman, not a girl, if you catch my drift, sir. Although, sometimes, it's difficult to tell age especially when the ladies get dressed up.'

'Did she have any distinguishing features, for example colour of hair or memorable jewellery?' Clement continued.

'No. Nothing like that. She had light brown hair taken up, as I recall. And as I say, she looked elegant, most refined. That's why I thought it odd she'd joined them.'

'Thank you, Mr Harrison,' Lowe added. 'If you remember anything else, no matter how small, please telephone the police station immediately.'

'Of course, Sir.'

'Is there a porter at the front door?' Clement asked.

'Of course, Sir, always. This is *The Australia Hotel.*'

'And would this man on duty today be the same man as last Thursday evening?'

'Yes, sir. We work similar shifts. Three o'clock in the afternoon to midnight, or seven in the morning to three in the afternoon. The night staff are separate. But of course, the bar is closed at night,' the barman said, glancing at Lowe.

'Thank you for your help,' Clement said.

Leaving the bar, they went outside and found the doorman. Clement described the trio. 'I remember them. I thought the young lady in green was not well. She seemed inebriated to me. The American serviceman and the other lady each had her under an arm. They were laughing rather loudly, or so I thought.'

'Did you see which way they went on leaving?' Clement asked.

'I believe they were collected, Sir.'

'You mean a taxi?' Lowe asked.

'No, Sir. A vehicle pulled up, and they all got in.'

'Anything unusual about the car?'

The doorman nodded. 'I thought it odd. It was a van, like a delivery vehicle. The woman in the evening dress seemed rather too sophisticated to travel in a tradesman's van.'

'Can you describe it?' Lowe asked.

'A van, filled in sides. No advertising banners on display, as I recall. I would say it was either dark green or black.'

'Thank you. If you remember anything else, please call the Central Police Station. It is of the utmost importance.'

Descending the front steps to the street, they climbed back into the police vehicle and drove away.

'Thank you for including me, Henry,' Clement said, as the car drove along Castlereagh Street. 'Could you drop me off at Circular Quay?'

'Of course. What about the briefing at seven o'clock?'

'It may have to be later. Check with the officer of the day. I'll let him know when it will be. I do, however, want to check on Miss Howard first though, then I'll join Tom in Newtown.'

127

'Regardless of the hour, Clement, I'd like to join you, if you don't mind. It could be useful to hear what they have to say.'

'Mrs Lowe won't mind?'

'She's a policeman's wife, Clement. Irregular hours go with the job.'

The police car drew up opposite the busy ferry terminal and Clement alighted. The place was congested with commuters all huddled under the awning, protected from the inclement weather. He checked his watch: half-past six. Fumbling in his pocket for the fare, he boarded the evening ferry to Cremorne Point.

Clement sat outside in the cold air where no one disturbed him. He thought about the woman in pink, as described by the barman. Harrison had described her as mature. If Win Hughes had gone anywhere with the woman, did it stand to reason that she knew her? Even though Mrs McKenzie had dark brown hair, could Harrison have been describing her? Clement stared at the waters, the white foam trailing behind the small craft as it scurried across the harbour, weaving its way between ships both large and small.

Despite the weather, he always enjoyed the outdoors, listening to the sounds of the sea and hearing the birds. And, for some unknown reason, he liked what some would consider inhospitable or even bleak places. Such places brought perspective to life, or so he believed. And it gave him time to think. He stared up at the waxing moon. It would be full in a few days' time, its brightness casting shadows and highlighting even the darkest corners of the harbour and making black waters sparkle with flecks of light.

Below him, he heard the reverse thrust of the engines. Then the thump of the gangplanks being lowered. Clement stood and made his way to the gangway, joining the stream of commuters as they descended to Cremorne Point Wharf. He hurried away, covering the distance to *Waverley Guest House* in ten minutes. Climbing the stone steps to the front door, he rang the bell. From inside, he could hear the strains of operatic music and a woman was attempting to sing.

The pale-faced Nigel answered the door.

'Good evening,' Clement said, raising his hat. 'Would Miss Howard be in?'

'Mother! It's that friend of Joan's!' the boy shouted.

The singing stopped. Nigel held the door open, and Clement stepped inside.

'She's in the sitting room,' Nigel said, pointing to a large room on his right. Clement walked in and found Evelyn seated between two men, one was grey-haired and portly, the other younger, and of a similar age to himself.

Evelyn stood when she saw him. 'Clement, may I introduce Colonel Reeve and Mr Bretton? And you've met our landlady, Muriel Pendleton.' The two men stood and shook hands with Clement. Muriel Pendleton floated towards him, her red lips twisting into a smile.

'Mr Wisdom. So nice of you to recommend our humble establishment to your friend. She and I are good friends already. Isn't that right, Evelyn?'

Evelyn emitted a muffled laugh.

'I just wanted to see that you've settled in well,' he said to Evelyn. 'I thought you may appreciate a short stroll around the area, just to acquaint yourself with your new neighbourhood.'

'But it's freezing out!' Muriel protested. 'She couldn't possibly go out-of-doors now!'

'This isn't cold, Mrs Pendleton,' Evelyn said. 'If you'd felt the icy wind of an English winter, you wouldn't call this bitter.' Evelyn stood. 'I'll get my coat, though.'

While Evelyn retrieved her overcoat, Clement stood and waited. Muriel Pendleton walked over to the grand piano, which dominated the sitting room. 'I'll entertain you with a song, while you wait. Some Puccini, perhaps?'

She didn't wait for a reply before launching into an operatic aria.

Evelyn appeared in the doorway and Clement took his leave. They stood on the front veranda of the house, Mrs Pendleton's voice penetrating the glass.

'Shall we?' Clement said.

'I'm not sure how much longer I can stand being here, Clement. Did you learn anything new?'

Clement told her about his visit to *The Australia* and the woman in pink. He also informed her about his conversation with Commander Long the previous day.

'Dear Lord! You think that the Japanese submarine attack and what's going on at WESC are connected?'

'I don't know, Evelyn. But if Mrs McKenzie is passing on information, she's running a dangerous game. And now she would know the security services are involved, it's only a matter of time before she's discovered.' Clement paused. 'Is Joan in tonight?'

'She isn't. John Connor called for her earlier, apparently. Not sure Veronica would approve.'

Clement smiled. 'Will you be alright here tonight? I'm sorry the guest house isn't to your liking, but it's only a few days.'

'Like you, I keep something up my sleeve,' Evelyn said, tapping her forearm. 'I'll see you tomorrow, at WESC.'

'God willing.'

She looked up at him. 'Meaning?'

'I think someone will return to check on the gravesite. If they discover the body has been exhumed, they will know they've been compromised.'

'How would they know to look?'

Clement pursed his lips.

'You think Peggy Seaton is the connection, don't you? But how would Peggy know about the exhumation?' Evelyn asked.

'Not sure. But she would know the police are looking for Veretti. And she lives nearby.'

'Could be coincidental.'

'Murder and coincidence are never accidental. Besides which, Bert Smith said one of them was a woman and that she walked away from the graveyard. I don't think for a minute that Peggy is the brains behind it all. But

Peggy and Mrs McKenzie know you moved to the same guest house Joan lives in. Perhaps you should move again. It could be safer.'

'Another move? Thank you for your concern, Clement. Best I stay put; it's only a few days.'

'If you're sure. But just in case, lock your door and keep those weapons close. I'll see you tomorrow.'

Escorting Evelyn back to the front door to the guest house, Clement hurried back to the wharf. In the darkness, he saw the lights from the approaching ferry. Above him, clouds were gathering, scudding across the sky and making the moonlight flicker. He pulled his coat around him as a gust of wind blew in across the harbour, making him shiver. Stepping aboard the ferry, he sat in his usual seat until a passing rain squall forced him to sit inside. At Circular Quay, he caught a tram downtown, then changed trams at Broadway for another to King Street, Newtown.

Just as Tom had said, King Street was long and narrow. On both sides, the shops that fronted the street were all closed. Clement kept to the footpath where he could get shelter from the overhead awnings in front of the shops. Few people were about. Finding Church Street, he hurried past the large brick rectory with its rusted ironwork gates, then crossed the road. As he turned into Prospect Street, the silhouette of a man was walking towards him. He knew the swagger.

'Tom!' Clement whispered.

Archer looked up. 'Struth, Clem! Frightened the life out of me!'

'Why are you here and not outside Miss Seaton's house?'

'She's been home for some time. Lights are out and everything's quiet. So, I wanted to see how close that church is from the house.'

'Where's her house?'

'Around the corner,' Tom paused. 'So this church is close?'

'It is.'

They walked back to Church Street in silence. The rain ceased, but the night was cold. Standing beside an old, twisted fig tree, Clement gazed at the outline of the church and its shadowy graveyard.

'It's like one of those grizzly fairytales,' Archer whispered.

'Did she go straight home?'

'Yep!'

'Meet anyone?'

'Nope.'

A sharp wind blew across the yard, sending the branches of numerous large trees swaying. There was nothing welcoming about this final place of rest. It told its own story of grim reality, privation and neglect. Clement pointed along the path, past the church to where the tombstone with the ship's prow lay waiting.

'Let's look around. But keep your hand on that knife I gave you.'

'No fear there, Clem.'

133

Passing the church, Clement found the ship's prow tombstone. Squatting beside it, Clement flicked on his torch and checked the time. Nine o'clock.

As soon as he did, a voice called from somewhere across the large graveyard.

'Come out and show yourself, Dick McCutcheon!'

Clement thought it was Bert Smith's voice. But he wasn't sure.

'I'll have a look,' Tom said.

'No, Tom. If it is the man I met at the police station, Bert Smith, he won't recognise you and he could make more noise. I'll go.'

Hunching low, Clement ran down the gravel path, then took to the long grass to cover the sound of his footfall. Ahead of him, he could see the silhouette of a man hunched beside a tombstone.

Crouching beside a nearby leaning headstone, he whispered, 'Bert?'

The man stood then ran onto the path, heading for the street more than a fifty yards away. Clement stayed still. If the man was Bert, he would find somewhere else to go. Clement hoped so, and not just for this night.

On the breeze, Clement heard the sounds of scrapping. He ran back to Tom. 'Did you get a look at the man who ran away?'

'Yeh. Looked like a hobo to me. Rope around his waist and more than a day's growth on his beard.'

Clement nodded. Then, on the night air, he heard footsteps crunching the gravel.

CHAPTER FOURTEEN

Monday 25th May 1942

Clement and Tom stayed low, crouching behind the tombstone as four dark figures passed them, their footsteps heavy on the gravelled path. Two carried shovels. No one spoke. They were heading for the gate to the street.

Clement signalled to Tom to skirt the path on one side. He took the other, hoping to reach the front gates before the men. But in the darkness, the way was strewn with hazards; fallen headstones in the long grass or concealed rectangular slabs of long forgotten graves. Tripping on one, Clement fell. Wrapping his arms around his head, he fell onto his side, his ribs finding the stone edge of a gravesite. He clenched his teeth as a searing pain shot down his left side.

The footsteps stopped.

'Who's there?' a male voice said.

Clement stayed prostrate in the long grass. Breathing through wide nostrils, he forced the pain from his side, clutching at his ribs, he lay still.

'You see who it is,' a male voice said some little distance away from him.

'Probably a drunk.'

'Well, have a look!'

Clement rolled over until he felt another tombstone, then rolled onto his side before crouching behind it. With the sound of approaching footsteps on the gravel, he withdrew his knife. Then all went quiet. He sensed his pursuer was now in the grass and close.

Holding his breath, he waited, his knife ready. But seconds passed and nothing stirred. Clement stood.

His attacker lunged.

An iron grip on his neck, sent shooting pain down his right arm, paralysing his hand. His knife fell from his grasp. His attacker's hold was strong, the massive hand on his shoulder was squeezing hard. Clement felt dizzy and light-headed as though he may faint. Then the iron grip loosened, and he felt something cold against his neck. Still holding his ribs, he tried to breath, his eyes wide. There was no escape this time. Then he heard the thud like cough. It was so close he could hear the rush of expelled gas from the barrel, and he knew exactly what it was. The cold metal on his neck vanished. Bending forward, and clutching his side, he gulped air. Archer stood in front of him.

'Time to go, Clem,' Archer whispered from behind his balaclava.

Clement saw the outline of a man lying on the ground behind him. Bending down, he rolled the man over and searched the face. The deep-set eyes were fixed in death.

Even in the limited light, Clement didn't know the man but he saw the dark trousers and short black coat. Still holding his ribs, Clement rubbed his neck. His attacker had been a very strong man. But he was not young. Clement could still feel the icy barrel of the pistol on his neck.

'Maybe now!' Archer whispered.

'Is he dead?' a voice shouted from some distance away.

'Yeah!' Tom shouted, his response quick and short.

Clement squatted down and felt for his knife in the long grass. Sheathing it, he searched for his torch. 'Stay here.' Clement said, then crept back to where he'd fallen, then he rejoined Archer.

'What now?' Archer whispered again.

'Wait.'

The insistent voice was shouting again. 'Come on. Leave him there whoever he is!'

'Skirt the drive and wait by the gate out of sight. And thank you, Tom,' Clement said his voice a mere whisper.

Clement ran diagonally forward and back onto the path, covering the distance between himself and the gate in seconds. A few yards short of the group, he heard Bert call out. 'What do you want? I haven't got anything.'

Clement stopped. He made an instant decision and holding the torch wide from his body, switched it on. In two seconds, he panned the beam over the group caught in its glare, then extinguished the torch and ran diagonally forward. In those few seconds, he'd seen four figures, three scattered into the shadows. The only person in the group who'd stood staring into the light, was Bert Smith. Dropping to the ground, Clement crawled behind a nearby headstone.

'Charlie?' a voice called.

'That's not Charlie,' another voice said.

'Who is it, then?'

'I'm not waiting to find out.'

Ahead Clement heard a scuffle. A long-anguished groan carried on the night air. Clement remained still. Then running footsteps again. Several minutes passed. Not far away, a motorcar engine started.

Minutes passed.

'Clem!' Tom's sharp whisper.

Staying behind the headstone, Clement paused before speaking. He wasn't sure they'd all gone. 'Here!' he said at length, then moved position to another tomb. Standing, Clement crossed the gravel drive and ran towards the high walls of the church.

Seconds later, Tom joined him. 'Have they gone?'

'I think so,' Clement said, breathing hard and rubbing his aching neck.

'You alright, Clem?' Tom whispered.

'I'll live.'

Clement stared into the darkness, then reached again for his torch. Holding it away from his body, he switched it on and flashed it quickly over the scene. Ahead and lying on the ground was Bert Smith. Clement flicked the torch around the gate and around the grass in front of him. No one. All Clement could hear was Bert's strident breathing. 'Get back to Miss Seaton's,' Clement whispered. 'As soon as I get help for Bert, I'll join you there. And Tom, be careful. Don't be seen.'

Tom disappeared through the gate and into the night.

Clement rushed forward and crouched beside Bert Smith. 'Hold on, Bert. I'll get a doctor for you.' Across from him, Clement could see a light on in the rectory. Taking his handkerchief from his pocket, Clement wound it into a ball, then lifted Bert's shirt. Even in the pale light, the amount of blood was large. He stared at the wound. There was little damage to the flesh, but blood was flowing with every pulse onto the ground. Clement knew the blade would have gone deep. Deep enough to sever major arteries and veins. Bert needed medical help and soon. Clement held the knotted handkerchief to Bert's flesh then, releasing the rope around his trousers with one hand, repositioned it over his handkerchief. Working quickly, he tied the knot tightly over the handkerchief, hoping it would apply sufficient pressure to the wound to stem the blood loss. Leaving him, Clement rushed to the rectory's front door and rang the bell multiple times.

Several minutes passed. 'Who is it?' Murray called from behind the door.

'Clement Wisdom. Bert Smith has been stabbed. Could you please call an ambulance?'

Clement heard the lock rotate. Murray stood in the doorway, his dressing gown tied around his waist and a torch in his hand.

'We should get him in here. Where is he?'

'On the path.'

Running, Clement led the minister to where he'd left Bert. He stared at the bloodstained ground. The man was nowhere to be seen. In the few brief minutes Clement had been at the rectory, Bert had vanished. Clement panned the torch beam around the graveyard, then ran to the gate to check the street. Nothing. A small pool of blood quickly seeping into the dirt was all that indicated anything had happened there.

An icy shiver coursed through Clement as the realisation hit him. He'd been watched. His thoughts went immediately to Tom. Had he run straight into a trap? And what of Bert? 'We need to call the police.'

'It may not be necessary. Perhaps Bert has gone because his injuries were not as bad as you thought. You should understand that while it's not a regular event, occurrences in the night hereabouts happen frequently.'

'I think they should be called.'

'Of course, if you think it is necessary. And you're welcome to sit in my study while we wait.'

'Thank you, but no. I need to check something.'

Clement dashed away, his heart thumping in his chest. Running along Church Street, he turned into Prospect Street and then Horden Street and stopped at the corner, his gaze on Peggy Seaton's house. Swallowing, he tried to steady his breathing and to stop the telltale clouds of vapour issuing from his mouth into the cold night air. His ribs ached and his mouth felt dry. He feared for Archer. Behind the drawn curtains, Clement could see a light was on in Peggy Seaton's front room. Clement looked around. 'Tom!' he whispered several times into the night. There was no reply.

He crossed the road and quietly climbed over the low brick fence onto the narrow front veranda. Leaning against the front wall, he craned his head around the window. The curtains were thick and heavy, but he could just see through the crack between them. Edging himself closer, he peered into the front room. Tom was sitting in a chair in the middle of the room, his arms tied back, and two men were standing over him their backs to Clement. Tom's shirt was torn open, exposing his chest. Clement couldn't see either the knife scabbard or the Welrod holster, and he wondered if Tom's captors had them. If they had, Tom's fate was certain.

'Who is he!' a voice shouted loud enough for Clement to hear. He waited.

'I don't know! I've never seen him before,' a terrified female voice shrieked.

Peggy Seaton came into view briefly, then crossed the room. Clement saw Tom's gaze follow the girl. In that moment, Clement was sure Tom had seen his eye through the gap in the curtain. And for a second, he believed he'd seen Tom wink.

One of the two standing over Tom landed a blow to the side of Tom's head, and Archer reeled sideways.

'What do you want?' Tom asked, his voice slurred as though drunk. 'What have you done to my old mate, Bert?'

'He's another hobo!' one of the men standing over Tom said.

141

Clement felt a rush of relief.

'He's not dirty enough!'

Clement swallowed hard. Archer wasn't yet out of danger, but at least they hadn't found his weapons. Somehow Archer had removed them. There was a long pause.

'That old nuisance has blabbed to the police.'

'How do you know that?' another said.

'Because the body's not there, imbecile! It could only have been him.'

'Good thing he's dead, then.'

'Where did you put him?'

'He's in the van. We'll throw him off North Head later tonight.'

'Where he'll be found by some rock fisherman, you idiot! We'll put him in the pit for now.'

There was a brief pause. Clement could hear Tom burbling. He seemed to be singing; the tune emitted in the short, muffled phrases of the inebriated. Clement half smiled at his quick-witted sergeant.

'Shut up!' someone shouted.

'He's another drunk from the cemetery. But what to do with him now?'

Tom lowered his head, as though drunk or asleep or both.

'Take him back to the graveyard. Let him sleep it off there. Chances are he won't remember a thing, anyway.'

'And if he does?'

'Maybe we put him in the pit too?'

Another long pause ensued.

In the distance, Clement could hear police sirens wailing. The two men beside Tom looked up, bewildered, their heads turned to another in the room not visible to Clement. Clement leaned back on the wall, his mind racing. If they panicked now and took Tom with them, he may never find Archer.

'What do we do?'

'If the police are stopping cars and they find him and the hobo in the boot, we're done for. I say we leave him here and get out before the cops arrive.'

Another brief pause followed.

Clement reached for his Welrod and began to plan how he might rescue Archer. A loud, frontal attack seemed the only way. As he hadn't seen any weapons in the hands of Tom's captors, Clement counted on everyone in the small room being rendered confused and immobile by a sudden and confronting attack. But with Archer tied to the chair, his life and Tom's counted on these men not having guns. If they didn't surrender to him, he'd be shooting to kill with no time for hesitation. It was a gamble he had to take.

'What do we do?' a voice repeated, this time the tone more insistent.

Clement edged his way to the front door, his boot ready to kick the door in, the Welrod held high and firm in his grip.

'You keep him here tonight, Missy. And make sure he's gagged. We'll come back for him in the morning.'

Clement lowered his weapon and returned to the window. With his eye on Tom, he waited.

'What? He could be dangerous! I could be murdered in my bed!' Peggy said.

'He's tied to the chair, you imbecile! Lock yourself in you room then, if it makes you feel safer.'

The sirens were close now.

'We should go.'

'What about Charlie?'

'If he's alive, he'll get himself back. If not. Well, he got paid, and he knew the risks.' There was a brief pause. 'If the police come knocking, you don't know anything. Understand Missy? I'm sure you won't do anything silly. Just remember the lovely Edwina.'

'We'll be back in the morning for whoever he is.'

'Maybe one of us should stay with her?'

'She's not going anywhere. She's not that stupid. Not with a thousand pounds under her mattress and all the clothes she's been given from the black market hanging in her wardrobe. She'd be banged up for years. Maybe even hanged.'

Clement heard the whimpering. But he couldn't see Peggy.

Then a door inside opened. Clement leaned back into the wall, his Welrod close to his chest. A few seconds later, he heard footsteps, then a door closed, and the front sitting room went dark.

Climbing back over the front fence, Clement sheathed the pistol and ran to the corner with Prospect Street. A minute later, a van sped away from a rear lane behind Peggy Seaton's house. Clement stared after it, trying to see the registration plate, but it was too dark.

Running, he returned to St Stephen's. A police car was already parked outside the rectory. Clement rushed to the front door and rang the bell. 'Are the police inside, Reverend Murray?'

Murray nodded, then held the door wide, and Clement stepped inside. Lowe was standing in the sitting room, his notebook in his hand.

'I think there could be a body in the graveyard, Inspector,' Clement said, then told Lowe what had happened.

'Preston, take Constable Roberts with you and scour the graveyard till you find this man. I'll go with Major Wisdom to Miss Seaton's house.'

'What do you want us to do with the body, Sir, if there is one?' Preston asked.

Clement cut in. 'You cannot leave him here, Henry. These people may return and remove him tonight. He's the best lead you have at present to identifying this group.'

'Put him in the boot of the police car, carefully, Preston, and wait for Major Wisdom and me here.'

'Yes, Sir.'

Clement turned to Murray. 'Can I use your telephone?'

'Of course. It's in the hall.'

Clement telephoned the officer of the day at Victoria Barracks. 'Could you please get a message to Lieutenant Watkins and Private Savage to rendezvous in the briefing room whenever they return to barracks? It may be late before I'm there, but please tell them to wait.' Clement hung up, then returned to the sitting room where Lowe waited. 'Perhaps I should knock at Miss Seaton's front door, Henry. She will recognise me and not consider me a threat. And remember Peggy Seaton doesn't know Tom Archer. As far as she knows, he's a drunken man who'd sought refuge in the churchyard and stumbled into whatever these men were doing there.'

'Could be dangerous. Is she alone?'

'I think so.'

'Well, we know she's involved now.'

'If she is there, it could be best if you arrested her. Safer for her that way.'

'You think she's run away?' Lowe asked.

'I should, given the same circumstances.'

'Right. So where is this house?'

Clement led the way back to Horden Street, and Clement knocked at the door. Several minutes went by, but no one came. Clement knocked again.

Still no one came. Lowe pounded on the door. 'Open up! Police!' They waited. 'Perhaps she's asleep.'

'Perhaps. But I think it's more likely she's gone. She's afraid. And she doesn't know who Tom is. If you have no objections, Henry, I can open it without causing damage,' Clement said. He reached into the inside coat pocket and withdrew two small metal instruments. Inserting them into the lock, he rotated the barrel until he heard the click.

'I'm not going to ask,' Lowe said.

'Best not,' Clement answered.

Clement stepped into the darkened front hall. It smelled of dust and cooking fat from years of life. Lowe pointed to the stairs. 'I'll check upstairs.'

Clement turned the handle on the door to the front sitting room, where he'd seen Tom tied to the chair. He nudged it open.

The room was dark, but he could see Tom slumped in the chair, his head forward, a handkerchief tied around his mouth. Upstairs, he heard the heavy footfall of Lowe's boots on the timber floors. Clement flicked on the light, then untied the gag and cut the ropes that held Tom to the chair.

'Tom! Can you hear me?' Clement whispered.

Archer lifted his head, his left eye so swollen it had closed. 'Can't see you too well, Clem. But I'd know that voice anywhere.'

'Can you stand?'

'She'll be right, Clem. Just give me a minute.'

Tom's face was badly bruised and cut, and his left eye was swelling quickly. Blood was oozing from the cut above his eye and running down his face and onto his chest. 'Don't worry about me, Clem. Takes a lot more than that to knock me out!'

Clement helped Archer to his feet. 'The inspector's car is in Church Street. Can you walk that far?'

Lowe met them in the hall. 'As you suspected, Clement. She's gone. I'll put a watch on this place, though.' Clement led Tom to the front veranda. Reaching for his lock picks again, he relocked the front door.

Lowe looked at Archer. 'Your sergeant looks bad. You stay here, and I'll bring the car around.'

'Wait on, Henry. Tom, what did you do with the Welrod and knife?'

'They're under some bushes in Church Street, near the corner with Prospect. That car we heard start, it was further down the street. I saw them put Bert in the boot. But I knew once they turned on the headlights they'd see me. So I tore open my shirt and removed the Welrod and knife.

'I'll get them, Clement. You stay with Archer.'

'Did you see any of their faces well enough to describe them?' Clement asked.

'The two who stood over me, yeah. The one in the corner sat in the dark so I couldn't see the face.'

'Anything unusual about the voice? An accent, perhaps?'

'I know it sounds mad, but it didn't sound natural. Low, but not low enough. I got the impression...' Tom paused. 'It just sounded fake.'

'In what way?'

'You'll think I've gone troppo.'

'Sorry?'

'Insane.'

'So?'

'I could be wrong. But I thought it was a woman.'

Clement saw the black police car pull up at the corner of Horden and Prospect Streets. Leading Archer, they walked towards the car and Clement opened the rear door.

'Did you find the man in the graveyard, Sergeant Preston?' Clement asked.

'Yes, Sir. His body's in the boot. And we retrieve Sergeant Archer's weapons.'

'Is the deceased known to you?'

'A little difficult to say, Sir, in his current state. Have to wait until Dr McCowage performs his tricks before I could say for certain.'

Clement glanced at Tom. He suspected Archer had fired the lethal shot but now wasn't the time to ask. 'Henry, could you take us to Victoria Barracks? Sergeant Archer needs medical attention.'

'Of course.'

Clement watched Tom from the corner of his eye. Archer was stoic but with his eye swollen and the repeated blows to his head, Clement believed he was suffering from concussion.

'Tell me everything you remember, Tom,' Clement asked, attempting to keep Tom conscious.

Tom repeated what Clement already knew. 'Tell me again about the person in the corner. Other than the voice, was there anything else that made you think it was a woman?'

'Couldn't be sure. But I thought I saw their feet.'

Clement thought of Edwina Hughes's missing shoe. 'What did you see?'

'Shoes. I would swear they were pink.'

CHAPTER FIFTEEN

Monday 25ᵗʰ May 1942

Clement left Tom in the infirmary and hurried towards the briefing room where he asked Lowe to wait. He'd been over half an hour while the doctor examined Archer, and he hoped Lowe was still there. He opened the door. Lowe was standing by the table staring at the map of Sydney Harbour.

'Sorry to take so long, Henry.'

'How's Archer?'

'They want to keep him in hospital under observation for a few days. But he's a strong man. He'll be fine.'

Lowe sat down heavily in a chair near the table. 'I took the liberty of using your telephone to speak with Preston. As the bullet used to kill our unknown man wasn't found at the scene, and perhaps never will be, we may never know what sort of weapon was used. But I will ask you if you believe Sergeant Archer shot the man found in the graveyard.'

'I can't answer that. Truthfully, Henry, I didn't see the person who saved my life.'

'Well, we'll leave it at that then,' Lowe said.

'What I do know is that whoever attacked me carried a pistol and had the strongest grip I've ever felt. My shoulder, as well as my ribs, will be sore for days.'

'How do you know he carried a weapon?'

'It was held at my neck.'

'A civilian with a pistol,' Lowe said.

'Any idea who he was?' Clement said, reaching for the back of a chair and sitting down.

'None. Preston took the body to our mortuary. The postmortem won't happen before tomorrow. Hopefully, once McCowage attends to him, we'll know more.'

'Anything known about Miss Seaton's whereabouts?'

Lowe leaned backwards, swinging on the chair. 'It will be interesting to see if she turns up for work tomorrow.'

'Will you arrest her?'

'Certainly. I'll be on the doorstep of number 10 Clarence Street at eight o'clock tomorrow morning. I'd like to get to the bottom of this one way or another before the Americans find out their boy isn't at WESC anymore.'

'It could also be safer for her if she's imprisoned.'

'She's not an innocent party in all this, Clement.'

'I know. But I can't help thinking she's in over her head. After all, I heard them say she was being bribed. And not just with clothes and trinkets. If the amount was correct, a thousand pounds is a lot of money. How would anyone come by such an amount?'

'Organised criminals.'

'Yes. Possibly.' Clement thought back to his time in Cambridgeshire where a German spy had landed. That man had been carrying over five hundred pounds, and Clement had heard about another who took twenty thousand pounds into Britain. 'Or an enemy desperate for information on a regular basis.'

A knock at the door halted the conversation. Joe walked in and sat down.

'What news, Joe?' Clement asked.

'Mrs McKenzie took the ferry to Cremorne Point. I followed her up Musgrave Street, and she went straight home.'

'She didn't see you?'

'No, I was careful not to sit anywhere near her. I was also first off the ferry and ran up Musgrave Street then hid behind a fence until she passed me. I'm sure she didn't see me. Then I followed her to her house. I waited across the road and out of sight until all the lights went out. I stayed a further fifteen minutes, but no one came, and she didn't go out again. In fact, she retires pretty early, so I decided to check that guest house on my way back to the ferry. Lights on all over the house. Even in the attics at the back. The whole place was lit up like a Christmas tree.'

'Any sign of Miss Howard?'

Joe shook his head. 'No. But the music was pretty loud.'

'Is there a jetty outside or near Mrs McKenzie's house? Would she have access to a path leading back to the wharf?'

Joe ran his hand over his brow. 'Sorry, Clem. I thought all the houses just fronted the water. She could have left the house by boat. I didn't think of that.'

Clement told Joe what they'd learned about Peggy Seaton.

'Is Tom ok?' Joe asked.

'He has some concussion and a few cuts and bruises. But nothing much stops him. The doctor says he just needs rest.'

'Are you any closer to learning what's going on?' Joe asked.

Clement leaned forward over the table and clutched his side. 'I believe someone at WESC has been passing information to our enemy. What I don't know is why Edwina Hughes was killed. Nor how many are involved. But you can be sure that it affects the security of this nation and perhaps the Allied war effort in the Pacific. And something else. There is something personal about all this.'

'What makes you say that, Clement?' Lowe asked.

'The postmortem rape. That's not about espionage. Nor, really, even passion. That's dominance or revenge. Or just plain lust. Likewise, the postmortem serrated stab wounds found on Veretti. That level of hatred? That's personal.'

'You think Mrs McKenzie is involved?' Lowe asked.

'Perhaps. Or she may be completely innocent and re-tired early just as Joe surmised.'

'What do they want?' Lowe asked, frowning, but he seemed to be talking to himself.

Clement answered anyway. 'Information about our ability to decipher their codes and names of the people involved in our Secret Intelligence Bureau, would be my guess. Joe, you said Hank Veretti was just a radioman. What specifically does a radioman do onboard a ship?'

'They send out and receive messages.' Joe paused. 'Oh, my goodness, they're also responsible for the handling and destruction of classified information.'

'So not just names of code breakers. Joe, perhaps you should speak again to Rudy Fabian. And I'll contact Long. It would be useful to know if FRUMEL has picked up any unusual radio transmissions in the Sydney area,' Clement said. In his head, he heard Long telling him about the Russian ship being attacked. If the Japanese were intending to invade, or repeat Pearl Harbor, it stood to reason they had sympathetic ears and eyes on the ground.

'What's FRUMEL?' Lowe asked.

'Just part of the Allied War effort based in Melbourne.'

'I'll call Fabian tomorrow,' Joe said.

The door opened, and Mick entered and removing his coat sat down. His eyes scanned those present in the room.

'Mick, anything to report about Miss Evans?' Clement asked.

'Tom not with you, Clem?' Mick asked.

Clement told him about St Stephen's church and what had happened to Tom.

'And our star witness, Bert Smith has been killed and Peggy Seaton implicated and vanished,' Lowe added.

'Struth! But maybe she's not alone.'

'What happened, Mick?'

'Miss Evans took the tram from Clarence Street to Glebe. I got on the same one and got off when she did. She went to the local shops, then I followed her home. I stood on a nearby corner where I could see the front gate. Around ten, a man knocked at the door. Twenty minutes later I saw them leave.'

'Did they leave together Mick?'

'Yeah.'

'Did you follow them?'

Mick shook his head. 'Couldn't. They drove away in a van.'

CHAPTER SIXTEEN

Tuesday 26th May 1942

'Did you get the registration plate number?' Lowe asked.
    'Sure did.'

'At last, a breakthrough,' Lowe said.

Mick passed a crumpled page to Lowe.

'I'll phone this through to the sergeant on duty tonight and get onto it right away,' Henry said. 'Mind if I
use this telephone again, Clement?'

'Not at all. And Henry, could you ask for any further
information on the deceased man found in the graveyard?'

'Will do.' Lowe reached for his fob watch. 'Even
though it's after midnight, Preston may still be at the station. McCowage won't be in till nine later this morning.'

'There's nothing further to be done tonight, then.'
Clement turned to face Joe and Mick. 'Thank you both
for your vigilance. I'm sure we are getting closer, and the
pieces will come together soon.'

'I'm sure sorry about the jetty thing, Clem. It never
occurred to me there'd be a way out at the back.'

'In fact, Joe, people whose houses are built next to a river, or any waterway, refer to the waterfront side of the house as the front.' Clement paused, a frown creasing his forehead. 'Did you see any garages there?'

'Come to think of it, no. But there are a few cars parked on the street outside.'

'Well, thank you both again. You should get some well-deserved rest now.'

Joe pulled on his coat. 'See you later then, Clem.' Without looking back, he walked to the door and let himself out. Clement stared after Joe. He wondered if Joe's seeming indifference had more to do with embarrassment. It was a simple mistake. But hopefully not a crucial one.

'I'd like to see Tom, Clem,' Mick said, standing.

'Of course, but the matron there may not let you in at this hour. Best to let him sleep and see him later this morning.'

Mick nodded. 'What do you want me to do tomorrow? I mean later this morning?'

Clement hadn't thought that far, but he knew he should. He tried to think, but exhaustion was clouding judgement. 'Come to the church in Clarence Street again at noon. I'll see you there.'

Mick nodded, then reached for his coat and, pulling it on, left the room. Clement waited for the door to close. 'Henry, as soon as you know about the postmortem results would you telephone me at WESC tomorrow?'

Lowe stared at Clement. 'You got something on your mind?'

'Just something I want to check.'

'Given what's been happening, best you don't go anywhere alone. You could have been killed tonight. And look what happened to your sergeant.'

'Yes, you're right.' Clement glanced at his watch. 'It's late and I need to be back at WESC tomorrow. Well, later today. Good night, Henry.'

Clement walked with Lowe to his car parked in the forecourt and watched it drive away. Locking the briefing room door, he went to his small room and set his alarm clock for five o'clock. If he were lucky, he'd get about four hours' uninterrupted sleep.

The alarm rang through his head like an express train. Rising, he quickly strapped his knife to his leg and the Welrod around his chest. The action was almost automatic for him now. Dressing quickly, he left the officers' quarters and walked out to Oxford Street. The early pre-dawn chill wrapped around him, penetrating his coat and making him shiver. It was still dark, although he could just see the palest of light tingeing the sky to the east. He stamped his cold feet on the pavement as he waited for the tram.

Alighting at Kings Cross, he walked down Macleay Street. There were few people on the streets. Some were late night revellers going home. Others were women still working the streets in that part of Sydney. But most were factory workers, street cleaners and garbage men. Among them were men dressed in heavy working clothes with strong boots and short black coats. Following them,

Clement walked north towards the harbour and the naval base at Garden Island. Even in the early hours of a dark winter's morning and still some distance away, Clement could see the blazing lights of the construction site at the dockyards which operated around the clock. So bright were these lights, he could see the silhouettes of the ships moored in the harbour beyond.

He followed a stream of construction workers walking towards the main gate. On approach, he reached for his *Most Secret* security pass and made straight for the guard on duty.

'I'll have to telephone the senior officer to get permission for you to enter,' the guard said.

'Are you sure you want to wake him at this hour?'

The guard glanced at the clock on the wall. 'How long will you be?'

'Ten minutes. Perhaps less.'

'Go on then. *Kuttabul* is moored on the right, the eastern side.' The guard nodded him through. Leaving the stream of workers heading for the new docks under construction, Clement searched among the many vessels tied up along the wharves. Checking the names of each ship as he passed, he saw the *Kuttabul* tied up on the eastern side. It was larger than he'd expected and resembled a double-ended passenger ferry. It had an enormous single stack funnel in the middle. Several lights were already glowing on the lower decks. A gangplank extended from the wharf to the ship. Stepping onboard, he quietly walked along the main deck. This deck, from the plaque above one corridor was for officers. Clement stepped into the corridor quietly and opened a door. Inside, he saw a man asleep in a bunk. As neither Connor nor Lockhart were officers, Clement returned to the entry and searched for the internal stairs that led to the lower deck. Taking them, he saw a multitude of hammocks. They were slung across the beams. A few lights on bulkheads were already lit. While some hammocks hung limp and empty, several held the bodies of sleeping sailors. Creeping between the rows of hammocks, he searched for someone awake. About halfway along the line of sleeping sailors, he found a naked man staring at him. In his hands, he held a toothbrush and a towel.

'Sorry to disturb,' Clement said. 'Do you know where I might find John Connor or Jim Lockhart?'

'I know Jim. Further along, in the bow,' the man said, leaving him.

Clement crept further along the rows, the resonance of snoring the only sound. Checking each face, he eventually found Lockhart.

'Jim! Jim!'

Lockhart stirred, then opened his eyes. 'Who is it?'

'Clement Wisdom from WESC. It's urgent. I need to speak with you.'

'Wait a bit,' Lockhart said. Then rising in one smooth action he sat up and swung his legs over the hammock. 'What time is it?'

'Almost six.'

Lockhart rubbed at his face. 'What can't wait till later?'

'Have you seen either Hank Veretti or John Connor?'

'Veretti?' Lockhart yawned. 'Haven't seen him since the first day at the school. I guess I thought he might have gone bush.'

'And Connor?'

'Yeah. Saw him yesterday at the school. But he isn't staying onboard anymore. He's found himself a bit of stuff. Staying with her, apparently.'

'Does this woman have a name?' Clement asked, hoping it wasn't Joan.

'He said it was a secret. But I think it's a girl from WESC.'

'When did he leave the *Kuttabul*?'

'A day or two ago,' Lockhart said, rubbing his eyes.

'And Veretti?'

'He's never been here.'

CHAPTER SEVENTEEN

Tuesday 26th May 1942

Clement hurried back along the concrete path towards the main gate and, waving to the guard as he left, hurried back up the hill to Kings Cross. The day had dawned, but it was still cold and a light, misty rain was falling, making the coming day bleak. The night shift of dock workers was filing out of the naval dockyards. Hundreds of men tramped their way back along the harbour front to Woolloomooloo. Clement stared at their clothes. While it wasn't a uniform, there were similarities to his attacker. He pondered the man in the graveyard called Charlie. Perhaps the clothes said more about his social position than the place of work.

As he climbed back up Macleay Street, Clement thought what Lockhart had said. It surprised him that Lockhart had never seen Veretti on the *Kuttabul*. Did that mean he'd never been on board? If he wasn't on the *Chicago* and he'd never arrived onboard the *Kuttabul*, where had he been? If the Americans thought he was on shore leave to attend the course, would anyone ask about him? And, Lockhart had said that John Connor had left the *Kuttabul*. Although at least Connor had told Lockhart where he'd gone.

Connor was a handsome man who would have no trouble finding a partner. And even though the country was at war, if John had found someone with whom to share his life, then Clement was happy for him. His thoughts returned to Veretti. Veretti's whereabouts was more than troubling. But before raising any alarms with the Americans, Clement wanted to question Connor about Veretti. In Kings Cross, he caught a tram for Oxford Street and Victoria Barracks.

Weak sunlight was breaking over the rooftops as he walked back towards his quarters. But his mind was too alive to sleep even for an hour. He sat on the veranda and tried to bring logic to the chaos of the past week, starting on the first day when everything changed. When the men arrived at WESC. Despite his attempts to concentrate, he felt utterly drained. And the cold had seeped into his bones. The previous day and night had been tumultuous. And this day promised to be no different. He ran his hand over his day-old beard. Dragging himself from the chair, he went to the showers, shaved and changed his clothes. While the warm shower had temporarily revived him, and were a welcome panacea for his aching ribs, what he really needed was hours of uninterrupted sleep, and he knew it, but first he wanted to eat, then see Tom Archer.

'Not too long, Major,' the nurse said.

Clement looked along the rows of beds and saw the only tanned skinned man in the ward. Standing beside Archer's bed, he stared at his loyal sergeant, the impish face swollen, and the deep purple hue of bruising was spreading across his face. 'How are you, Tom?'

Archer sat up, his face contorting, trying to smile. 'Right as rain, Clem.'

'So I see.'

'Don't let that worry you. I'm just as pretty on the inside.'

Clement laughed. 'I think it best you stay here for a few days, Tom. I don't want to receive complaints about you scarring young children.'

'She'll be apples, Clem. Just give me a day and I'll be back on my feet. I've been worse. Although you should've seen the other bloke.' Archer's grin faded. 'Saw Mick last night. The night nurse let him in. She's a bonza sheila. Sorry. Good sport.'

'Glad you made that clear. Tom, about the man we encountered in the churchyard last night,' Clement paused and turned to see if anyone was listening. 'Was there anything about him you can remember? Anything at all?'

'Sorry Clem. Too dark and all too quick. How's it going?'

Clement allowed a long sigh to escape his lips. 'It was a busy night. Veronica Evans may not be as innocent as she portrays. Nor Mrs McKenzie.'

'Yea. Mick said. At least he got the registration number of that van.'

'Yes. Inspector Lowe is checking on that. I should go, Tom. I'd like to see that body for myself and to hear about the van. Rest. And that's an order. I need you back.'

Archer beamed through the swelling.

Hailing a taxi on Oxford Street, Clement arrived in Central Avenue about fifteen minutes later. He nodded to Constable Roberts who indicated for him to go to Lowe's office on the second floor.

'Good morning, Miss Simpson. Is Inspector Lowe in?'

'With Doctor McCowage, Major.'

'Do you think it would be alright if I were to join him there?'

'I'm sure it will be, Major Wisdom. I bought some tea and biscuits yesterday, if you'd like some on return?'

'Most kind.'

'I'll put an extra cup on the tray then.'

Clement strode to the lift and took it to the lower ground floor. Stepping out, he walked to the double door of the mortuary and pushed it open. McCowage and Lowe looked up as Clement entered.

'Mind if I join you?' Clement said from the door.

'Come in, Clement.'

McCowage returned to his work. 'Close range shot. No stippling, so the weapon was held against the skin. A professional at work with a professional's weapon, I'd say.'

'Anything to identify him, Henry?' Clement asked, avoiding McCowage's remark.

'Curious. And not something most victims have on them at the time of death. But then he wasn't expecting to die. He had a pistol, an odd-looking thing, and a grappling hook. That suggests he works in the wool industry. But as there aren't any farms hereabouts, I'd say he was a wharfie.'

Clement stared at Lowe.

'A docker,' McCowage added.

Clement glanced at McCowage. 'Mind if I have a closer look?'

'Go ahead.'

Clement stared at the body. Not old, but not young either. Lifting the hands, he turned them over, wondering if this was the hand that gripped his shoulder until the muscles went into spasm. The palms showed the skin and callouses of a manual labourer. 'How old was he?'

'Mid-forties would be my guess,' McCowage said. 'Despite his evident strength from well-developed musculature, especially in his upper arms and thighs, he's had a lifetime of manual work. He's got early signs of arthritis in his joints and considerable crepitation in his knees. I'm guessing I'll see some compression in the spine and perhaps a few fractures. Goes with the job.'

'Can I see the pistol?'

'In there,' McCowage said, his blood-soaked gloved finger pointing to the room off to one side. 'Clothes are there too. I figured you'd want to see them.'

Lowe and Clement walked into the adjacent room. The pistol was slim with a grooved pistol grip and a narrow barrel. 'It's reminiscent of a Luger. But the barrel's narrower.' Clement held it in his palm. Engraved along the hilt were four Japanese characters. He thought of Evelyn who doubtless could translate it. 'I've seen nothing like it before.'

'Would Colonel Ravenscroft be able to identify it?' Lowe asked.

'More than likely. It is possible, Henry, that it was kept as a souvenir from the last war. Even though the Japanese were on our side then, a lot of men brought home mementoes. But Ravenscroft should know about it.'

'I'll get it checked,' Henry added.

'Has it been fired?'

'Yes. Only seven bullets in the magazine. It holds eight,' Lowe said.

Clement thought back to the previous night in the graveyard. But if this man had been shot by Archer's Welrod and Bert Smith had been stabbed by someone near the gate, when had this pistol been fired? 'And the grappling hook?'

'Standard equipment, if he's a waterside docker moving cargo, especially wool bales. I'll get in touch with the union. If he's been employed at the wharves for years, they'll know who he is.'

Clement shifted his gaze to the clothes. The trousers, complete with bracers, were made of heavy blue cloth as was the shirt. A black woollen and leather short coat and heavy workman's boots lay beside the trousers. Both showed years of use and wear. Clement thought back on the men he'd seen leaving the Garden Island Dockyards. But while it was concerning, it wasn't hard proof that

Charlie had worked there. 'Can you let me know about any forensic tests? Especially if there are any mould spores or traces of engine oil?'

'Of course. Where will you be today?'

Clement looked at his watch. 'I should attend WESC today.'

'Good. I want to see if Miss Seaton had shown up yet. I sent Preston first thing this morning.'

'Was she there?' Clement interrupted.

'No.'

'Will you be talking to Veronica Evans and Mrs McKenzie about their movements last night?'

'Yes. I can go now. I'll give you a lift, if you like.'

Clement followed Lowe downstairs to the car, and they drove across town to Clarence Street. It was almost ten when they pulled up outside. Alighting, Clement opened the door, and he and Lowe climbed the stairs to the middle floor.

Clement stared at the office door. It was closed. Through the glass panel, he could see Mrs McKenzie's coat and hat on the stand in her private office beyond. But the coat-stand in the front office where Peggy Seaton usually sat, was empty, as was her chair.

'She's done a runner, that's for sure,' Lowe said. 'I'll put out a description of her to all the police stations. She can't have gone far.'

'I don't see Veronica's green coat and hat on the stand either. Sit in here, Henry. They must be upstairs. I'll let them know you'd like to speak with them.' Hurrying, he went to the upper floor. Through the door, he could see Mrs McKenzie standing in front of the class.

'I'll be taking class today. Miss Evans has called in sick. Tune your transmitters to UHF frequencies and we'll begin.'

Clement returned to the middle floor and told Lowe that Veronica wasn't there.

'You stay in the class, Clement. I'll pick up Preston from the police station and then go to Glebe to interview Miss Evans.'

Lowe returned to the street, and Clement went upstairs and took his seat. Behind him, he saw Joe. Seated in the back row were Jim Lockhart and John Connor.

It surprised Clement that, although he felt exhausted, his hand scribbled down Kana Morse with the efficiency of an expert. He'd struggled with standard Morse Code for months, but suddenly, even Kana seemed like second nature, and he was actually finding the task easy. Thirty minutes later, Mrs McKenzie collected the transcripts and announced a morning tea break. Joe stood, then pulled his chair beside Clement's.

'How's Tom?' Joe whispered.

'He'll live. He's a tough man.'

'Any news?'

'The deceased from the churchyard is most likely a dock worker. He had a Japanese pistol on him.'

Joe frowned. 'Well, that confirms your theory about espionage.'

'Perhaps. Has Mrs McKenzie shown any sign of her knowing you were watching her?'

'None.'

'Hello again,' John Connor stood beside them. 'Jim says you visited him on the *Kuttabul* very early this morning. Anything wrong?'

'I'll ask you the same question, John. When was the last time you saw Veretti on the *Kuttabul*?'

'I've never seen him there. But then I haven't been there for a while myself. My father's in town, so I've been staying with my auntie in Annandale.'

Mrs McKenzie entered the room and walked straight up to Clement. 'Could I have a word, Mr Wisdom?'

Clement shot a glance at Joe.

'My office I think.'

Clement followed her to the middle floor. Opening the office door, Mrs McKenzie switched on the light and led him through to her office, closing the door. 'Major, I'm anxious about Veronica. She isn't ill. At least not that I know of. When she didn't arrive in time to start the class, I stepped in. I thought it unusual, but perhaps with all that's been going on she'd slept in and would arrive later. But when morning tea came, and she still hadn't arrived, I telephoned her home. It just rang and rang. In light of all the recent events... I'm so worried about her.'

'Can I use your telephone, Mrs McKenzie?'

'Of course.'

Clement picked up the receiver and dial the number for Central Police Station. 'Inspector Lowe, please. Major Wisdom speaking.'

'I'm just on my way, Clement. Something urgent?'

'Veronica Evans did not arrive at work this morning. And when Mrs McKenzie telephoned, no one answered.'

'You think she didn't return home last night?'

'More than possible,' Clement said.

'So, is she involved?'

'I couldn't say.'

'Ah! You're being overheard. I'll collect you in five minutes.'

Clement went straight outside and waited on the footpath. Minutes later, the police car pulled up and Clement got straight in. Lowe sped along the street, then onto a bridge heading west.

'It's not far. Just past the greyhound racing track.' Lowe drove quickly, taking narrow streets and through areas of Sydney Clement had never seen. Turning into Gottenham Street, he parked the car some distance from the house. Clement alighted and walked to the end of the road while Lowe went to the front door and knocked. At the corner Clement saw a short flight of steps where he guessed Mick had stood when he witnessed a man and Veronica Evans leave. In one direction, Marlborough Street led back to Glebe Point Road. In the other, down a narrow lane, was the main access street, Bridge Road. Five minutes later, Lowe stood on the footpath and looked in both directions. Seeing Clement, Lowe walked towards him, joining him at the corner.

'No one there. And I couldn't see anyone inside through the front window. Nothing looks disturbed. I'll check the rear lane.'

Clement joined Lowe as they walked around to the rear of the house. A locked gate secured the property from the lane. Lowe pulled himself up to see over the high brick fence. 'No sign of forced entry that I can see.'

'I don't think you will, Henry. Mick said she went with him. Did you trace the van?'

'Yes. It's registered to a butcher in Goulburn. And reported as stolen three months ago.'

'Where's Goulburn?'

'It's about a four to five-hour drive south of Sydney.'

'What happens there?'

'Farming community. Sheep and cattle, mostly. There's a railway and a prison, quite a few pubs and it's freezing in winter.'

'It's vital we find this van. Do you have any leads on the identity of the deceased?'

'A union bloke is coming in around noon.' Lowe checked his watch. 'We should get back. Central Avenue or Clarence Street, Clement?'

'Central Avenue, if you please, Henry.'

'I thought you might say that.'

Clement sat in Lowe's office. A minute before twelve, Lowe's phone rang. 'Escort him to the mortuary, would you Preston? We'll meet you there.' Lowe hung up. 'After you, Clement.'

McCowage met them at the door. Clement could see the union official was a large man, thick set with heavy jowls and rough hands.

'Ever seen a dead body before, Mr...' McCowage asked.

'Keenan. Only my old mother.'

'Not quite the same. This way then, Mr Keenan,' McCowage said, opening the door wide.

'I'm Inspector Lowe. This man is my assistant,' Lowe said, indicating Clement.

Clement nodded but didn't speak.

McCowage drew back the shroud. 'Holy Mother! It's Charlie Manning.'

'Does he have a family? Wife?'

'She died a few years ago. No kids that I know of. I'll take a collection for his funeral and wake. We'll see him done right.'

'Know anything of his private life?' Lowe asked.

'Not much,' Keenan shrugged. 'He lived in Woolloomooloo. Above the pub. Kept to himself.' Keenan scratched his head. 'Although, once I saw him collected from work in a car by a very swanky woman. I remember wondering what she would want with him. He had nothing much, expect brawn. Strong bloke.'

Clement rubbed his shoulder. 'Do you know where he was working recently?'

'He was at Garden Island with about a thousand others on the night shift.'

Clement caught a tram back to Clarence Street. In view of the circumstances, he hoped Mrs McKenzie wouldn't be too upset with him absconding from class for an entire morning. Alighting in York Street, he strode

173

towards the WESC. Opening the door, he went straight to the upper floor. Mrs McKenzie was rubbing the blackboard clean.

'Mr Wisdom? Any news?'

Clement gazed at the empty room. All the chairs were placed up on the desks for the day. 'She wasn't at home,' he said, watching the woman. 'But Inspector Lowe is looking for her. I'm sure she'll be alright. Perhaps she is unwell and went to a relative's house. We'll find her.' Clement again surveyed the empty room. 'You've cancelled the class for today?'

'I've had to. Miss Howard didn't arrive.'

CHAPTER EIGHTEEN

Tuesday 26th May 1942

Without waiting, Clement ran down the stairs to the office and telephoned the Central Police Station. His hand was shaking when he dialled the number and asked for Lowe.

'Right! I'll pick you up in a few minutes,' Lowe said. 'We'll try the guest house first.'

Clement's heart was pounding. Despite his exhaustion, adrenaline was coursing through his body and his mind. Running from the WESC building, he remembered he'd told Mick to meet him in St Phillip's church. He checked his watch. It was already one o'clock. As he ran to the church, he kept one eye on the street for Lowe and the other on his running feet. His mind was on Evelyn. He'd always wondered if she was the intended target or just an added bonus to some other more intricate enemy plan. As he approached the church, he saw Mick patiently waiting in the porch. 'Mick, sorry I'm late.'

'Thought you may have forgotten. But then I said to myself, no Clem wouldn't do that.'

'Thank you for your confidence, Mick. I have to go with Inspector Lowe. Go back to the barracks. Stay in the briefing room. I'll telephone you there if I need you. And, Mick, have your weapons with you, including that rifle you brought with you from Brisbane.'

Leaving Mick, Clement returned to WESC and stood pacing the pavement outside the entry. 'Think!' he told himself. Evelyn. Where was she? Did they know her importance? In his mind, he tried to remember everything he'd overheard outside Peggy Seaton's house. It wasn't much. What little there was centred only on Tom's identity. Evelyn hadn't been mentioned once. If she were the intended victim, why had they taken Veronica? Clement truly believed WESC was pivotal. He just didn't know how. Looking up, he saw the police car coming down Clarence Street.

Lowe's car drew up beside him, and reaching for the door handle, Clement got in. Sitting in the police car, with the siren blaring, he leaned his head against the window. He was beyond needing sleep now. Adrenaline was keeping him going. He knew enough about Evelyn Howard to know she wouldn't go anywhere willingly without someone knowing where she was. Especially so, in view of recent events. If she had been taken, he also knew she would do everything in her power to leave some sort of trail. He gazed at the ironwork arch above his head as they crossed the Harbour Bridge and headed for Cremorne. 'Perhaps I should enquire about her, Henry? And I think we should turn the siren off as we get closer.'

'You think she's there?'

'I don't know where she is. But if something is going on there, we don't want to alert them prematurely.'

'Agreed.'

Lowe cut the siren on approach, then parked the police car higher up Musgrave Street. Getting out, Clement walked to the imposing house. As he climbed the front steps, he prayed she had a cold and had gone to bed. He pressed the doorbell.

'It's you again,' Nigel said, his hand on the door.

'Who is it, Nigel?'

Clement heard the woman's voice call from somewhere in the house.

'It's Mr Wisdom. Who are you here to see this time?'

Clement stepped into the vestibule. The door to the sitting room was closed, and the house was silent. Mrs Pendleton appeared and glided towards him. She was drying her hands on a small towel, which she rolled into a ball then shoved it into an apron she was wearing.

'Is Miss Howard in?' Clement asked.

'Miss Howard? Why no! She left as usual for work this morning.'

'What time would that have been?'

'A little after eight, I think. I don't keep tabs on my guests.'

'Did anyone see her go?'

'What's this about?'

'She didn't arrive at work this morning. So any information you can give would be helpful. Do you recall what she was wearing?'

'An overcoat and hat, I think. I didn't pay that much attention, I'm sorry.'

'May I see her room?' Clement asked, his gaze on the stairs to the upper floor.

'Absolutely not! I don't allow members of the public to just wander around my guests' rooms. What an extraordinary request! Now if I've answered your questions, I have work to do.'

'Of course. When she returns, would you please ask her to telephone WESC? It is important.'

'Very well. Nigel, show Mr Wisdom out.'

Clement left the house. He walked away up the street towards the police car. Lowe was still seated behind the wheel when Clement got in.

'Well?' Lowe asked.

'Very cold reception! Mrs Pendleton says Evelyn left for work this morning as usual. But she wouldn't let me in to see her room. If we haven't heard from Evelyn before tonight, I think you should search her room. But you'll need a warrant to do it.'

'I'll arrange it this afternoon. Where would you like me to drop you?'

'Victoria Barracks, please Henry. I want to check on Archer and I need a few hours' sleep. You'll check on Evelyn as soon as you have the warrant?'

Lowe nodded. 'If she hasn't contacted either you or me by ten tonight, I'll put out a missing person report. Once I have the warrant, I'll search her room. It's odd, don't you think, that Miss Howard and Miss Evans have both disappeared?'

'Not forgetting Miss Seaton. It isn't coincidental, Henry.'

Thanking Lowe for the lift, Clement walked into the barracks and went straight to the briefing room.

'Mick, thank you for being here. Leave your weapons here, I need to speak to you and Archer. Walking across the barracks, they entered the infirmary. Tom was lying on his side in the bed reading *Smith's Weekly*. Clement thought he looked bored to ribbons.

'How are you, Tom?' Clement asked.

'Better than you, by the look of you, Clem.' Tom sat up straight and stared at Clement. 'I've seen that look before! What's up?'

'Are you well enough to do a job?'

'Yep. Where and when?'

'Tonight. I need you and Mick with me.'

Four hours later, the alarm woke Clement, and he rose from his bed. He'd fallen asleep almost immediately after putting his head on the pillow. Going straight to the briefing room, he telephoned Lowe.

'Any news of Evelyn?'

'Nothing.'

'Right. Did you get the warrant?'

'Yes.'

'Will you go tonight?'

'I'd planned to.'

'Can you give me a few hours?'

'You think she's there?'

'I'm hoping she is. But I think it may be best not to alert Mrs Pendleton.'

There was a long pause. 'By delaying, you could jeopardise her safety,' Lowe said.

'I have given this much thought, Henry. She is trained in self-defence, and she has a Fairbairn Sykes knife. Not one I supplied.'

'Right.' Lowe paused. 'A few hours.'

Clement replaced the telephone receiver then checked his watch; five o'clock. Hoping Mrs McKenzie was still at WESC, he dialled the school number.

'Hello?' Clement recognised Mrs McKenzie's voice.

'It's Clement Wisdom speaking. Mrs McKenzie, other than myself, was there anyone else missing from class today?'

'In fact, two people, Major. Joan Olivant and John Connor.'

Leaving the barracks, Clement, along with Tom and Mick, took the tram to Circular Quay. The sunset had come and gone, its pale light quickly disappearing. Clement bought three return tickets for the six o'clock ferry. Handing a ticket each to Tom and Mick, they boarded the Cremorne Point ferry and sat in different places around the small ship. Clement scrutinised every face he could see. But he didn't recognise anyone. At Cremorne Point Wharf, he strode down the gangplank and started walking up Musgrave Street. From the corner of his eye, he saw Tom and Mick following. Once away from the wharf and evening commuters, he waited by the entrance to the side pedestrian path for Tom and Mick to join him.

'That's the guest house,' Clement said, pointing. 'Tom, you wait at the bus stop. Mick, you go further up the street. But don't lose sight of this path. I'll signal you if I need you from here.'

Clement walked along the narrow lane leading to the street behind. It was well used despite the overgrown shrubs that bordered it. He remembered Joe telling him about a garage there. Rounding the corner, he saw it. It was an old, dark brick building with a tiled, pitched roof and windows at the top of the double garage doors. Both these windows were made of frosted glass, and both were covered in brown paper. The wooden garage doors facing the street were secured with a padlock. Clement studied the scratched concrete Joe had told him about and knew the doors opened outwards and were in regular use. Beside the garage was a high brick fence. Clement looked around to see if he was alone. But now it was dark, and the moon wasn't high enough in the sky yet to cast its light over the scene. He felt sure, even if someone was looking out their window, he wouldn't be seen. Reaching up, he grasped the top edge of the brickwork and pulled himself slowly up and looked over the edge. Beyond, he saw into a large rear garden. No one appeared to be there. In the centre of the lawn was a small circular flagged stone sitting area under a pergola. There were several deck chairs there. On the other side of the garden and nearer to the rear of the garage, was a washing line. Beyond, the house looked as though all doors and windows had been closed in anticipation of a cold night. From the glare of lights from the house, it was possible for him to see the rear garden clearly. His gaze moved along the windows and doors. While most curtains were drawn, several had cracks of light where the curtains didn't close properly. The blackout restrictions were, evidently, not strictly enforced by the landlady. He stared at the house in disbelief. None of the doors or windows that faced into the rear garden had been covered in brown paper. In fact, lights blazed everywhere. Lifting his gaze, he saw three attic dormer windows set into the roof line. These rooms were not visible from the front of the house. He frowned. None of these windows were covered either. In fact, not one window in the entire house was covered. Frowning, he focused his eyes on every window on the middle floor, studying each, wondering which was Evelyn's room. He stopped, his eyes wide. An icy shudder spread through him. At the end window, he saw something on the windowsill. Clement jumped down and ran back along the footpath to Musgrave Street. Signalling Tom and Mick, they joined him in the laneway.

'What is it?' Tom said.

'Do you have any binoculars on you, Tom?'

'No, but Mick does. A telescopic sight he always has with him.'

'Belonged to my grandfather. So it's not army issue. When you want a clean shot, you learn it's always useful to see the target up close.'

'Well done, Mick. May I borrow it?'

Mick reached into his overcoat and withdrew the item then handed it to Clement.

'Stay here, Mick!' he said. 'Tom with me.'

They ran around to the rear of the house. 'I'll give you a hoy up,' Tom said.

Clement stared. 'A what?'

'You know, a lift up. Like a stirrup,' Tom said, intertwining his fingers.

'Right.' Clement put his left foot into Archer's cupped hands and hoisted himself up the wall then propped his left elbow against the brick fence. He peered over the wall, then placed the sight to his right eye, and focused it on the last window. He felt his face fall. On the windowsill was a single shoe.

Clement dropped to the ground. 'Tom, that shoe you found in the park opposite the school; did you ever find the pair? Did you look for it at the time?'

'I had a quick look for it under the nearby plants, but I didn't find it. Why?'

Clement grinned. 'She's there. And I'm guessing not by choice. She's found the connection between these people and Edwina Hughes.'

'What?'

'Edwina's other shoe.'

'How are we going to do this?' Archer asked.

CHAPTER NINETEEN

Tuesday 26th May 1942

Clement crouched in the side lane as darkness fell around them. Music was coming from inside the house. It surprised Clement how loud it was. With Tom and Mick each patrolling the perimeter fences in opposite directions, they crossed over every six minutes. Clement ran to the front and crouched in the shrubs. Before him, he could see the front veranda. All the windows to the sitting room on the right now had the curtains drawn. The room on the left where he'd spoken to Joan was dark. He lifted his gaze to the upper floor. Several lights were on in rooms on the right side of the house, but again the drawn curtains prevented him from seeing anyone. One light was visible behind a closed blind on the left-hand side. Leaving the front, he returned to the rear and studied the house. From the rear boundary, he could see three attic windows where there were no curtains and where lights blazed. Below them, the upper floor windows were dark, except the two end rooms. Clement lifted the scope again and stared at the shoe placed on the sill. 'Get Mick, Tom.'

Tom disappeared into the side lane. Looking through the scope, Clement focused it on the shoe. 'Clever woman,' Clement whispered. Minutes later, both Archer and Savage stood beside him.

'This is what we'll do.'

Scaling the fence, Clement and Mick dropped into the rear garden and, hunching low, crossed the lawn. Clement signalled to Mick to stay hidden in the shrubs near the garage and from where he knew Mick would have a good view of the rear of the house and all the windows facing the garden. Staying low, Clement ran along the northern side of the house to the front. Waiting only seconds, he climbed onto the front veranda and went straight to the window into the front room on the left. Using his lock picks, he slipped the window lock, then waiting only seconds, pulled himself through it. Standing in the cold room, he crept around the furniture and tiptoed towards the door to the front hall and listened.

The music was loud, but he could hear voices and the occasional burst of laughter. Closing his eyes to concentrate, he listened for any activity in the hall. Nothing. Rotating the handle, he opened the door a crack and peered out. The front hall was bright and the sitting room opposite was lit, an open fire glowed in the grate. Easing the door open, he stepped into the vestibule, his eyes wide, his hand reaching for his knife. To his left was the staircase. It was old with timber treads which Clement knew would creak under his weight. Keeping his feet on the edge of each step, and climbing two at a time, he silently went upstairs, pausing on the top step. Easing his head around the corner, he looked down the corridor in both directions. Below him, he heard a door open. Staying close to the wall, he peered over the banister. The boy, Nigel, was carrying a tray and heading for the stairs.

Clement stepped into the upper hall and, tiptoeing, hurried down it to his left, towards where he hoped he'd find Evelyn. On his left, and opposite the end bedroom was a small alcove that held two closed doors. He slipped into it, his ears straining for sounds of footsteps. Quickly trying the handles and opening each in turn, he found one led into a bathroom, the other to the lavatory. Stepping inside the bathroom, he stood behind the door and listened. The footsteps seemed more distant. Clement breathed out, realising Nigel had gone to the opposite end of the house. Opening the door, he slipped into the short hall and pressed himself against the wall. Edging his head around the corner, he could see Nigel standing outside a door further along the corridor. In one hand he held a tray, in the other were keys. As the door opened, Clement heard the shattering scream.

Pulling back into the alcove, he held his breath as the terrifying sound carried down the hall. It lasted less than thirty seconds then silence. Staying where he was, he waited. A few minutes later, he heard a door open again. Edging his eye around the corner, he saw Nigel returning to the stairs, carrying the tray. Clement left the short hall and went to the room at the end where he hoped he'd find Evelyn. Using his lock picks, he rotated the barrel, then slowly opened it and slipped inside.

A knife was at his throat. But the arm around his neck was a woman's. 'Evelyn?'

She stepped in front of him. 'You took your time, Clement.'

'Get your coat, then we'll leave by the rear door.'

'Not without Veronica and Joan.'

'They're both here?'

'Not sure about Joan. A woman is definitely here. I've heard her screaming. I don't know who it is. Like me, she's probably locked in. But I know Veronica is here. She was coming out of the bathroom as I was leaving the lavatory. She was tricked into coming. A man went to her home and told her he was Peggy's uncle. Said she was ill and persuaded Veronica to help. She found the shoe in the van. I'm sure we'll find it matches the one Tom found in the park.'

Clement checked his watch. 'We need to hurry. Do you know where Veronica is?'

'No, but I think there is someone next door. But there's someone else upstairs.'

'In the attic?'

'Yes.'

'We don't have the time to check, I'm sorry.'

'Why? What's happening?'

'Tom will pound on the front door in five minutes. We must leave now.'

Evelyn grabbed her overcoat and put it on. Clement opened the door to the corridor a crack and peered out. Seeing it clear, they both stepped into the hall and Clement, using his lock picks, relocked the door. Listening for any sounds, Clement crept to the next door.

'Veronica? It's Evelyn,' Evelyn whispered through the door.

Inserting the lock picks, Clement slipped the lock and pushed open the door. Evelyn stepped into the doorway. Veronica was standing by the window, a wooden desk chair raised and firmly grasped in her hands. 'Veronica don't scream! It's me. Grab your coat and come now.'

'Is this a trick?'

'No! We're being rescued, but we need to hurry.'

Clement waited in the hall by the door, his gaze fixed on the top of the staircase for anyone approaching, his Welrod in his grip. Evelyn and Veronica stepped into the hall. Then a light went on downstairs, illuminating the upper hall.

'Inside,' Clement whispered, and they returned to Veronica's room. Clement locked the door. Without moving, they waited. Clement heard the footsteps in the corridor, but they too seemed to be going to the other end of the house.

'Are they bringing you supper?' he whispered.

'Not me,' Veronica said.

'Nor me. That boy brought me some food at seven, if that's what they call it. The thinnest gruel I've ever seen.'

Clement's thoughts went to the pathologist's report of Hank Veretti's stomach contents. Listening again, he heard the footsteps return along the corridor.

Clement checked his watch. 'We have to go!' he whispered. Opening the door, he peered into the corridor again. The light in the upper hall had been switched off. Beckoning behind him, they crept along the corridor to the staircase, and Clement peered over the banister into the front hall below. From the light in the lower front hall, Clement could see the door to the sitting room was closed.

Leaning against the wall, they crept slowly downstairs. Music was once again coming from the sitting room. Although Clement hadn't previously been in the house further than the entry foyer, he guessed there was a back hall. Moving more quickly now, he opened each door, until he saw the rear door to the garden. Ushering Evelyn and Veronica inside, he closed the door to the hall.

As they moved swiftly towards the back door, a side door from the scullery into the kitchen opened. Nigel stood facing them, his surprised expression mirroring Clement's own. Clement stared at the tray in Nigel's hands. It held a kidney-shaped dish with several cotton wool swabs in it. Lying beside it was a full syringe.

Clement withdrew his knife and stepped closer to the startled boy. 'One sound and it will be your last.'

In that instant, Clement heard the pounding on the front door. Nigel dropped the tray, the contents crashing to the floor.

'Hold your knife on him, Evelyn?'

'With pleasure.'

Clement locked the door to the hall. 'Veronica, pick up that syringe on the floor and bring it with you. Be careful though. Time to leave.'

'And Nigel?' Veronica asked.

'Sit down Nigel,' Clement said. 'Who is upstairs?'

'Mother!' Nigel screamed.

Clement lunged forward, sending the boy falling to the floor. Evelyn grabbed the syringe in Veronica's hand and stabbed the contents in Nigel's thigh. Leaving the boy on the floor, screaming for his mother, Evelyn wrapped the syringe in a tea towel, and pocketing it, they left the house. Without looking back, they ran across the lawn to the rear fence.

Ahead, Clement saw Mick had placed an upturned wheelbarrow against the fence. Smiling, Clement pointed to it as Evelyn and Veronica ran towards the stone wall.

'There's a side lane to your left. Wait there,' Clement called.

'Where are you going?' Evelyn asked.

'To help Tom.' Clement doubled back, heading for the side garden. 'Mick, with me!'

Rounding the corner of the house, they climbed onto the front veranda. Then a single shot rang out.

CHAPTER TWENTY

Wednesday 27th May 1942

'Mick! Wait three minutes, then come to the front door.'
Clement climbed through the overgrown bushes at the
side of the house and ran along the front veranda, his
Welrod in his hand. The front door was open, the door
and lock splintered. Staying close to the door, Clement
crept in. Keeping his body close to the wall, and checking
the stairs to his left, he edged himself towards the door
to the sitting room and leaned his head around the archi-
trave. To his right he could see Tom in the sitting room,
his Welrod raised. In front of him were two men Clement recognised as Colonel Reeve and Mr Bretton. Both
looked terrified. To one side, standing by a small open
Davenport desk was Muriel Pendleton. Her left arm
rested on the desk's slope, her hand edging towards the
drawers.

Clement kicked the door wide and rushed into the
room. 'Take your hand away from the desk and stand
with the others,' he said, pointing his weapon at the
woman.

Muriel's eyes widened, her gaze fixed on Clement. In a second, she flung open the drawer, and withdrew a pistol. With no time to aim, and the weapon in her left hand, she pulled the trigger. Clement lunged forward, grabbing the woman, his hand reaching for the pistol. As she struggled, the pistol discharged, the bullet lodging in the ceiling.

Tom rushed for the pistol. Clement held the woman, her arms pinned behind her body. 'Sit with the others!' Clement said, moving Muriel Pendleton to the piano stool where the two men sat. Clement turned the pistol over in his left hand. He saw the Japanese characters engraved in the weapon. 'This will see you hang.' Clement pushed the pistol into his belt then shifted his gaze to Tom. 'There's a telephone in the hall. Call Inspector Lowe.' Clement faced Mrs Pendleton, his Welrod gripped in his right hand. 'Who are you keeping prisoner upstairs?'

Muriel laughed. 'And why would I tell you that?'

'Because they may not shoot you, but I certainly will!' a female voice behind him said. Evelyn stood in the door, Mick's Welrod in her hand.

'Yes, I think you could. Well, you have me,' Muriel said, her lips curling into a smirk, the gesture defiant. 'But nothing now will stop our plans. Kill me, if you wish. I'm not important.'

From somewhere in the house, Clement heard a door slam. He stepped closer to the woman. 'Who else is in the house?'

Muriel beamed. 'No one. Now.'

'Where is Joan?' Evelyn asked.

'Joan? Joan Olivant! I'd like to know that myself. She owes me rent.'

Leaving Tom and Evelyn to watch the group, Clement walked into the front hall. There he saw Mick and Veronica. 'Mick, can you wait outside for Inspector Lowe?'

'I can do that, Mr Wisdom. Private Savage and I heard what just happened. I'll look after Inspector Lowe. We also heard that door slam. Someone is definitely upstairs.'

Clement waited until Veronica was safely outside.

'Mick, stay here at the bottom of the stairs. Detain anyone who comes down. With force if necessary. I'll call if I need you.' Clement ran up the stairs. The upper hall was dark. He listened for any sounds of a presence. But nothing came to him. Finding the light switch, he turned on the hall lights and looked along the corridor in both directions. Still no sound. He thought back to what Evelyn had told him. She said she'd heard sounds from the room above hers. Creeping along the corridor, he first checked the bathroom and lavatory, then opened the door to Evelyn's room. He stood in the centre of the room and listened. Nothing. Was it possible whoever had been upstairs had now moved? Were they still in the house? He paused in the doorway to Evelyn's room with his gaze on the corridor and listening for any movement. Stepping back into the hall, he felt a rush of cold air. Hurrying, he relocked Evelyn's room and crept along the corridor. The cold draught lasted only a few seconds. It was replaced with an eerie silence. He suspected someone had opened and closed a window. With his Welrod raised, he crept to the next room; the one occupied by Veronica. He unlocked it and stepped inside. While it had an identical layout to Evelyn's, unlike Evelyn's room, there were no personal items there. He knew immediately that Veronica had told the truth. She had been imprisoned there. But not for long. His gaze rested on the window. Walking towards it, he tried the latch. It was locked. Standing by the window, he looked out. But in the darkness, he saw no one.

Relocking Veronica's door, he stood in the hall and listened. Below him, he could see Mick at the base of the stairs. Mick's gaze was on him. That left three more rooms. His eye went to the closed doors of each. One faced to the rear of the house. The other two faced the front.

Trying the handle to the first room facing the front, he unlocked the door. Stepping inside, he saw immediately the room was used by a man and a man who lived there permanently. Photographs sat on bureaus, trousers hung over a valet stand. Clement reached for one photograph. He could see it was of Colonel Reeve and Mr Bretton, although years younger and taken on a stage surrounded by theatrical props. Clement walked to the wardrobe and opened the door. It was filled with men's clothes. Turning around, his eye surveyed the cluttered room. To one side was a door. Going to it, Clement found it unlocked. It led into the other room facing Musgrave Street. It, too, was occupied by a man. Clothes were scattered around the room. Going to the wardrobe, he opened it. Inside, there appeared to be theatrical costumes. Brightly coloured and elaborate.

Closing the wardrobe door, he returned to the corridor. He stood, listening. Again nothing. He stared at the door to the room that faced the rear garden. Holding his Welrod, he leaned against the wall, his hand reaching for the doorknob. This door was unlocked. Twisting the handle, and using his foot, he kicked it open.

Pointing the pistol into the room, he stood in the open doorway. The room was empty. He looked at the window. From where he stood, he could see it was closed, and the handle latched. He felt an icy shiver. Checking behind the door, he stepped into the room and quickly surveyed it. Here the furniture was arranged differently, and the bed linen appeared crumpled as though it had been occupied for some time. He walked over to the bed and pulled back the bedcovers. There was a small patch of dried and fresh blood on the edge of the sheets. On the bedside table was a bowl of thin soup. Clement stared at it then put his hand on the bowl. It felt warm. Whoever had occupied this room had left in a hurry. Or been removed. Crossing the room, Clement opened all the drawers in a chest under the window. Nothing. A suitcase sat in the corner. He placed it on the bed and prized open the lock. A blue coat and hat lay crumpled on top of several other items of women's clothing. He recognised the blue coat immediately. He felt his heart sinking. But where was she? And what of Joan?

Outside the room, Clement heard the floorboards creak. Running back to the open door, he waited before stepping into the hall. A shot at close range rang out, the bullet whizzing past his face and lodging in the door frame. Clement drew back and waited. His heart was pounding. He edged forward, his face peering around the doorframe. Another shot. Pulling back again, he heard running feet.

'Mick!' Clement shouted from the inside the doorway.

'Coming!'

Clement heard Mick's running feet in the hall. He ran into the bedroom. 'Clem? You alright? I heard a couple of shots. Where are they?'

'You didn't see anyone? In the hall?'

'No.'

'Dear Lord! We've missed them!' Clement understood in a second. The second shot had made him call Mick and as soon as Mick had joined him, whoever had been hiding had disappeared downstairs.

Rushing to the window, he threw it open and peered out into the darkened garden below. There, he saw two men and a woman running across the lawn. Dashing out of the room, Clement raced down the stairs to the kitchen door and ran outside. In the street beyond, he heard a vehicle driving away.

CHAPTER TWENTY-ONE

Wednesday 27th May 1942

Keeping his Welrod in his grip in case anyone remained there, he slowly opened the small door to the garage. With his Welrod raised, he craned his head around the edge of the door and peered into the space. It was dark and a strong wind was blowing into the garage from the street. He stared at the open doors swinging in the wind. He'd be so close! Only a few minutes sooner and he'd have caught them. Sheathing the Welrod, he closed the large garage doors, then returned to the house.

Lowe was inside when Clement walked into the front hall. He told Lowe what had happened.

'Did you get a look at their faces?'

Clement shook his head. 'I'm sorry, Henry. If I'd been a few minutes sooner, we'd have the ring leaders. You still have Mrs Pendleton?'

'She's not going anywhere,' Lowe said.

Clement followed Lowe into the lounge. Seated in a row on the long piano stool, with their hands secured in police handcuffs, were Mrs Pendleton and the two men, Colonel Reeve and Mr Bretton. Clement scrutinised the two men. They appeared genuinely frightened and from their expressions, he was inclined to believe they were innocently caught up with a group of traitors. But experience had taught him; when it comes to traitors, nothing can be left to chance. And good spies are excellent liars.

He shifted his gaze to the boy Nigel who sat on a low chair, his hands cuffed and his head downcast. Lowe had separated the boy from his mother. Clement stared at the lad. He guessed the boy to be about sixteen. But something about the lad made him appear childlike. Almost infantile. He was agitated, his cuffed hands wringing in his lap, his head twitching. Clement surmised him to be accepting of his situation and no longer a threat to anyone. He glanced at Muriel Pendleton. The woman sat bolt upright, her expression one of resolute defiance. Clement continued to watch her. Not once did she glance at her son. Clement had wondered why Lowe had separated mother from son, but perhaps Lowe recognised something about their relationship he'd seen before. Whatever that was, Clement knew Lowe would have his reasons.

'I know nothing about any of this,' Colonel Reeve was protesting.

'Save it for the interview,' Lowe said. 'Preston. Take these two men and the boy in the police car and put Mrs Pendleton in the police wagon. You'll have to support the lad. Whatever was in that syringe has affected him.'

'Henry, it's possible another is upstairs in one of the attic rooms. Archer and I will check.'

'Not without me, Clement,' Lowe said.

They climbed the stairs to the upper floor. 'Tom, even though I've checked all the rooms on the first floor, check them again. Whoever left just now was moving between rooms. Someone could still be here. And check the bathroom and lavatory hall. Open all cupboards and keep your Welrod in your hand. Be careful! Once you've checked there, come upstairs to the attics.'

Clement and Lowe climbed the narrower stairs to the attic level. Lowe withdrew his pistol. Pausing on the top step, Clement peered around the edge and along the hall. He saw no one. Neither did he feel any icy draughts. Waiting there, he listened for any sounds of movement, but all was silent. In front of him were the three closed doors to the rooms that overlooked the rear garden. He pointed for Lowe to stand to one side of the first door. Leaning against the wall, Clement reached his hand around to the handle. It was locked.

'Open up! Police!' Lowe called.

No one responded.

But Clement felt the icy presence, like the steely gaze from a portrait. They waited in the hall. A full minute lapsed, and nothing stirred.

'I think you may have to use your special skills here, Clement,' Lowe whispered.

Clement heard the tread on the stairs. He glanced sideways and saw Archer join them. 'Anything?' Clement whispered.

Archer shook his head.

Archer held his Welrod at the door as Clement stood to one side of it to pick the lock. Rotating the barrel quickly, and staying on one side, he kicked the door open. Archer rushed in, followed by Clement then Lowe. No one was there. Clement's eyes scanned the room. It wasn't a bedroom. Newspapers were strewn across the floor. A meal tray with used crockery and cutlery was on the table and a radio sat by an armchair. Clement stared at the tray, a frown forming. A small chop bone sat on the plate. Whoever occupied this room had left in haste. And the chop bone suggested this occupant was a guest, not a prisoner. Clement bent to pick up a newspaper. He checked the date, then reached for another paper, then another. The occupant of this room had been there at least a week.

Clement walked over to a door. Standing to one side, he tried the handle. Again locked. Archer raised his boot and kicked it open. The lock gave way in a second, shattering and splintering the door and timber frame. No one called out or screamed, and no shots were fired. Clement stepped into the room. No one was there, and it looked as though no one had occupied the room in a very long time. On the opposite wall was a single bed, a chest of drawers was under the dormer window. A wardrobe leaned against the side wall. Clement gazed around. No personal effects, no photographs. He walked to the wardrobe and opened it. It was full of clothes. Clement ran his hand along the shirts. All pale blue. Two pairs of dark blue trousers hung at the end. Clement's mind was racing. He'd seen similar clothes before, on the body of Hank Veretti.

Lowe stood beside him. 'What's your thinking on this, Clement?'

'I don't know, yet.'

Without waiting for Lowe to respond, Clement walked back into the corridor and strode towards the third and final door. With his pistol raised, he kicked open the door. Again no one was there.

The room contained a table with a straight-backed wooden chair. Nothing was on it except a pencil. Clement realised what had been there. He walked towards the table and ran his hand over the tabletop. Positioning the chair by the window, he reached forward and opened the latch. Pushing it wide, he stood on the chair, then climbed onto the table, then sat on the windowsill. Drawing his legs up, he stood, his back to the garden and, holding the window frame with his left hand, he leaned out. Extending his arm, he ran his fingers along the upper edge of the window.

'Pass me your torch, Tom?' Clement called.

Still grasping the window frame, he held the torch in his right hand and shone it over the wall. He saw the wire attached to the window's timber frame. Keeping the beam on, he traced it upwards to a hole in the eaves. 'Henry, can you check the roof cavity tomorrow in daylight? I suspect you'll find an aerial there.'

'Of course. And I'll check on how Preston is going with that lot downstairs,' Lowe said. Clement climbed back into the room and closed the window. He could hear Lowe calling to his sergeant downstairs.

'Tom, I want to see inside that garage before we go tonight. It may still hold a clue.'

'Like mould and engine oil?'

Descending to the ground floor, Clement and Tom left the house via the kitchen and walked towards the garage. Opening the door, they stepped inside.

'Would you find the light switch, please, Tom?'

A second later, a light came on. Clement stood by the door and gazed at the garage's interior. Shelves holding tools and machine parts lined the walls. In the middle of the floor, was a grate. Clement walked towards it.

'Struth! A mechanic's pit. That would be lined with oil,' Tom said.

Clement shone the torch onto the grate and peered in. He gasped, the action involuntary. His mouth opened, and he could hardly speak. 'Tom, get Inspector Lowe.'

Tom joined him and stared into the pit. 'Bloody hell!'

'Get Inspector Lowe, would you?'

Archer nodded and left.

Clement stared at Peggy. He knew she was dead. Her face had the deathly pallor of rigor mortis, and her eyes were fixed, wide open. He could see her dilated pupils staring into nothingness, and he felt the crushing impact of wasted life.

He closed his eyes, forcing himself to breathe. The image of Veretti and his oil-stained clothes flashed in his mind. Was this where Veretti had drawn his last breath? Clement believed McCowage would find Veretti's blood here. He remembered overhearing mention of a pit when Tom had been held captive inside Peggy's house. Edwina's shoe, found in the van explained how Veretti's blood had been found on her clothing.

Clement ran his hand through his hair as he thought about the four murders. As horrifying as each was, none of it explained Edwina's death. Or why Veretti had been killed? Staring at Peggy Seaton's body, he silently recited the Lord's Prayer. In a world consumed with madness and destruction, why had naïve young women been sacrificed? What cause justified this? Clement felt his jaw clench. Mrs Pendleton held the key. He visualised her defiant expression. It said so much. That she'd been caught didn't seem to matter to her. Clement visualised Nigel, downcast, agitated. Not even her son's plight mattered to her. Whatever was planned would go ahead with or without her.

He returned to the garden to await Lowe. He couldn't look anymore at the tiny body curled up in such a disgusting place. Whichever way Clement thought about it, something major was about to happen. And on a large scale. The wires he'd found extending from the attic room to the eaves confirmed the existence of a radio transmitter. If Mrs Pendleton was spying for the Japanese, she would hang.

'Tom tells me there's a body here,' Lowe said, walking towards Clement.

'Yes. It's Peggy Seaton.'

'What a business!'

'Do you think you can get Mrs Pendleton to tell you what's going on?' Clement asked. 'Because whichever way I look at it, Henry, this is not just murder, it's espionage. And even if she was the woman at *The Australia* who enticed Edwina away, we still don't know if she is the ringleader.'

'I'll do my best, Clement. But there's not much I can do if she refuses to speak.'

Clement pulled his coat around him, then checked his watch. It would be dawn soon. He wondered why this time of night was always so cold. His memory flashed to the ridge above Winchelsea Beach in East Sussex in England and a cold pre-dawn when he and Arthur Morris had lain in wait for a German submarine to rise out of the English Channel. That had been half a world away when he'd first joined the SIS. It seemed a lifetime ago. Pushing his hands deep into his pockets for warmth, he stamped his feet on the damp ground, his memories of the German U-boat surfacing. The very look of them made him shudder. Sinister. Silent. Malevolent. Clement felt the icy finger of foreboding as a seed took root in his brain. He checked his watch. 'Henry, can you get someone to drive me to Mascot?'

'Mascot? To the airport? Where do you want to go, Clement?' Lowe asked.

'Melbourne.'

CHAPTER TWENTY-TWO

Wednesday 27th May 1942

Thanking Lowe for the lift, Clement hurried into the airport. The place was becoming familiar. He slumped into the nearest chair and removed his hat. He knew he must look dishevelled. But what troubled him couldn't wait. His exhaustion could. And, he could sleep on the aeroplane. He stared vacantly at the growing crowd gathering for the flight. It surprised him to see so many people there. Business went on regardless of war. On the wall opposite, he saw a public telephone. He checked his watch. Just after seven. He wanted to telephone Commander Long, but it was unlikely that Long would be in his office yet. He decided to call anyway. Closing the door to the telephone booth behind him, he dialled the memorised number.

'Victoria Barracks,' a quick female voice said.

'Would either Commander Long or Miss Copeland be in currently?'

'Hold the line.'

Clement heard the telephone ring. But it wasn't answered.

A minute later, the receptionist spoke again. 'Is there anyone else who can help you?'

'Do you know if Commander Long will be in today?'

'Hold the line.'

Clement waited.

'Yes. About ten this morning.'

'Thank you. Could I leave a message?'

'Of course. Go ahead.'

'Could you please let Miss Copeland know that Major Wisdom would like to see Commander Long later this morning?'

'Very good.'

Clement hung up, wondering if the message would get through. Regardless, he intended to go. Opening the door, went to the Australian National Airways counter and purchased his ticket.

The flight to Melbourne was scheduled for nine o'clock. With no luggage, he waited in the lounge and stared through the large glass window to the tarmac beyond.

He felt numb. Debilitation and confusion were clouding his judgement. He closed his eyes and thought back on his past; the eighteen months he'd been with the SIS. Once his life had been simple, predictable. When all he had to think about growing potatoes and writing his sermons. But with the war, his life had changed so much and, probably would never be the same again. His thoughts turned to his late wife Mary. He visualised her face, trying to hear her laugh. But while his memories of her would never disappear, they weren't as clear anymore. Screwing his eyes tight, he banished those cherished times from his mind. At least for now. Exhaustion made him maudlin. He stared out through the window at the growing light of a gloomy day. In the distant sky, he caught the instant flash of daylight on the silver metal aeroplane. He watched it descend then land. The high-pitched noise of the aeroplane's engines roared as it approached the terminal, the wind from the rotating propellors sending anything loose scurrying across the tarmac.

Once, air travel had been a novelty. He stood and wandered towards the gate. In Australia, it made sense to fly. Distances were vast and time short.

Minutes later, the descending passengers crossed the wind-swept tarmac and hurried towards the warmth of the terminal building. Most wore military uniforms. His mind went to the aeroplane he'd seen fly over the city five days previously. He hoped that if it had been an enemy aeroplane, the air raid sirens would have sounded.

The loudspeaker broke his thoughts. The flight was boarding. Wrapping his coat around him, he walked out across the tarmac towards the waiting aeroplane and climbed aboard. Taking his seat, he strapped the seatbelt in place, then leaned his head against the porthole window. He was asleep in seconds.

The hostess roused him as they commenced their descent. From the window, he saw the open pastures. The cows still grazed near Essendon Airport. As he stepped from the aeroplane and crossed the tarmac, he saw a car at the side of the enormous hangar that belonged to the *Australian National Airways*. Recognising the WRAN who collected him the last time he flew to Melbourne, he walked towards her. 'Miss McManus, isn't it?'

The girl beamed. 'It is, Major. Nice to see you again, Sir. Any luggage?'

'No. I'm only here today. At least, I hope I'm only here a day.'

'Commander Long is expecting you. I'm to take you straight up as soon as we arrive at the barracks.'

Almost an hour later, they drove into Victoria Barracks, Melbourne. The stone building looked the same as he'd previously seen it earlier in the year, except now it was winter and the Virginia creeper that covered the building had lost its leaves, leaving a strange web-like mesh on the building.

Stepping inside, he smelt the familiar odour of the halls of power: cigarette smoke, bees wax and human endeavour. In the corridors, American uniforms mingled with Australian and Royal Navy and people rushed along scrubbed corridors.

He took the stairs to the upper floor. Long's secretary greeted him. 'Commander Long is in the War Room, Major. You are to go straight in.'

'Thank you, Miss Copeland. And I apologise for my dishevelled appearance.'

'No apology required, Major Wisdom. We all have a job to do.'

Long was standing gazing out the window when Clement walked in. The man's naval jacket hung loose, and he rocked slightly on his feet. He spun around as Clement knocked on the door.

'Ah! Wisdom. What was so urgent it brought you here in person?'

'I need to speak with someone called Lieutenant Rudy Fabian.'

'Take a seat and tell me all about it.'

Clement sat at the long, highly polished war room table and brought Long up to date with events.

'I'm so pleased Miss Howard is safe. The others are a tragedy, but Miss Howard's loss would be disastrous. What's your theory?'

'This is only my opinion and, as yet I cannot prove it.'

'Go on.'

'There is one person who is pivotal in all this. And his name was Hank Veretti.'

'Was?'

'Yes. He was murdered.' Clement informed Long about Veretti's wounds and the method of his death. 'But aside from the double attack, it is my opinion the dead man may not be Veretti.'

'You think he's alive?'

'I don't know. But it's possible someone here does.'

'Who?'

Clement told Long about Joe Watkins's inclusion in the course at WESC and why Joe was there. 'Can I meet this Rudy Fabian?'

'He's a difficult customer, Clement. Secretive.'

Clement laughed.

'Even more secretive than me. He doesn't share information willingly. The Secret Intelligence Bureau has changed since you were last here.'

Clement heard the note of regret in Long's voice, or perhaps it was despair. 'The nation's security may depend on him identifying Veretti. I have a photograph of the deceased. Although it was taken posthumously.'

Clement reached into his coat pocket and handed the envelope to Long.

Long stared at the photograph. 'Not a pretty sight. I'll call Fabian now. You can wait here. I'll ask Miss Copeland to find you something to eat.'

'Would Eric Nave be in his old office?' Clement asked, hoping to reacquaint himself with the code breaker.

'No. They've moved out of Victoria Barracks a little while ago. He and Fabian have a fractious relationship. Best not to have them both in the same building let alone the same room.'

'I'm sorry to hear that,' Clement said.

Long left the room to call Fabian. Clement noted there was a telephone in the War Room, but Long had chosen not to use it. Clement believed Long didn't want him overhearing what was probably going to be a terse conversation with the American lieutenant. Ten minutes later Miss Copeland arrived with a tray of tea and sandwiches.

Clement smiled, then ate the sandwiches.

It was some time before he heard the American accent in the corridor.

'This better not be a waste of my time, Long,' a booming voice said. A short and not unattractive man with neatly combed hair strode into the War Room where Clement was waiting. 'What's this all about?'

Clement stood. 'As your time is so valuable, I won't waste it telling you all about this matter. If it is of interest to you, I'm sure Commander Long can fill you in. I have a photograph of a man who we believe may or may not be Radioman Hank Veretti. If you can confirm his identity, I can return to Sydney.'

'What makes you think I know this guy? I'm an officer, for God's sake.'

'My apologies, Lieutenant. And I should introduce myself. I am Major Clement Wisdom of SIS. I understand you have an interest in this man. It will only take a second, if you'd be so kind as to look at it.' Clement withdrew the picture from the envelope. 'Of course, it was taken in the mortuary, so it may be difficult for you to recognise him. But I have it on good report that as you are interested in this man, and his Purple Heart, you would have a thorough knowledge of him and his service record. And possibly a photograph of him taken at the time of his enlistment.'

'Pretty sure of yourself, Major. I'd sure like to know how you know about my interest in this guy.'

'Sometimes sharing information will deliver a quicker end result, Lieutenant. And usually mutually beneficial.

Especially if the nation's security is on the line. So, if you would take a look, we can both get on with our jobs?'

Fabian pursed his lips, then held the photograph up. 'You see that under the chin, Major. It's small, but it's there. A mole, as big as a dime. Was noted at his medical. Despite what he looks like here, unless that's been painted on, that's Veretti alright. And as far as my interest is concerned, not that it's any of your business, I'm always suspicious of anyone who does anything alone. Especially when that someone has access to highly classified information, and whose actions are more like a guerrilla fighter than a radioman, if you catch my drift.' Fabian looked at Clement in the eye, then thrust the photograph back. 'So, I'm glad he's dead. Because now I don't need to worry about him being a Jap spy.'

Clement returned the picture to the envelope.

'Well, if that's it, Long, I've got important work on right now,' Fabian said.

'Anything you're sending to Leary?' Long asked.

'If Vice-Admiral Leary wants you to know about it, he'll be in touch.' Fabian left the room, his determined footsteps echoing down the hall.

Long drew in a long breath. 'Does it answer your question, Clement?'

Clement raised his eyebrows. 'Doesn't he have to share information with you?'

'It goes first to Vice-Admiral Leary, Commander of Allied Naval Forces in the South-West Pacific. If he deems fit we should know about it, then he gets in touch.'

'Extraordinary! Is he based in Melbourne?' Clement asked.

'Yes. It's not quite what I envisaged when we set up the Combined Operational Intelligence Centre in '40. But while having to pass everything to Leary first does slow everything down, decryption is a slow process anyway, Clement, as I'm sure you recall from your time with Nave. However, there is something else I can share with you. I received a report from FRUMEL about a Japanese submarine continuing to patrol our East coast. This message was intercepted three days ago. And it's still going through detailed decryption. However, it isn't so much about submarine sightings this time. It appears to be a report on the shipping in Sydney harbour, including numbers of aircraft hangars at Mascot. You could well have been right to be concerned about that aeroplane you saw the other day. If I learn anything more, or if indeed you do, please get in touch as a matter of urgency.'

Clement nodded. 'Of course. Can you let me know what the decrypt says when it is completed?'

'You've met the head of that department.' Long paused. 'I'll let you know once I've been informed, if I am. You're welcome to get a billet here, then McManus can take you back to Essendon tomorrow morning.'

'There isn't a flight this afternoon?' Clement asked.

'I'm afraid not. In fact, our national airline is lucky to have any aeroplanes at their disposal. Our own government and the Americans have seconded four DC-3's just today.' Long put his hands into his pockets. 'I may be able to get you a seat on the flight tomorrow or Saturday morning. Just check in with Miss Copeland. I mean this in all sincerity, Major. Clement. You look exhausted. An enforced break will do you the world of good. It's not only good for the body, you know, it does wonders for the brain.'

Clement smiled. He knew Long was right. 'Can I telephone my team and let them know I won't be back tonight?'

'Of course. Miss Copeland will place the call for you. Good luck, Clement. Find out who's behind these abductions and murders.'

'I'll do my best.' Clement walked with Long as far as Long's office. Long disappeared into his inner office and closed the door.

'I have the Officer for the Day at Victoria Barracks, Sydney on the telephone for you, Major,' Miss Copeland said. 'And I'll book your return flight to Sydney, hopefully for tomorrow.'

She handed Clement the receiver and Clement left a message for Archer to notify them of his delay.

CHAPTER TWENTY-THREE

Melbourne
Thursday 28th May 1942

Clement wandered towards the red brick building at the rear of Victoria Barracks in Melbourne. It had been in those tiny offices that he'd first met Commander Eric Nave, Code Breaker and Intelligence expert. Now the building housed records and some accommodation for visiting personnel. It saddened Clement to hear that Nave and the American Fabian had a problematic relationship. As he climbed the stairs to the newly refurbished rooms, he heard a door close. Looking up, he saw a man in naval uniform closing the door to Nave's former office. The man turned around. 'Clement?'

'Eric! How very good to see you. I heard you'd moved out?' Clement said. He shook hands with Nave.

'We have. I just came to see if I'd left anything here by mistake. I'm due at a meeting this afternoon with Long. Are you billeted back here?'

'No. In fact, I'm flying back to Sydney when I can get a seat, hopefully tomorrow.'

'Dinner then. In the mess.'

'I'll look forward to it.'

Nave took the stairs to the lower floor and Clement found the room Miss Copeland had allocated for him to get a few hours' rest. Opening the door, he found a pair of cotton pyjamas at the foot of the bed. He marvelled at women like Miss Copeland. Her ability to get things done reminded him of Mary.

Clement lay on the bed and allowed his mind to drift. Perhaps Long was right about enforced relaxation. Although, relaxation wasn't really the correct word. Until the ringleaders were caught, his mind couldn't completely rest.

He allowed a deep sigh to escape his lips. His ribs only hurt now if he breathed too deeply. He thought about Tom Archer and his admirable loyalty. He owed Archer his life. His mind turned to Evelyn and Veronica. He didn't doubt that the injections of whatever drug the syringe held was intended for them. But perhaps the attack on Evelyn was only to frighten her off. Peggy would have passed on her name and that she taught Japanese. She would also have known that Evelyn worked for Signals Intelligence in Melbourne as part of the Secret Intelligence Bureau. Perhaps that knowledge was enough to see them want her removed and someone had been sent to scare her into leaving WESC. But why had Veronica been kidnapped? Had she been destined for the same fate? Or was she purely a red herring designed to confuse him and Lowe. Clement shook his head. If that was their intention, then it had worked.

At six, he went to the washroom to freshen up then to the mess to meet Nave.

'Long told me you'd moved from the barracks,' Clement said as they sat down.

'Yes. Things have changed. And, in my humble opinion, not for the better. Jack Newman took offence when the British wanted control. That is largely why they didn't come to Australia. Now we have the Americans throwing their weight around. They treat us as though we are rank amateurs. But we press on. I'll miss Evelyn when she's gone. As I imagine you might too?'

Clement felt himself slightly flush. He hoped Nave didn't see it. 'She's an intelligent woman. A lot like my late wife, in many ways. Practical and competent. Also incredibly brave. Do you know anything of her pre-war life, Eric?'

'Not really. She comes from Dorset, I think. It's sad, isn't it. We know so little about the people with whom we work so closely. It's the war.'

Clement glanced around the dining room before speaking. 'I don't suppose you've deciphered anything about Japanese submarine movements around the east coast?'

'What's you interest?'

Clement told Nave about the events of the last ten days.

'My goodness! And you think these people are in contact with the enemy?'

'It would appear so. They are prepared to kill to carry out their plans. Whatever they are. I didn't find the wireless transmitter at the guest house, but I am sure there was one there.'

'If I hear anything, where can I contact you?'

'Victoria Barracks in Sydney. Or through Inspector Lowe at Sydney Central Police.' Clement paused. 'I'm grateful, Eric. I don't want to see you get into any sort of trouble over it, though.'

'For that to occur, Clement they would have to acknowledge I exist.'

CHAPTER TWENTY-FOUR

Friday 29th May 1942

Clement met McManus at the entry to Victoria Barracks Melbourne. It was still dark outside, and the morning air was below freezing. McManus was wrapped in a heavy overcoat and wearing thick gloves. He'd forgotten just how cold winter in Melbourne could be. It was as cold as any winter in East Sussex. He stepped outside and was almost blown off his feet. She smiled as he climbed into the rear seat. It was not yet five o'clock and sunrise was still hours away.

The flight was surprisingly smooth and from the port-hole in the aeroplane he'd seen the last glimpse of a near full moon before the daylight extinguished its glow. A bright, full moon always worried him. It was when the enemy were at their most unpredictable.

The aeroplane landed in Sydney just on daylight. Archer was there to meet him.

'Learn anything useful for us?' Archer said as they walked outside the terminal.

Clement hailed a waiting taxi. 'I've learned that the body in Inspector Lowe's mortuary is Hank Veretti.'

'Didn't we already know that?'

Clement ignored the remark. 'Has Lowe found the people who left the guest house?'

'Not yet. Mick and Joe spent Wednesday night and last night there watching in case anyone came back to the guest house.'

'And did they?'

'Not Wednesday night. Don't know about last night yet. What do you want to do now?'

'Are they both at the barracks now?'

'They'll be back soon. Inspector Lowe has been sending some of his men to watch the place during the day. Mick and Joe get back around eight.'

They travelled back to Victoria Barracks in silence. Clement paid the fare, and they walked inside. Clement checked his watch. It was too early for the mess to be open.

'Can you get me some breakfast, Tom?'

'Sure thing, Clem. What would you like?'

'Eggs and toast would be nice.'

'What did Commander Long say?'

'Two eggs, thank you, Tom.'

Clement walked towards the briefing room as the sun broke over the rooftops of Sydney's eastern suburbs. He stared up into the morning light. He thought about the full moon he'd seen during his flight back from Melbourne and despite the wintry weather, he knew a full moon cast so much light that everything below was bathed in a monochrome display. It was an ideal time to launch a raid. Frowning, he opened the door to the briefing room and, lifting the receiver, dialled the memorised number. 'I know it's early, but I need to speak urgently with Commander Long.'

'He's not in today, Major,' the telephonist said.

'It is urgent.'

'I'll call his home number. Hold the line.'

While he waited, Clement heard a faint roar. Frowning, he listened. The familiar sound of a piston engine grew louder. Lying the telephone receiver on the table, he ran outside and stood next to the parade ground, looking up into a cloudy sky. Through the low clouds, he saw the wings. An aircraft flew low overhead, heading west over the city. Squinting, he tried to see any markings, but the aeroplane disappeared into a bank of thick clouds further to the west. He ran back to the briefing room and reached for the receiver as the line connected.

'What is it, Major?' Long said.

'I apologise for calling so early, Commander. We need to triangulate any wireless transmissions from unknown origins in the Sydney area. I think the Japanese are planning a raid on the city and possibly the ships in port. Soon, if not today, then in the next few days while the moon is full. And, as we speak, an aeroplane is flying over Sydney. Just this minute, it flew directly over my head. Can you find out if it's one of ours?'

'Where can I reach you today, Wisdom?'

'If I'm not at the barracks, call Inspector Lowe of Sydney Central Police.' Clement pressed the dial tone buttons, disconnecting the call. He wanted to speak to Lowe, but it was still early. Too early for Lowe to be in his office. Tom opened the door. Carrying a tray, he put in on the table. Clement reached for the plate of two eggs and toast as Tom set a mug of hot tea on the table beside him.

'Did you hear that plane just now, Clem?'

'I did, Tom.'

'One of ours?'

'I don't know.'

'You reckon the Japs are going to do what they did in Darwin?'

'It's certainly possible.'

'What did Commander Long say?'

'You are beginning to know me too well, Sergeant. As soon as it's nine, I want to speak with Lowe.'

Archer sat at the table but didn't speak as Clement ate his breakfast. 'You've eaten, Tom?'

'Yeah.'

'You're rather quiet this morning.'

'Can I ask you a question, Clem?'

'Yes,' Clement said, reaching for the tea.

'Where are you going after here?'

Clement stared at the tanned face. 'Home, I imagine.'

'Then what?'

'Like you, Tom, I do as I'm told.'

'Not quite the same as me. Can I come?'

Clement laid his knife and fork on the plate. 'I'm not sure that's possible. But why would you want to?'

'I've got to know you. We work pretty well as a team. You, me and Mick.'

'Mick too? Does he know about this?'

'Yeah. We talked about it yesterday while we watched that guest house. Mick's not all that bright. But he's a real good sniper. And a good bloke covering your back.'

'It's cold where I'm headed next, Tom.'

'So you do know.'

'I should have gone last December.'

'That's summer then.'

'Not exactly.'

'Ah yeah. Northern Hemisphere.'

'Yes. And very cold in December.'

'Where?'

'Shetland.'

'Where's that?'

'It's a small group of islands to the north of Scotland.'

'That suits me. I'm sick of the tropics, anyway.'

'I thought you didn't like the cold?'

'These islands, do they have big cities or is it outback country?'

'There is nothing there like the Australian outback. But the Shetland Islands are rather barren. The main city, Lerwick is a lot smaller than even Darwin.'

Archer nodded. 'Alright. I'll do it.'

Clement laughed. 'I don't know if you can come, Tom. Let alone Mick too.'

'She'll be apples. Commander Long will make it work. Just need you to ask.' Tom stood. 'I'll tell Mick.'

'Tom! I cannot give you guarantees. It's up to Commander Long and my people in London. And, Tom, no talk about Shetland. And that's an order.'

Archer grinned, his white teeth gleaming. He tapped the side of his cheek. 'Doesn't hurt to smile anymore, either.'

As Archer stood to leave, Mick, and Joe entered.

'Nothing happening at the guest house through last night, Clement,' Joe said. 'If you don't need us, we could do with a shower and something to eat.'

'Of course. And thank you, both.'

Clement finished his breakfast. That Archer and Savage wanted to come with him made him smile. Their loyalty was genuine. And they had proven themselves to be excellent soldiers. He just didn't know if it were possible. Putting he knife and fork together on the plate, he wondered if he wanted them along. He would be responsible for them. He thought of his former team in East Sussex. While some of those men had proven to be courageous, others had not, and some had died. Perhaps taking Archer and Savage wasn't a good idea.

Clement watched the hands of the clock till it was nine. Then he telephoned the Central Police Station. 'Inspector Lowe, please.

'Clement? I was about to call you. I'm heading back to that guest house now it's daylight. Would you like to come?'

'Yes. I'll wait at the gate here, if you can pick me up.'

Leaving the briefing room, he walked towards the main gate. It was cold and a strong wind blew in across the parade ground. The morning had dawned fine, but rain clouds were gathering. As the minutes passed, he stared at the greying sky and remembered the early morning aeroplane. Surely no one, not even the enemy, would attempt to invade in such blusterous weather. He prayed the wintry weather would continue for days. From the corner of his eye, he saw Lowe's car drive in.

'Morning, Clement.'

'Henry.' Clement closed the passenger door. 'Any news?'

'Nothing. Mrs Pendleton isn't saying a word. Likewise, the son. Although I think he is the weaker. I'm hopeful he'll crack soon. Lads like Nigel don't last long in prison.'

'May I ask you a question Henry, about Nigel?'

'Yes.'

'Why did you separate him from his mother?'

'Did you see the lad's eyes?'

Clement shrugged.

'That's drugs. He's only sixteen, so he didn't find them himself. She's kept him that way.' Lowe paused. 'She's a piece of work, that one.'

'Why would a mother do that to her son?'

'Not every mother is gentle and loving. In my experience, some mothers create a dependency. It's mutual. She supplies him with the drugs that make him feel good, and she has someone who'll never leave her.'

Clement frowned. He couldn't imagine such selfishness. Especially selfishness masquerading as love.

The car drove over the harbour bridge and took the back roads to Cremorne.

'Any news about the van?'

'No. My guess it's parked in a garage somewhere hereabouts. It could be anywhere.' Lowe paused. 'I've arranged rooms for Miss Howard and Miss Evans at The Metropole Hotel for the time being. They can walk to WESC from there.'

'Thank you, Henry.'

The car pulled up outside the guest house. Clement looked up at the building. It sat high on the hill overlooking the other houses and the waters of Sydney Harbour. 'Is there anyone here?' he asked Lowe.

'Yes. Although not in the house. I've had the local lads patrol around the area since eight this morning.' Lowe pushed open the gate, and they went to the front door. Lowe rang the doorbell, just in case, but no one came.

'Do you still have the two older men in custody?'

'Yes. Colonel Reeve and Mr Bretton. Although they deny any involvement, I wanted to see this place and search their rooms before releasing them. They can return to collect their belongings later when I'm satisfied they're not involved, and we've collected all the evidence.'

'Do you have a key?'

'Don't need one. You're here.'

Clement smiled, then reached for his lock picks.

Inside was still. No loud music played, and no voices could be heard. 'While you check downstairs, I want to see the attic rooms again.'

'Any reason?'

'I'd like to see the view.'

'I wasn't expecting that!' Lowe said. As Clement climbed the stairs, he heard Sergeant Preston's voice.

'Doctor McCowage is on his way, Sir. He said not to touch anything till he gets here.'

'Of course,' Lowe said, walking into the sitting room.

Clement climbed the stairs to the top floor. Entering the room, he walked over to the window where he'd climbed out onto the sill and found the wires to the aerial. The view was of the roofs of houses that presumably fronted the next bay, Mosman Bay. But he could not see the water. He lifted his gaze to the next promontory; the land occupied by the famous zoo and in front of it, a glimpse of the open bay known as Athol Bight. There, moored in the bay and in the centre of his vision was *HMAS Westralia.*

CHAPTER TWENTY-FIVE

Friday 29th May 1942

Clement stood staring at the ship moored in Athol Bight, its grey bow pointing directly towards him. Jim Lockhart was assigned to the *HMAS Westralia* before moving to *HMAS Kuttabul* in order to attend WESC. Was Lockhart part of the conspiracy? Could he have been in contact with whoever was sending out messages from the guest house? Perhaps using a torch light flashed through a lower deck porthole? That he was no longer onboard this ship may have been an unforeseen hiccough. Lockhart gave the impression he was a straightforward lad whose ambitions were to be an electrician. Nothing more. Nothing less. Clement closed his eyes, trying to remember everything the young man had said. But there was nothing suspicious about Jim Lockhart. Did that make him the epitome of a master spy?

Leaving the room, Clement went to the floor below and to the room where he'd seen the blood-stained sheets. Something other than the obvious troubled him about this room. Frowning, he turned to leave but stopped and stood in the doorway, staring out into the corridor. Directly opposite this room was the door to Bretton's or Reeve's room. That door was open, and he could see Lowe standing inside. How was it that neither of these men heard the screaming? The proximity of the rooms made that unlikely. Had she only ever been drugged during the day when both men were absent from their rooms? Or did they know?

Clement joined Lowe.

'No accounting for taste,' Lowe said. 'The other room is the same.'

Clement's gaze slowly surveyed the elaborate room. It was filled with photographs, some on the wall, some on tables, and others anywhere one could fit. Large Victorian furniture occupied every space. And memorabilia of a theatrical life were everywhere gathering dust. Clement walked into the connecting room. From the number of personal items in both rooms, it was evident these men resided permanently at the guest house. And the rooms were larger and the furniture more elaborate than any other bedroom on the floor. Clement returned to the first room, the one opposite the room Peggy Seaton had been kept in. 'Do we know whose room this is?'

'No. But from the photographs, they evidently knew each other. Well.'

'Yes. For many years, it seems,' Clement said. He walked towards a dressing table. In the centre, beside several pots of lotions and creams, was a silver framed photograph. He picked it up. The picture, taken perhaps twenty years before, showed both men dressed in elaborate costumes with a small child similarly dressed. He didn't know much about the theatre, but it was evident from the costumes and make-up they were all wearing that it had an Oriental setting.

'Do you know what show this could have been?' Clement asked Lowe.

Lowe stared at the picture, then shrugged. '*The Mikado*?'

Clement replaced the picture on the bureau. 'That's Gilbert and Sullivan, isn't it?'

'Yes. But I'm not the one to ask. McCowage and his wife go to those sorts of things. Best to ask him about it, if it's important.'

Studying the dressing table, Clement scrutinised the items there. He'd never met an actor. While he understood the need for make-up on the stage, he wondered about the fake beards, rouge pots and tubes of flesh-coloured sticks arranged there. He picked one up and sniffed it. It had a distinct odour. Grease paint, they called it. It smelt like nothing he'd encountered before. He wondered if it was still in daily use. Clement stared through the window to the street beyond, wondering about his own assessment of these men. Was transforming or even hiding the natural features of the face just part of an act, or was it an act of self-preservation or self-denial? He remembered the first time he'd seen Muriel Pendleton with her thick make-up and bright red hair. Had that been a wig? He considered masks fell into the same category. Or was the make-up used on someone else?

He walked back and picked up the photograph again. 'Henry, could you ask Bretton and Reeve about this?

'What's your thinking?' Lowe asked.

'How long ago was it taken? What was the show? And who is the child?' Clement thought for a moment. 'How old would you say they are now?'

'Fifties. Sixties.'

'And in this photograph?'

Lowe stood beside him and studied the picture. 'Twenty or thirty years younger.'

'So the child would be in his or her twenties or thirties now.'

'Is it important, Clement? I can't see that it helps find our killer.'

Clement smiled and replaced the picture. 'You're probably right.'

Clement walked out and stood in the hall, a lazy, cold breeze filling the corridor. He walked back to the stairs and felt the icy draught. Upstairs, one of the attic windows had been opened. Climbing the stairs, he went to the room where he'd found the radio transmitter wires. Sergeant Preston climbed through the window.

'Did you find anything, Preston?' Clement asked.

'The wire goes into the side of the attic window, Sir. So there must be access into the roof cavity from this room.'

Clement looked around. A chest of drawers stood to one side. Pulling it away from the wall, they saw the small

231

door. Preston opened it and crawled through. A second later, Clement saw the man switch on a torch.

'Anything?'

'Oh yes. There's a metal contraption in here, Sir. I'm guessing that's the aerial.'

Clement bent down and peered into the confined space. The cage-like structure was large. He pondered the transmitter's range. But were the transmissions sent thousands of miles or just a few?

Crawling out, he returned downstairs to the first floor bedrooms. From the stairwell, he could see Lowe talking with McCowage in the entry hall below. He wandered back into Peggy's room, his eye falling on her suitcase. He knew she'd left Horden Street in the middle of the night. But where had she gone that they'd found her so quickly? If she had no family in Sydney, it stood to reason that she'd gone to a local hotel. And in Newtown there were several. Checking them wouldn't have taken long.

Clement wandered across the hall and took another look at the bedrooms occupied by the two men. Cluttered. Untidy. Filled with theatrical memorabilia. He returned to the hall and stared at the doors along the corridor. He felt himself frown. Where was Muriel Pendleton's room and Nigel's? Leaving the upper floor, he went downstairs to find Lowe. Doctor McCowage had arrived and was in the kitchen. Clement walked in.

'Wisdom. Thought you'd be here somewhere. I'll do the postmortem on the girl later today.'

'Thank you. Henry are there any bedrooms on this level?' Clement asked.

'Yes. Two along there. Surprising, really. I would have thought the owner, and her son would have occupied the two best rooms upstairs. But no. She and the boy were in the old servant's quarters.'

Clement walked along the corridor and stared into the tiny rooms. The one occupied by the boy Nigel was almost institutional. A single bed, a chest of drawers and a collection of moths and flies pinned to a board hanging on the wall. Leaving it, he walked into the other room. Given the woman's flamboyant tastes, the room was almost bare. Only the dressing table had collections of pots and powder. A mask with feathers hung from the mirror along with a fan decorated with birds and flowers. Two yellowed and often-fingered cards were tapped to the mirror's edge. Clement read them. Both were messages of congratulations for a performance.

He returned to the kitchen to find Lowe. 'Henry, can you find out about Mrs Pendleton's financial affairs?'

'Your reason being?'

'Just exploring possibilities.'

'You think she may have become involved for the money?'

'It's one reason people commit treason.'

'I'll get Preston on to it this afternoon.'

'And while he's checking Mrs Pendleton, could he look into the background of Jim Lockhart?'

'Who?'

'A lad doing the course at WESC. He said he was on the *Westralia* but he's on the *Kuttabul* at present. Is it co-incidental that the *Westralia* is moored within sight of this guest house?'

'If you think it's important, Clement.' Lowe paused, his hands in his coat pockets. 'I realise that while my job is to find a killer, you have a different role. But, I'm afraid, Clement, I cannot tie up valuable police resources with enquiries that don't have a tangible connection to the murders.'

'Of course. And I apologise, Henry. I'll check Lockhart myself.' Clement walked out the kitchen door and stood in the rear garden. He understood Lowe had a job to do and his focus was finding a killer. For Clement, however, finding the killer was only half the story. His gaze roamed around the garden as he recalled the image of two men and a woman running across the back lawn. One man was carrying a suitcase. 'No prizes for what that contained,' Clement muttered to himself. He was convinced that even though he was shot at in the hallway upstairs, only one person had been there, the other man and woman he believed had hidden downstairs in Mrs Pendleton's room, waiting to make their escape together. He wandered over to the garage. Stepping inside, he stared into the mechanic's pit. He felt the nausea well up, the memories and sight of Peggy lying there filled him with grief. Even without McCowage's test, he knew they'd find fungal spores and machine oil. But how long Hank Veretti had been imprisoned there?

Clement strolled back into the garden and stared at the house. He thought about Muriel Pendelton and her motivation. Was it purely money? But if not financial gain, what would motivate anyone to betray their country? In his mind's eye, he saw the stab wounds in Veretti's body. Two lethal. Three vindictive.

Hank Veretti.

'Clement!'

Clement tuned at the sound of his name.

'If you've seen enough, we'll go,' Lowe said.

'Do you know if McCowage has taken samples from the mechanic's pit?'

'Already done,' Lowe said, returning inside.

Clement sat in the front seat as they drove back to the Central Police Station.

'You're quiet, Clement. Care to share your thoughts?'

'There's someone I need to speak to.'

'Not saying who?'

'Can't at this stage, Henry. Can you drop me off at WESC?'

'Of course. No hard feelings about earlier?'

'None whatever.'

'You will let me know if you learn anything relevant to these murders?'

Clement smiled. 'Of course. And you'll let me know what Preston learns about Mrs Pendleton's financial affairs?'

Lowe pulled up in Clarence Street. 'Where will you be later?'

'Here or Victoria Barracks.'

Thanking Lowe, Clement stepped from the car and walked the short distance to the front door to WESC. He went straight to the top floor and peered inside.

Veronica Evans was seated in front of the class. Evelyn was standing at the blackboard, speaking. Avoiding eye contact with them, he slipped quietly into his seat. Behind him, he saw Joe, and behind Joe was Jim Lockhart. His gaze lingered on the man. Beside him, John Connor's chair was empty. His gaze went immediately to where Billie and Joan usually sat. Billie was present, her head down, and it seemed to Clement that she was scribbling on a page, her attention distracted. But Joan's seat was vacant.

At the afternoon tea break, he went to see Billie.

'Billie?'

'Mr Wisdom? I thought you'd left.'

'I had a few things to do.'

She nodded.

'Do you know where Joan is?' Clement asked.

'It's not the same, is it? I mean with Win dead and Joan gone who knows where.'

'Have you spent any time with Jim Lockhart?'

'Why would you want to know that?'

'Just curious, I suppose. Jim arrived here the same day as John Connor, and I see he's not here either.'

'I know. Do you think he and Joan are together?'

'Is that what you think?'

'I don't know what to think, Mr Wisdom. And I don't know if Joan and John are together.' She paused. 'We'll be finished Kana soon and I'm being posted to Brisbane, so I'll probably never see them again, anyway.'

'Well, I'm glad to have met you, Billie. Take care and God speed wherever they send you.' Clement returned to his seat. He wanted to speak with Joe.

'Got a minute?'

'Sure thing.'

'Could you do some digging?'

'As long as it doesn't involve Captain Bode.'

'Well, it might. Can you ask if I could speak with Bode? Or at least the intelligence officer onboard *Chicago*?'

'It may be best to see that British guy, Muirhead-Gould. After all, he's supposed to be in charge of the military here.'

'Could you also ask Lieutenant Fabian if FRUMEL has heard anything about Japanese ship or submarine movements in the area?'

Joe raised his eyebrow. 'You got a death wish, Clem? First Bode now Fabian.'

'Thanks, Joe.'

Clement checked his watch, then stood and pulled on his coat.

'You coming back here?' Joe asked.

'It depends. I want to attend the postmortem on Peggy Seaton.'

'Sure. I'll let you know later tonight if I have any luck with either of your requests.'

Clement hurried down the stairs and out onto the street. He walked several blocks before hailing a cab.

Alighting at the corner, he went straight into the police station and took the stairs to the lower floor. Pushing the door open, he saw McCowage standing by the corpse of Peggy Seaton.

'No stab wounds here. No recent sexual activity either. Very little to suggest anything but sedation, followed by a massive dose of morphine. Did you know Preston found another six vials of the stuff in the scullery. I'd venture to say that he was about to administer several more lethal doses.'

Clement visualised the syringe on the tray that Nigel had dropped in the kitchen. He felt the icy shudder. He thought of Veronica and Evelyn. He could hear Commander Long's voice telling him that Evelyn's loss would be catastrophic.

'Do you think there's enough evidence to convict Nigel for Peggy's murder?'

'That's Henry's department. The boy is a minor. Doesn't prevent him from being convicted of murder but the evidence isn't enough. He may have been taking the stuff to the room for someone else to administer.' McCowage reached for Peggy's left arm. 'Have a look at here.' Five puncture marks ran down her arm. 'You will also notice some bruising around her wrists and ankles. These were not postmortem. The girl was restrained. Perhaps she screamed out. I'm told the music was loud enough to cover her screams, so it's likely no one heard her. Sergeant Preston asked me to inform you that he'd like to show you something they found at the house. As it doesn't involve the deceased, you'll need to see him about it.'

'Do you know where he is?'

'Ask at the front desk.'

Clement left the mortuary and took the lift to the ground floor. Preston was in reception when Clement arrived there. 'I understand from Doctor McCowage you have something to show me.'

'I do. If you'll come this way.'

Preston led Clement along the corridor towards a room on the left. 'It's in the evidence room, Major.'

'Preston. Could you do something for me?'

'As long as Inspector Lowe doesn't object.'

'Where does Peggy Seaton's family reside? I'm assuming a relative will need to identify her body formally.'

'We'll have her next-of-kin address taken from her employee file from WESC, Major.' Preston opened the door and Clement walked in.

'This was found in Colonel Reeve's room. Inspector Lowe says you'll know what you're looking at.'

Preston opened a bag and pulled out a pink dress made of satin and lace. Under it was a pair of pink shoes.

'Now here's the interesting thing,' Preston said. 'The shoes don't fit Mrs Pendleton.'

CHAPTER TWENTY-SIX

Friday 29th May 1942

Clement stared at the garments. 'Has Mr Harrison at *The Australia* identified them?'

'Yes, Sir. But it's not enough to convict. I'll get that address for you, if you'd like to come with me.'

Clement followed Preston along the corridor towards the lift. 'Do you have family, Sergeant Preston?'

'Just a mum and dad, Sir.'

'You are a great asset to Inspector Lowe. And I'm sure will one day make a very good inspector yourself.'

'Thank you, Sir. Policing is all I've ever really wanted to do. But it isn't conducive to family life.' Preston opened the cage doors to the lift, and they went to Lowe's office on the second floor.

'Miss Simpson, could I have the file on Miss Seaton?' Preston asked.

Preston opened the file and Clement read the names. *Daisy and Wilfred Seaton, Grafton Street, Goulburn.*

'Have they been notified?'

'Yes, Sir. They are expected to arrive here tomorrow around noon, I believe.

'Could you let me know when they arrive? Oh! And sergeant have you had a chance to look into Mrs Pendleton's financial affairs?'

'Not yet, Sir. We need official approval to access bank records. Aside from which it's too late now and the banks won't be open again till Monday.'

'Of course. Thank you, Sergeant.'

Clement needed to think, and for that he needed complete solitude. Leaving the police station, he took the tram back along York Street and walked to Clarence Street and St Philip's church. Entering the quiet, dark place, he sat in a pew at the back of the church and closed his eyes, trying to empty his mind of clutter.

He thought of the people. Of Mrs McKenzie who would have known that Peggy Seaton grew up in Goulburn. And Veronica Evans, who had access to all files at WESC. He wondered if Peggy or her parents were more involved with the group than he'd believed. In his mind's eye, he saw her lying in the mechanic's pit. So cruel. Curled like an infant, easily manipulated and naïve. She had surely been exploited and the manner of her death showed utter contempt. That Evelyn and Veronica were to suffer the same fate, an overdose of morphine, implied that Veronica was innocent of any involvement with the group. But it wasn't a certainty. Did this exonerate Veronica and Mrs McKenzie? His thoughts turned to the obsequious Mrs Pendleton, the curled bright red lips, the red hair and exuberant manners. And her small, austere bedroom.

She was certainly complicit. But, it now appeared, she wasn't the woman dressed in the pink cocktail outfit and wearing pink satin shoes. That these items had been found in Colonel Reeve's room implicated the two men. But, Mrs Pendleton or Nigel could have planted the dress and shoes there and neither Reeve nor Bretton would have known about it. But one thing was beyond doubt: the van. It had been used to bring Veronica to the guest house, where it was doubtless garaged since being stolen from Goulburn. And Veronica had found Edwina's shoe in it. The van not only connected Edwina to Hank Veretti, and Veronica, it also confirmed Mrs Pendleton's complicity.

CHAPTER TWENTY-SEVEN

Saturday 30th May 1942

Hank Veretti. And a van from Goulburn. Clement had had a sleepless night. Where exactly was Goulburn? Rising, he dressed and went to find a map of New South Wales. Enquiring of the Officer of the Day, he took the map to the briefing room and spread it out on the table there. He stared at the name: Goulburn, so many miles away. Other than what Lowe had told him, all he knew was that the van had been stolen from there three months ago. Lifting his gaze, he thought about the theft. What if it hadn't been stolen? What if the butcher had reported it stolen to disguise the fact that it was no longer there? Clement stood and reached for the telephone and dialled the number. 'Inspector Lowe, please.'

'Not in at present, Major Wisdom. And I don't expect him for some time. He's gone to see Rear-Admiral Muirhead-Gould,' Constable Roberts said. 'Can I take a message?'

'Could you ask him to telephone me either at WESC or at the barracks when he gets in?'

'Of course.'

Clement hung up. He rubbed at his forehead, thinking about the owner of the van. Could Peggy's father have been one of the two men he'd seen running away across the rear lawn of the guest house? He recalled the image. From their running gait, neither man was old. Could he have been the man Mick saw collect Veronica Evans from her home? Glancing at the clock on the wall, he lifted the receiver again, and dialled the extension number for the Officer for the Day.

'How can I help, Major?' the officer said.

'Can you get a message to Sergeant Archer?'

'I believe your sergeant is still on base, Major. Would you like him to see you?'

'No, just get this message to him, please.' Clement dictated the message and hung up. *Your sergeant*, the officer had called Archer. Perhaps that was right. It certainly was beginning to look that way. Returning to his quarters, he gathered his hat and coat and hurried out to Oxford Street and hailed a taxi. He had fifteen minutes to get to WESC.

Just before the lunch break, Clement heard the footsteps on the landing outside the classroom. He looked up and saw Archer dressed as a delivery man standing in the doorway.

'Parcel for a Miss Evans,' Tom called, his eyes roaming around the room.

Veronica went to the door and stood in front of Archer. Clement did not know what was said between them, but Veronica seemed to go along with the performance.

'Put it on the desk in the office downstairs. And next time, leave any deliveries at the office. Mr Wisdom would you please show this man where to go,' she said, turning on her heel.

Clement stood and left the room, following Tom downstairs. 'Well?'

'I gave him a long, hard look. The bloke at the back, right?'

'Yes. Jim Lockhart.'

'Never seen him before.'

'You're sure.'

'When you're being punched black and blue, you don't forget that face.'

'Thanks, Tom.'

'Also there's a message for you. Commander Long wants you to call him as soon as you get back to the barracks. There's also a message for Joe.'

'Right.'

'Anything else for us to do, Clem?'

'Yes. Can you and Mick go to a hotel called the Woolloomooloo Hotel? It's a bit rough, sorry.'

'Shouldn't worry us, Clem.'

'Ask about a man named Charlie Manning. I understand he lived there. Find out anything you can about his private life.' Clement watched Tom walk away. Returning upstairs, he resumed to his seat.

'What was Tom doing here?' Joe whispered.

'I'll explain later. But thanks for not indicating you knew him. Archer told me there's a message for you at the barracks. Can you let me know if that message is from Fabian?'

'What time will you be in tonight?'

'Not sure, but not late.'

The clicks resumed in his ear, but Clement's mind wasn't on the task, and he made numerous mistakes. An hour later, he handed the transcripts to Veronica. He saw her scowl as she perused his transcripts. She stood up from her desk and walked towards him.

'Not your best work, Mr Wisdom,' she said.

'May I ask you a question?' Clement said, quickly taking in if anyone was within earshot.

'Perhaps.'

'The man who convinced you to go with him from your home, did you recognise him?'

'I'd never seen him before.'

'Was he young or old?'

'Not young.'

'Was there anything different about him? An accent? A beard? Anything?'

'It was dark. He said Peggy was in trouble and would I help? He said he was her uncle.' She paused. 'He wore gloves. And a hat. Which he didn't remove. I'm sorry I can't be more helpful, Mr Wisdom.'

'And you've never seen him before?'

'No.'

'Did he say how he knew where you lived?'

'He did not. I assumed Peggy had told him.'

Clement nodded. Perhaps Peggy had been forced to reveal Veronica's home address. But it was also possible Peggy had passed on all the addresses on file.

Just after five, Clement left Clarence Street and walked to Circular Quay to the building that housed the Combined Defence Headquarters. It was an imposing structure built of stone and one designed, he surmised, to remind the populace of the importance of the people within. Showing his *Most Secret* security pass to the guard on the door, he stepped inside and asked to see Muirhead-Gould.

'He's not in,' an officious lieutenant said.

'It's urgent. It may involve the security of the city, if not the country,' Clement said.

'And you think you are better informed than the Rear-Admiral?'

'The Rear-Admiral may not have all the facts,' Clement said.

'Come back on Monday, Major. The Rear Admiral is celebrating his birthday this weekend. I doubt he'll have time to see you before then.'

Clement pursed his lips and left. 'Gatekeepers!' he muttered as he left the building. What was it about some junior officers? And why was important intelligence so frequently ignored? He just hoped they'd investigated the aeroplane that had flown over yesterday morning. He checked his watch. Nearly six and he still hadn't heard from Lowe. He hoped Lowe had had better luck seeing the Rear-Admiral. Taking the tram from Circular Quay, he returned to the barracks. Going to the briefing room, he dialled the number for the police station.

'How did you get on with Muirhead-Gould?' Clement asked.

'Clement. My apologies. I've been rather busy. As for Muirhead-Gould, I was soundly put in my place. Told to stick to policing and leave the defence of Sydney to him. Arrogant man. Typical stuck-up toffy Englishman!' Lowe paused. 'Sorry, Clement. That accusation doesn't apply to you.'

'No offence taken. And just so you know, I've had my fair share of dealing with opinionated Englishmen. One other thing, Henry. Did you know Peggy Seaton's parents live in Goulburn? Where the van was stolen? What if it was only reported as stolen?'

'Good question. I'll let you know.'

Clement hung up. The group would arrive soon, and he needed to call Commander Long. Right on seven Joe walked in.

'What news Joe?'

'That plane you saw yesterday did it have one wing or two?'

Clement thought back. 'I can't be completely sure, Joe. It flew over the barracks, heading towards the city. I only watched it for a few seconds because I was on hold waiting to speak with Long in Melbourne.'

'Apparently you're not the only one asking questions.'

'What's the significance of the wings?'

'There's a report in from a battery nearby that said it's an American Curtiss Falcon floatplane. Now I can tell you, Clem, I've just learned from FRUMEL there was a Curtiss Seagull observation plane captured by the Japs in the Pacific some weeks ago. Maybe we should speak with Commander Long again?'

'Something I needed to do, anyway. Long requested I call him when I got in this evening.'

Clement picked up the telephone receiver and dialled the number in Melbourne.

Ten minutes later, he replaced the telephone receiver, an icy shudder coursing through him. He turned to face Joe.

'Dear Lord! What is it, Clem?' Joe asked.

'He's received multiple reports about that aeroplane. It was assumed it was a US Navy *Seagull*. But upon investigation, the only ship in the area carrying *Seagulls* is the *Chicago* and all four of her aeroplanes are currently onboard. He also told me about the one the Japanese stole.' Clement stared at the map of Sydney laid out on the table. All the ships in the harbour were sitting ducks. 'Why did you ask me about the wings?'

'A *seagull* is a biplane; it has two wings. A Japanese *Glen* however is a monoplane.'

'But how would a Japanese plane get this far south without a safe place to refuel?'

Joe shrugged. 'Who knows? How long is it since you've eaten, Clem?'

'I had some breakfast this morning. At least, I think it was this morning.'

'Then I'm going to treat you to the best dinner in town!'

'Really? Where?'

'The Officers' Mess.'

Clement laughed.

That night, he lay in his bed and allowed his mind to drift. So much depended on those in charge in the city and on whatever information the newly created FRUMEL could intercept. But as important as any Japanese attack was, why had a sweet and innocent girl like Edwina Hughes been killed? What possible connection was there between her death and a solo aeroplane flying over the city? Twice!

CHAPTER TWENTY-EIGHT

Sunday 31st May 1942

The knock at the door was loud. Clement started, then rising wrapped his dressing gown around him and opened his door.

'There's a man to see you at the gate, Sir. Says it's urgent.'

'Who is it, Corporal?'

'Says his name is Jim Lockhart. Says you know him.'

'Thank you. I do. While I dress, would you show him to the briefing room I'm using? But don't let him in. And please stay with him until I get there.'

'Sir.'

Clement dressed quickly. He didn't yet know if Lockhart was involved, and he felt ambivalent about the young man showing up at the barracks. Skirting the parade ground, he strode towards the briefing room. Lockhart and the corporal stood beside the door, waiting. Lockhart's expression was grave.

'Jim? What's happened?' Clement asked, wondering if the scowl was an act.

'Can I ask you a question?'

'Certainly. Just wait here a minute.' Clement unlocked the door and stepped inside. He hastily rolled up the maps of Sydney Harbour and Goulburn, then returned to the door and let Lockhart in. Clement saw the man's eyes dart around the room.

'You're more involved than just a concerned student of Morse Code, aren't you?'

Clement stared at the young man, his concerns mounting. 'What's your question, Jim?'

'What happens to someone who goes absent without permission?'

The question surprised Clement. 'I suppose that depends. In the last war, a British soldier who left the front without leave was shot, if he were caught. Now, I imagine it's a court martial and perhaps imprisonment. I'm not sure about Australian soldiers or sailors.'

'Mind if I sit down, Sir.'

'Not at all,' Clement said, his eye on Lockhart. Clement reached for a chair and sat as well. He stared at the young man. Lockhart fidgeted and seemed almost reluctant to talk about what had brought him to Victoria Barracks.

'Thanks, Sir. I've been really worried about it. I didn't know who to speak to without getting him into trouble.'

'Who, exactly, are we talking about?'

'John. John Connor. He and that girl have eloped.'

Clement's eyes widened. 'You mean Joan Olivant?'

Lockhart nodded.

'How do you know this, Jim?'

'He telephoned me at WESC last thing yesterday. Mrs McKenzie wasn't pleased about me taking private calls. Said he wasn't coming back. Said they'd married and intended to disappear.'

'Did he say where they are?'

'No. But it was a long-distance call. I heard the operator connect us.'

Clement thought for a second. If Lockhart was genuine, then it was surprising news. If not? Was it a clever deception? 'Have you ever seen John and Joan together?'

Lockhart's expression changed from concern to incomprehension. 'Come to think of it, no. But perhaps they didn't want anyone to know.' Lockhart was shaking his head. 'I never saw them together at WESC.' He let out a half-laugh in bewilderment. 'They were careful about that, weren't they? Her friend, Billie didn't even know.'

'Thank you, Jim. I will have to report what you've just told me. But I'll put in a good word for them, and hopefully they'll be found before any need for disciplinary action.' Clement stood and walked towards the door. Opening it, he held it wide for Lockhart to leave. 'Don't worry about John anymore, Jim. Best you concentrate on being the best morse code operator in the navy. But thank you again for telling me. With luck, John will come to his senses and return. Stay safe, Jim, wherever they send you.'

'You not coming back to the class either?'

'Perhaps. But there's a lot going on at present.'

'I hope you find them first,' Lockhart said. He loitered by the door.

'Is there something you want to ad?'

Lockhart held Clement's gaze. 'I know John's a bit older than me but men like John, Sir. They're different. Street wise, my mother used to call it. Clever. Sometimes too clever.'

'What do you mean by that, Jim?'

'Just a feeling.'

'Sometimes those feelings are right,' Clement urged.

'We had a drink together one afternoon after class. Strange, really. He's one of those blokes who answers a question with a question. I always felt he was looking down his nose at me. You know, thought himself better than everyone else.'

'You didn't like him?'

'It's difficult to put into words. Just a feeling, really. I never felt at ease around him. And now I think about it, I'm not sure I knew anything about him at all.'

'Some people are naturally secretive. I wouldn't place too much importance on it. But going absent without leave is a serious matter and he, they, must be found, and before he's in serious trouble.' Clement walked with Lockhart to the main entrance then watched him walk away, down Oxford Street.

If Clement hadn't seen the *Westralia* moored in Athol Bight, he may not have been so suspicious of Lockhart. Was he trying to deflect suspicion and cast doubt on Connor? As serious as going absent without leave was, John Connor's disappearance was the least of Clement's worries. Or was it? 'You're becoming a very suspicious old man, Clement Wisdom,' he muttered. He stared up at the sky. It was a bitter grey day. He felt his stomach rumble. Locking the door, he walked towards the mess. It was nearly lunchtime, and he hadn't heard from Tom yet if anything further had been leaned about Charlie Manning from the publican at the Woolloomooloo pub. He decided to check with the Officer of the Day if Archer had returned.

'Not yet, sir. Is there a problem?'

'Not at all. I'll see him later.'

Half an hour later, he walked out onto Oxford Street and caught the next tram for Liverpool Street and the Central Police Station. He wanted to read the postmortem results for Peggy Seaton.

Preston was at the front desk when Clement walked in. 'Do you know if Inspector Lowe has the postmortem report on Miss Seaton yet?'

'It's still with Doctor McCowage, Major. I'm heading there, myself to collect it for Inspector Lowe.'

'Mind if I join you?'

'Not at all.'

Clement walked with Preston to the lifts. 'May I know your first name, Sergeant?'

'William,' he said. 'But most people call me Will.'

'Not Bill?'

'My dad's name.'

Clement smiled. He liked Preston. He was a good policeman and clearly devoted to his calling. Preston let him into the mortuary. Clement sat in McCowage's office and read the reports before Preston took them upstairs. The engine oil and fungal spores that had been found in the mechanic's pit were a match with Veretti's stained trousers. Clement felt the despair the poor man must have felt; caged and vulnerable. He visualised Veretti, so young and exuberant about life. Clement felt a twinge of guilt for having thought him so obnoxious. He also thought of Edwina; sweet, innocent and so cruelly killed. And Peggy. Her postmortem report had said she'd died from a massive dose of morphine. Clement rubbed unconsciously at his forehead. 'What are you missing?' he whispered to the air.

It was near two when he returned to Victoria Barracks. Going straight to the briefing room, he found Archer and Savage sitting there. Mick was cleaning both Welrods, Tom was eating sandwiches.

'There you are! We wondered where you'd gone. Got something for us to do, Clem?'

'Learn anything from the publican last night?'

'Oh yeah! Cost us quite a few beers and we didn't leave till closing time. But Charlie Manning had recently come into money. Enough to buy a small boat. The publican said he'd disappear on his days off for hours and would often bring back a fish or two for his dinner.'

'Anything else?' Clement asked.

'Simple man, simple tastes.'

'Any ladies in his life?'

'I asked about that. The publican said he never saw Charlie with a woman. But I can tell you this, Clem from first-hand experience in the graveyard at St Stephen's, he may have been strong with an iron grip, but he was no streetfighter. And he could have been a bit deaf, too. Because he never heard me behind him. Even when I grabbed him around the neck, he didn't put up a fight. I don't think he knew what hit him. It's possible that Jap gun was planted on him by someone who had used it.'

'Or given to him as payment for services,' Mick interrupted.

'Yeah. That's probably more like it,' Tom added.

'I think you are both right,' Clement said.

'Well, if you don't need us anymore, Clem, we'll get some tucker.'

Clement stared at an empty plate sitting on the table. All that remained there were breadcrumbs. He wondered why soldiers were always so hungry. 'One more thing, Tom; did the publican say where Charlie kept this boat?'

'Yeh. Other side of the harbour, apparently. Somewhere called Athol Bight.'

CHAPTER TWENTY-NINE

Sunday 31st May 1942

'Did the publican also say how he got to it, if he lived at the pub on the south side of the harbour?'

'I asked that, too. Said he had a mate in the navy who took him across.'

'Did the mate have a name?'

Archer shook his head. 'I did ask, but he wasn't sure. Said he met him once, but he didn't remember a name being mentioned.'

'Thank you, Tom. You get something to eat, then return here.'

Archer and Savage left the room. Clement unrolled the map of Sydney Harbour and spread it out on the table. Placing his finger on the map, he drew an imaginary line from Garden Island Dockyard to Cremorne Point and Athol Bight. It ran almost due north and, in fact, was the shortest distance between Garden Island and any of the headlands in the immediate vicinity on the northern side of the harbour.

He looked at his watch and hoped Lowe was in his office. Lifting the telephone receiver, he paused before dialling. Lowe had made it clear he thought him too interfering with the investigation. Or too demanding. Perhaps both. But what he'd learned from Archer and Savage and the extraordinary visit from Lockhart about Connor and Joan, was information Clement considered Lowe should know. He dialled the number.

Clement told Lowe about Manning's boat and that John Connor and Joan Olivant had eloped. 'Can I help with anything, Henry?'

'I'll put out a request for information about them in the regional areas and in the city. But I think the boat worth investigating. I'll ask the local lads to have a look for it. I only have a skeleton staff on Sundays, but I'll see what we can do. And Clement, let me know what you find out about Lockhart.'

'I will. Any news about Peggy's parents?'

'Not much we didn't already know. It was Peggy's father, Wilfred Seaton who reported the van as stolen. You may remember he's a butcher. But as yet, we don't know if he has any involvement with our killers. One more thing, Clement; Colonel Ravenscroft identified the pistol as a Japanese Nambu model 14.'

'As I recall, it had been fired once?'

'That's correct. Held eight in the chamber, but only seven there. So far, we don't know what he fired at. Or who.'

'Perhaps it wasn't him who fired it, Henry.'

259

'Have you ever thought of a career in the police, Clement?'

'That has been suggested to me before, Henry. Perhaps. After the war. Assuming we win.'

He heard Lowe laugh.

Clement went to his quarters. For the first time in a long time, he had time to think. He lay on his bed staring at the ceiling, wondering about what would motivate a butcher in Goulburn to become a Japanese spy.

Rising, he walked out onto the veranda. Storm clouds were gathering. A shiver coursed through him. It was the cold weather he told himself. But he knew it wasn't. Something sinister was brewing. He could feel it. Standing, he returned to the briefing room to stare at the map, willing it to tell him what connected Hank Veretti to a guest house in Cremorne Point.

A knock at the door broke his concentration. Archer and Savage walked in. 'Guessed you'd be here. Anything we can do for you, Clem?'

'Perhaps you can, Tom.'

'Anything.'

'Perhaps you can both just listen. Take a seat, would you?'

Clement paced the room as Archer and Savage sat listening. He went back over events, but despite Tom and Mick adding small details that Clement already knew, something still evaded him. Something small. Either an event or something someone said. He knew Veretti was the key. Veretti was a radioman on the *Chicago*. Joe had told him that part of a radioman's duties were to collect and destroy sensitive information. What if he hadn't destroyed it? What if that information had been or was to be passed to the Japanese? Clement frowned as he paced. But if Veretti was a traitor and working with collaborators, why had he been killed? Muriel Pendleton would know, but she was prepared to go to the gallows to protect what she knew.

Clement turned suddenly and stared at Archer and Savage.

'Clem?'

'Tom. Mick. Thank you, both. I need to find out something. Have the rest of today off, but don't go too far away from the barracks.'

Clement grabbed his coat and hat and ran to the main gate. He hoped either Lowe or Preston would still be at the police station. Hailing a passing taxi, he went to Central Police Station. Asking at the front desk, he was told that Sergeant Preston was available but not Inspector Lowe.

Clement waited only minutes before Preston joined him at the front desk. 'Afternoon, Sergeant. Could you find out, as a matter of urgency, if Muriel Pendleton had any other children besides Nigel?'

'I'll need to contact the Department of Births, Deaths and Marriages for that, Sir. And as you know, today is Sunday. Not only the banks close on the weekends, but most public servants don't work on Sundays either. Even with a war on.'

'As soon as you can, please. Is she still here?'

'Mrs Pendleton? Yes, she isn't going anywhere soon.

She'll appear before the Magistrate tomorrow.'

'And the two men? Are they still here?'

'In view of finding the pink dress and shoes in their rooms, yes, they are. In fact, Inspector Lowe is with them now. Would you like to watch the interview?'

'May I?'

'Follow me, Sir.' Preston led Clement to the first floor where he'd seen the interview rooms. But this room had no glass panels to the corridor. A single door opened into a room with one window where a curtain was drawn over the glass. Another door led into the interview room. Preston draw back the curtain.

'Can he see me?' Clement asked.

'No. From the other side and with the lights on, all he'll see is a mirror.'

Preston drew back a sliding timber hatch. It was covered with a mesh screen, and Clement could hear Lowe speaking.

'Your full name?'

'Colonel Archibold John Reeve.'

'Date of birth?

'23rd March 1885.'

'Place of birth?'

'London.'

'Current address?'

'You know where I live.'

Lowe wrote in the address. 'How long have you lived there?'

'About three years.'

'Occupation?'

'Actor.'

'Much call for that at present?'

'I'm retired.'

'You use a military title, where did you serve?'

'Is this really necessary? I don't know what Muriel is involved in.'

'Just answer the questions,' Lowe said.

'India. I served in India.'

'Is that where you met Mr Bretton?'

'Yes.'

'We found quite a few unusual costumes in your room. Is this yours?' Lowe asked, holding up the pink dress.

'I've never seen it before.'

'And you don't know how it got into a trunk in your room?'

'What! No.'

Lowe stood.

'Can I go?'

'No. Until you tell me about the pink dress, you're not going anywhere.'

'I've told you, I've never seen it before,' Reeves shouted as Lowe left the room. Lowe closed the door to the interview room. 'Clement?'

Sergeant Preston said it would be alright for me to listen. Do you believe Reeve?'

'Not entirely. Too early to tell.'

'And Bretton?'

'He's in the next room. Like to join me?'

Clement nodded and accompanied Lowe to the next room. Inside, Clement saw a man sitting at the table. He was devoid of expression, verging on boredom. And the complete antithesis to Reeves.

'Full name?'

'Stephen Bretton.'

'No middle name?' Lowe asked.

'My father didn't believe in them.'

Lowe asked the same set of questions he'd put to Reeve. When asked his occupation, Bretton said, *doctor*.

'Of medicine?' Clement asked.

'Yes.'

'And presumably you would know the correct dosages of injectable drugs?' Lowe asked.

'Naturally.'

'Are you still practicing?'

'Only in an advisory capacity.'

'To whom?' Clement asked.

'Archie and I have been together for years. We were both in India. We were with the entertainment corps and aside from singing in the chorus, I was also the assigned doctor for the troupe.'

'How is it he has the rank of colonel?' Clement asked.

'It's an honorary title.'

'In other words, made up!' Lowe said. 'Falsifying a military rank is a punishable offence.'

'Then charge him. He's a harmless man who lives in his dreams. Let him have them. He's not hurting anyone.' Betton leaned back in the chair and crossed his arms, his steely gaze on Lowe. 'I've come across men like you before. You're a real bully, aren't you, Inspector.'

'That'll be enough from you.'

'How is it you reside permanently at the guest house?' Clement broke in.

Bretton's eyes shifted to Clement. 'It has a nice view.'

Clement wondered about the response. 'Is there a reason you don't call yourself Doctor Bretton?'

'Specialists are referred to as *mister.*'

'What's your date of birth?' Lowe snapped.

'January the first, 1900.'

Clement studied Bretton as the man answered Lowe's question. His responses were quick but told them little. His dark eyes were focused and determined, yet imbued with snide indifference. And if he wasn't lying about his date of birth, he was also fifteen years younger than Reeve. And where Reeve had been indignant throughout Lowe's interrogation, Bretton was almost sarcastic.

'What is your relationship with Muriel Pendleton?' Clement asked.

Bretton shifted his gaze to Clement. 'I know her not!'

'And the child in the silver framed photograph in your room?'

'None of your business.' Bretton leaned back in the chair.

Lowe stood and he and Clement left the room. 'He's lying, Henry.'

'Yes, he is. We'll ask Reeve about the picture.'

Following Lowe, they returned to the interview room where Reeve waited. Lowe pulled out the chair and sat.

'There is a photograph of you and Mr Bretton in a silver frame in his room at the guest house. Who is the child in the photograph?'

'I don't know. No one. Just a child actor. I don't remember his name.'

'So it is a boy under all that make-up?' Clement said.

'I'm not saying anything more.'

Clement and Lowe left the room and stood in the corridor outside the interview rooms. 'They're both lying.'

'I agree. We'll let them sweat a bit,' Lowe said.

'You'll keep them here?'

'Neither of them is going anyway, have no fear of that, Clement.'

Preston walked towards them. 'Excuse me, Sir. We've found some letters in the room of Messrs. Reeve and Bretton at the guest house. It appears that at least one of them speaks fluent Japanese.'

'Well done, Preston!' Lowe said.

CHAPTER THIRTY

Sunday 31st May 1942

'Do you have them?' Lowe asked.

'On your desk, Sir.'

'Can you read Japanese, Clement?' Lowe asked.

'No, but I know someone who can.'

Lowe pulled his fob watch chain and glanced at this watch. 'I could drive you to The Metropole. I'm sure she'll be there now.'

Clement smiled.

Going to Lowe's office, Lowe handed Clement the small parcel of letters. They were tied together with a blue ribbon, and none seemed to have envelopes. Clement turned the bundle over in his hand. There were five letters in all.

Leaving the police station, they drove to the Metropole Hotel. Lowe parked the police vehicle outside the front entrance. As they walked in, Evelyn was in the foyer, standing facing them as they approached.

Clement smiled when he saw her. 'You were expecting us?'

'Saw the car pull up. With no siren blaring, I assumed you came to see me. How can I help?'

'We need your linguistic skills, Evelyn,' Clement said.

'We should sit inside.' Evelyn led the way to a group of chairs in a reading lounge off to one side of the foyer where it was quieter. No one was there.

'Can you translate these?' Clement handed the bundle to Evelyn.

She pulled the blue ribbon and carefully opened each page then laid them side by side on a low table in front of them. 'No envelopes?'

'No. Just the letters, so we don't know who the intended recipient was or where the letters were sent from,' Lowe stated.

For some minutes she studied them, then lifted her head. 'I'll try to get them into chronological order.'

Clement and Lowe waited while she pored over the letters. 'They're not in code or enciphered. But they are personal. Written to someone who knew the sender well. And, written by a man to a woman.'

'You're sure they weren't sent to a man?'

'When I explain, you'll understand, Inspector.'

'What do they say?' Lowe urged.

'The earliest dated one refers to a night of passion that he'll not forget. The next is a month later when he's ardour has definitely cooled, saying that distance had made any future between them impossible. Then this,' she said, holding up the third letter. 'It's written two months later, and he's telling her not to write to him again and that he can't help her.' Evelyn looked up at Clement and Lowe.

'I don't think you'll need much imagination to work out what that's about. The fourth is a further two months later again. But the tone is quite angry. Don't contact me again, etc. etc. And the fifth is a threat. I want nothing to do with you or the child and if you ever contact me again, there'll be trouble. Although it doesn't say what form that trouble would take.'

'Is it signed?' Clement asked.

'First name only. *Tony.*'

'How long ago were these letters written?'

Evelyn flipped them over in her hand. 'Over twenty years. The first is dated August 1919, the last June 1920.'

'Henry, can you ask one of your men to get the photograph of Bretton, Reeve and a small child from the guest house?

'The one in the silver frame, where they're all wearing Oriental costumes?'

Clement nodded.

'I'll ask Preston to go now.' Lowe stood and walked towards the hotel reception desk to telephone the police station.

'How are you, Clement?' Evelyn said.

'I'll survive. You? How's your shoulder?'

'I'm fine. Although I'll be pleased when all this is over. Are you close to finding out what it's all about?'

'It's confusing. It's definitely espionage, but there is something personal about it all.'

'That's what makes it confusing. Is WESC in danger of being closed down?'

'I think the work Mrs McKenzie and Veronica are doing there is too important for that. They are very good at teaching Morse Code. Besides the armed forces need the women graduates with so many men serving now. And, with the Royal Australian Navy sending men as well, it's vital work. Besides which, I'm not convinced the organisation itself is involved.'

'Wasn't Peggy Seaton passing on names and addresses?'

'It seems likely. But that doesn't explain Hank Veretti's death.'

'And the others? Edwina and Peggy?'

'Edwina may have witnessed something. I'm sure Peggy was used to pass on information, but that's all. She made a mistake. Two in fact, the first was getting involved and the second was leaving the house in Newtown.'

'Why was leaving that house a mistake?'

'Because it showed them she was no longer willing to do their bidding. Too great a danger she may go to the police.'

'But?'

'Sorry?'

'Clement, I've known you long enough to know when you're either planning something or you know something that others don't. So would you care to explain your sudden interest in a photograph of Bretton and Reeve with a young child?'

'There is a picture of them taken approximately twenty years ago with a child. They are all wearing Oriental costumes and the photograph seems to be of a theatrical performance, possibly the *Mikado*. I'm hoping there may be something secreted in the frame that will identify the location or the child. That child would now be in his mid-twenties.'

'You know it's a boy?'

'Yes. Reeve said so.'

'How does it help?'

'Truly, I don't know. It is evident they had, or still have, a radio transmitter. The van was in the garage at the guest house and, Hank Veretti, who seems pivotal to all this, was for some time imprisoned in the mechanic's pit there. But Mrs Pendleton doesn't fit the pink shoes.'

'What about a drink, Clement?'

Clement stared at her. 'I rarely drink alcohol.'

'I think this is the perfect time for you to let your hair down, Clement Wisdom. Tea just won't do this time.' Standing, Evelyn walked over to the bar and ordered two glasses of whisky.

Lowe returned and sat heavily in the chair beside Clement. 'Preston will get it.' Lowe checked his watch. 'I should get home. My wife has been wanting me to assist with moving some furniture. Why the house needs rearranging is beyond me. Perhaps she wants it looking nice for the Japanese invasion.'

'I'll see you tomorrow, Henry.' Clement watched Lowe leave the hotel, then took another sip of whisky. 'Is Veronica still with you?'

'Yes. Although she wanted some extra clothes from her home, so took the bus to Glebe this morning.'

'Do the police know she did this?'

'I don't know. Do you still suspect her?'

'In truth, Evelyn, I don't know who to trust other than yourself, Joe, Tom and Mick.'

'How is Archer?'

'Much improved.' Clement sipped the whisky. The warmth of the heating in the hotel and the alcohol was comforting.

'What's about to happen, Clement?'

'I may fall asleep.'

'Not quite what I meant.'

'Evelyn, it's so complicated. Perhaps I just can't see the wood for the trees, as the saying goes.' Not far away and man started to play a piano. 'I'd better check on Archer and Savage. Do you know they want to come with me, when I return home?'

'Archer! In England!'

'I know. Incongruous as it sounds, I wouldn't mind having both of them along next time.'

'The sight of Archer and Savage will certainly confuse the Germans.'

Clement laughed aloud. 'You're good for the soul, Evelyn. Have you finished at WESC?'

'Yes. I'm just waiting now for clearance from Inspector Lowe to leave. Despite the circumstances, it has been good seeing you again. Will you stay here in Australia?'

'I think that unlikely. I'm supposed to do a job in the north of Scotland during the northern winter. And, unless I hear to the contrary, I still am expected back to do that.'

'Northern Scotland. I have not missed our winters since living in this part of the world.'

'I think you will notice a big difference at home. It's grim. Food shortages. Little petrol. Trains are painted black and overcrowded. And then there's the bombing raids.' Clement paused, then folding his napkin, stood. 'I should go. It's getting late. Thank you for the drink.' Clement looked through the window to the street beyond. People were running, hurrying to get out of the rain, their umbrellas bent against the wind.

'I'll walk with you to the door,' Evelyn said. 'Goodbye, Clement. Look me up when you get home.' Holding his forearm, she kissed his cheek.

'May God be with you, Evelyn.' Placing his hat on his head, he walked away. Outside, he walked towards Castlereagh Street to catch a tram.

It was just after five, and the short winter twilight was gone. Rain pattered his hat, and he felt the strong wind rushing between the buildings. On Castlereagh Street, he saw an approaching tram and waved it down. Stepping onboard, he shook the rain from his hat and coat.

'Which stop?' a bright voice beside him said.

'Victoria Barracks, please,' Clement answered.

The young woman flipped a handle on the ticket dispensing machine slung around her hips and handed him the ticket. 'Can I help you with your coat, dearie?'

Clement smiled. 'Thank you, but I can manage.' He sat near the window on the lower level, his coat in his lap. The young woman returned to her spot near the stairs to the upper deck. The tram was crowded.

His mind oscillated between Evelyn and Muriel Pendleton. Evelyn's company he enjoyed. Muriel Pendleton was another matter. He didn't understand women like her. What motivated people to kill? He visualised her sitting on the piano stool. So defiant. And silent. Why was she prepared to remain silent and possibly face the hangman's noose? He felt he was correct about maternal instinct. It was a strong motivational force. And one that would certainly keep a mother from implicating her child. Sunday. As frustrating as it was, he had to wait for the government departments and banks to reopen on Monday. At least Muriel Pendleton was in custody.

He sat on the veranda at Victoria Barracks and stared into the dark sky. They'd been so close. At night, especially in his dreams, the sight of two men and one woman running away from the kitchen door of the guest house played and replayed in his head. He decided to retire early. He had a headache.

CHAPTER THIRTY-ONE

Sunday 31st May 1942

A tremendous explosion lit up the night sky over Sydney, blowing the windows of Clement's room wide open, the glass smashing and spraying over the carpet. Cold air poured in. Instantly awake, he grabbed his dressing gown, then checked the time. Just before half past ten. Rushing, he went to the veranda. Below him, the parade ground was quickly filling with men. Clement looked up. Searchlight beams crisscrossed the night sky. But he saw no aeroplanes caught in their glare. Returning to his room, he dressed and went straight to the briefing room.

Within minutes, Tom and Mick entered. 'What's happening, Clem? The invasion?'

'I don't know, Tom. But get all your weaponry, some rope, binoculars, and anything else you think we may need and meet me back here in five minutes. Mick bring that rifle and your grandfather's scope. A grenade or two wouldn't hurt. And dress warmly.'

Archer and Savage left. Clement lifted the receiver and dialled the police station number.

'Can I leave an urgent message for Inspector Lowe?' Clement asked.

'I don't expect him before tomorrow, sir. But of course you can leave a message.'

'Did you hear the explosion just now, Constable?'

'Yes, sir.'

'I think it is more than likely Inspector Lowe will be in soon. Please tell him that Major Wisdom and two of his team are going to Garden Island Naval Dockyard. Did you get that, Constable? This is top priority! He must meet me there.'

'Yes, sir.'

Clement hung up just as Archer and Savage returned. 'What do you want us to do?'

'Follow me,' Clement said, pulling on his overcoat. He checked his Fairbairn Sykes knife and Welrod. Locking the door, they hurried through the main gate.

Running, they left Victoria Barracks. Clement kept his eye out for any passing taxis, but with the explosion and the search lights, people had come out onto the street and all available taxis already had passengers. Panic was quickly gripping the city.

Forty minutes later, they crouched on the hill in Macleay Street, the sentry box into Garden Island Naval Base in the centre of Clement's vision. Beyond, the construction lights were still blazing, flooding the darkness and turning night to day. Clement stared in amazement at the ships moored in the harbour. Silhouetted against the night sky by the intense lights at the dockyard, they lay at

276

anchor like sitting ducks in a side show alley. Then *Chicago* began to fire. Traces, like fireworks lit up the night and thick pungent smoke smelling of cordite spread across the harbour.

'Struth! What a sight!' Archer said.

Clement's gaze searched the skies, but he still saw no aeroplanes.

'What are they firing at?' Mick asked.

'From the angle of the tracers, it must be a submarine!' Archer said.

'Or several,' Clement added.

Another loud detonation reverberated around them, the earth shaking from the intensity of the blasts. A ship adjacent to the *Chicago* also started to fire. Around them, the harbour was total mayhem. 'Come on!' Clement shouted above the uproar. Running on, they ran down the hill and through the main gate to the Naval Base. Clement couldn't see the sentry. Chaos had ensued, and men were running all over the dockyards. Clement signalled for them to slow to a walk. 'This way,' he whispered, and keeping together, they headed for the eastern side of the wharf where Clement knew the *Kuttabul* was tied up. Clement made straight for some cargo on the wharf and hid behind it. Below him, several smaller craft were tied up there. In front of the *Kuttabul*, a small motorboat was tying up. One man, bent over, was tying a rope around the shoreline that led from the *Kuttabul* to the wharf above.

Clement waited, his eyes fixed on whoever came onshore. Within minutes, two men climbed onto the wharf.

'Wait!' Clement whispered again as another loud explosion blasted from a gun on a ship anchored not far away.

Clement kept his eye on the two men and the small motorboat. A third man stayed on board the vessel. 'Thanks. Make sure the boat is tied securely. Wait until they surface before making contact. Then come as soon as you can. See you there.'

The voice was loud, loud enough for Clement to hear above the barrage of explosions and chaos around him and on the harbour.

Staying low, he watched the two men walk briskly along the wharf, heading for the main gate. Neither carried anything. And both were wearing blue trousers and shirts with heavy jackets, exactly like the ones he'd seen hanging in the wardrobe at the guest house.

'Tom, you and Mick stay behind them. I'll circle around and confront them near the main gate. As soon as you see me, close in around them.'

Darting between the cargo, Clement hurried back to the main gate. He hoped the sentry was back at his box, but the man was nowhere to be seen. Clement saw the two men approaching the boom gate and withdrawing his Welrod, stood at the entry, his eyes fixed on the approaching men. Behind them, he could see Archer and Savage quietly closing in behind them.

He heard the screech of brakes behind him.

'Clem!' Tom screamed, his voice loud, the scream long and hard-edged. Clement heard the terrified warning and dropped to the ground as multiple gunshots rang out. The two men before him ran towards the gate. Then another shot. In front of him, he saw Mick lying on the ground, a rifle in his hands and his eye to his grandfather's scope.

Clement rolled over and over until he was near a stack of boxes, then stood. His eyes scanned the scene, looking for Archer and Savage. Savage was still on the ground, his rifle to his eye. Archer was behind the sentry box. Clement looked out towards the street. A car had pulled up and the rear door was flung open. The two men were running towards the car. Mick's carefully aimed shot had hit one man in the leg. The other man grabbed his injured partner and together they hurried towards the waiting car. Mick lay still, preparing for his second shot. As he fired, the car door slammed and drove away at speed.

Clement ran forward. 'Either of you hurt?' he yelled.

'No,' Tom shouted.

Mick stood. 'I got him in the leg and maybe the chest. Not sure about the second shot. It could have just hit the car.'

'I owe you both my life.'

'See, Clem. You can't do without us!' Tom said, grinning.

Clement looked up at the sky, then back towards the city buildings. Rain was falling, but the turmoil on the harbour had not diminished. Smoke from all the explosions was settling over the scene, and with the wind, the dense clouds were lessening but the smell of gunpowder was all pervasive. An eerie moonlight from the near full moon highlighted a scene of confusion and disorder.

'What on Earth is happening?' Tom said.

'I don't know. But that boat won't take itself back across the harbour.' Clement followed by Archer and Savage ran back towards the *Kuttabul*. All around them, people were running. With the help of the light from the dockyard works, Clement could see the small boat had gone. 'Can you pass me your scope, Mick?'

Removing it from the rifle, Mick passed it to Clement. Holding it to his eye, Clement panned the frantic scene. In front of him, the *Chicago* was still firing into the water, the bright traces spectacular in the night sky. Searchlights flooded the skies with beams of piercing light, and boats of all sizes and types were crisscrossing the turbulent waters. Smoke from the incessant firing of guns continued to fill the night and mixed with the inclement weather. Think! he told himself. Where would they go? Training the scope on Cremorne Point, he slowly panned the scope across the bay towards the *Westralia* in Athol Bight. A small craft was approaching the bay at high speed.

'We have to get across the harbour.'

'What now?' Tom said.

Below them, another larger launch was tied up near the *Kuttabul*. It had a good-sized deck and was larger enough to have sleeping quarters below. Clement jumped onboard.

'I am Major Wisdom of Special Forces. Can you take us across the harbour? To Athol Bight?'

'Tell me why and I'll see,' the owner of the boat said.

'I need to get a closer look at a small motorboat that left here a few minutes ago. Did you see it?'

'No. We were watching the barrage from here but not venturing out, in case a bomb landed nearby.'

'I don't have much time. But it is of national importance that I board that motorboat.'

The man nodded. Within a few minutes, the launch's motor roared into life and with the aid of the three other men onboard, they cast off and motored into the dark waters.

'I think whoever is on that boat will rendezvous with the enemy. We need to find them. How long to get across, do you think?' Clement asked.

'I don't want to go anywhere near the *Chicago* or the other big ships. If they are the target, we could be blown to pieces. With any luck there'll be a ferry leaving Circular Quay. We'll tag along behind them. It may take us the best part of an hour, though.'

'An hour! Can we make it sooner?' Clement knew that whoever was onboard the small boat once owned by Charlie Manning got into Athol Bight or Cremorne Bay, without being seen, he'd never find them.

'Do you have a radio onboard?'

'Of course.'

'May I use it?'

'It's a public frequency. Whatever you say will be overheard.'

'I understand. I don't suppose you have a morse code key for sending messages?'

'I've no reason to. Sorry. This isn't a naval vessel. I was only tied up at Garden Island because a mate of mine works there currently, and I offered him a bunk for the night. He's usually on the *Kuttabul*. But it's pretty spartan. I'll show you where the radio is.'

Clement followed the man below to the wireless. Holding the handset and depressing the button, he called for anyone at Victoria Barracks to respond. After five attempts, he heard a voice.

'Who is this?'

'Major Clement Wisdom. I need to get a message to Inspector Henry Lowe of Sydney Central Police.'

'Clement! Clement! It's Joe. Don't give your location, just listen. Heard from FRUMEL. Urgent you return here.'

CHAPTER THIRTY-TWO

Monday 1st June 1942

Clement checked his watch. It was well after midnight, and they were just off the fortress like structure built on a rock in the middle of the harbour, Fort Denison. Clement thought for a moment. Athol Bight was still a distance away. While he wanted to catch the man on the motorboat, he realised it was now well ahead of them, and chances were that whoever had been onboard had already tied it up somewhere and vanished into the night. 'Do you mind returning?' Clement asked the bewildered skipper.

A roar so loud shattered the night. A fiery ball of explosives and water shot into the air, sending a column of sea water heavenward. Visible from the light of the adjacent dockyards, Clement saw the *Kuttabul* fly upwards as though tossed by a giant hand. Then it slammed back into the harbour, fracturing the large wooden ship in two and sending shards of timber and other debris in all directions. In that second, the lights of the dockyard went out. The skipper and Clement stared at the fireball that was now quickly consuming the *Kuttabul*. In the glare of the flames, Clement could see men running.

'Struth! No one could survive that!' Tom said.

The owner of the launch stood beside Clement and Tom. 'We'll go anywhere you want, Major. If we'd still been tied up next to the *Kuttabul*, we'd all be dead.'

'Perhaps we could go to Circular Quay. It will be less congested, and we'll only be in their way of rescuing anyone still alive there.' For one moment Clement thought of Jim Lockhart. If he'd been aboard the *Kuttabul*, there was little likelihood he'd survive.

Thanking the owner of the motor launch, Clement with Tom and Mick headed out into the streets bordering Circular Quay. People were everywhere. 'This way,' Clement called to Archer and Savage. Pushing his way through the crowd, they headed for the trams on Castlereagh Street.

It was nearly two o'clock when they walked into Victoria Barracks. Clement went straight to the briefing room hoping Joe would be there.

'Clement!' It was Joe's voice.

Clement turned.

Joe was running towards them. 'Are you all alright? When I heard that explosion, I feared the worst.'

'We're fine Joe. What's the message from FRUMEL?'

'They've picked up a signal within a three mile radius of the city.'

'Do we know what it says?'

'It was strange. And made no sense. So maybe they got the decrypt wrong.'

'What do they think it says?' Clement urged.

'*Operation Butterfly, on standby*. That's what was transmitted. And it was signed *Sorrow*.'

'*On standby* surely implies there's a rendezvous and I think I know where, but what we don't know is when.' Clement paused. 'Can they find out exactly where the signal came from?'

'Triangulation puts it in the city.'

Clement opened the door to the briefing room and threw his coat over a chair. He slumped into a chair. His mind was spinning, and every muscle ached. 'A three-mile radius, Joe! Could be coming from anywhere on either side of the harbour! It would be like looking for a needle in a haystack!' The telephone in the corner rang, its insistent ring boring into Clement's already throbbing headache. He reached for the receiver.

'Clement?'

'Speaking.'

'Clement. It's Eric Nave here.'

'Eric? I'm guessing you know what's happening here. What is it?'

'Just thought I'd let you know. I'm aware of the message FRUMEL decrypted earlier, but I think I can add something. There was a message intercepted three days ago that didn't make much sense this end, so it was ignored here. But in view of today's transmission, it may be significant. It was just a group of co-ordinates and a time. I've checked the precise location, and it's in the middle of a bay, which is why it was disregarded as incorrect.'

'Where, Eric?'

'A place called Athol Bight. The time mentioned is 0400.'

Clement felt the icy finger course through his body. 'Thank you, Eric.'

'Anything else I can help with, Clem?' Joe asked.

'Stay by the radio. And thank you, Joe.'

Pressing the dial tone, Clement rang Sydney Central Police Station and asked for Henry Lowe.

'Inspector Lowe is here, Sir,' Preston said. 'With all that's going on, every policeman in Sydney has been ordered in. He got your message and went to Garden Island, but by the time he got there, the whole harbour was in uproar. He guessed you'd contact him when you could. I'll put you though now.'

Clement waited only a few seconds before the call was connected.

'Henry?'

'Clement? Where the devil are you?'

Clement relayed what had happened and what he'd learned from both Joe and Eric Nave.

'What do you want to do, Clement?'

Clement thought for a moment, then glanced at his watch. It was already after three. With the harbour still in total confusion, notifying the authorities would take hours, even if the telephone lines were not either down or jammed. And even more time for them to consider whether it was important enough for them to bother with getting someone to Athol Bight. 'Can you pick us up in five minutes? We need to go to any public mooring in the Athol Bay area. And Henry, we'll need a boat.'

Clement along with Archer and Savage waited by the main gate. Overhead, the thick smoke clouds from the explosions had long since vanished and the full moon was casting its blueish light over an empty parade ground. Neither could he hear any more of the deep booming sound of ships' guns. He stamped his feet on the hard surface to mitigate the cold. He felt they were close now.

Looking up, Clement's eye caught the flashing blue light of the approaching police car. Running towards it, Clement, Archer and Savage, jumped in and the car sped off, heading for the Harbour Bridge. As they crossed the ironwork structure, Clement saw the large American ship, *Chicago,* had slipped its mooring and, doubtless was heading out to sea as indeed were other ships. In the eerie moonlight, the whole place was a seething mass of shipping all on the move. The danger of running into another ship was great, especially at night and in the confines of Sydney Harbour. Clement also realised that he'd not seen or heard a single aeroplane, despite the hours the search lights had illuminated the sky about the harbour city. It could only mean one thing; the attack had been solely from enemy submarines. Just like the German Uboat-47 that had entered Scapa Flow back in '39, so the Japanese had entered Sydney. But how many submarines had come and where from? More importantly, were they still there, lying on the bottom of the harbour waiting to wreak havoc? These were questions Clement couldn't answer. Nor did he need to. But he surmised the dismissive Rear-Admiral Muirhead-Gould would have to, either this night or sometime in the future to a board of enquiry.

As the car pulled up near Athol Wharf, he saw a small dinghy tied up there. 'Belongs to one of our local lads, uses it for fishing apparently, but it should do for our purposes,' Lowe said, striding along the jetty.

Clement followed. 'Mick, stay here and kept your telescope trained on any buoy in the bay where there is only one small launch tied up there,' Clement said, pointing out over the dark waters.

Mick lay on the wooden jetty and gripped his rifle, his eye pressed to the sight. 'There's one tied to a mooring,' Mick said, his finger pointing out into the bay. Clement crouched down beside him, and Mick passed the rifle to him. There in the sight was the launch he'd seen tied up by the *Kuttabul*. A man stood near the helm.

'That's it,' Clement said, passing the rifle back to Mick. 'Can you see the person clearly?'

Mick held the weapon still and focused on the launch. 'Yep.'

Just at that moment, across the harbour, they could hear the barking of orders over a ship's loudspeakers, and coming from one of the larger ships leaving port.

'I see him. He's distracted by what' happening on the harbour. Want me to take him out, Clem?'

'No, Mick. We want him alive. And I don't want him wounded either unless absolutely necessary. He could

288

make enough noise to frighten away whoever he's meeting. I'll signal you if you need to fire.'

'What do you want me to do, Clem?' Tom asked.

'Henry, Tom should row. You sit in the stern with me in the bow. That way, you can stand and arrest him. I'll keep a pistol on him. And Mick is under my orders to keep him in his sights from the jetty.'

Climbing into the dinghy, they settled themselves. Using the oar, Archer pushed the craft off the jetty, then quickly placed it into the rowlocks and began to pull. With the distraction of the large ships manoeuvring on the harbour, Clement believed the man on the launch was totally unaware of their presence. Archer dipped the oars quietly into the water. About thirty feet from the launch, the dinghy began to rock in unexpected choppy waves. Holding the gunwales, Clement looked around for the cause. He couldn't see any shipping. Then, in the strong moonlight, he saw it. Rising like a dagger through the waves, a periscope glinted in the nocturnal light. Then the black metal hull of a submarine quietly rose before them.

CHAPTER THIRTY- THREE

Monday 1st June 1942

Clement stared at the rising mammoth. It silently emerged out of the inky water before them. It was beyond belief. He leaned forward to whisper to Tom. 'Pull the starboard oar in, quietly!' Hunching low in the bow, Clement gripped the oar, and kneeling in the bow, he paddled using a figure of eight movement. Silently he manoeuvred the craft alongside the launch. There they waited in the motorboat's lee as the submarine surfaced on the other side of the launch.

On the wind, Clement heard the conning tower hatch open. Then someone spoke in Japanese. Another responded. A few seconds later, the conning tower hatch closed.

As the submarine sank, it caused the water to rush forward, the waves around the submerging sub suctioning the motorboat towards it and making the dinghy roll and slap the surface waves. The dinghy bumped the side of the launch, as the two vessels bounced off each other.

In a second, Clement pulled himself onto the launch and rolled under a canvas cover lying on the deck.

From where he lay, he saw Tom pull the Welrod from this shirt. The man on board stood on the deck, staring into the waters.

'You're under arrest!' Lowe said loudly.

'He's got a gun,' Tom shouted.

The man fired, but with the rocking of the jostling boats, the shot went wide. Clement lifted the cover and quietly stood, the man's back was towards him. Archer was holding the man's attention with his Welrod held high and pointed directly at the man's chest. Clement inched forward, the Welrod in his grip and held it to the man's back.

'Move and you will die,' Clement whispered, his Welrod in his right hand still firmly against the man's back. 'Raise your arms, slowly!' Clement reached up with his left hand and wrenched the pistol gripped in the man's hand, then tossed it into the waters of Athol Bay.

Lowe shone a torch into the face of the man.

'Well. Well. I'd recognise that face anywhere, not to mention that fist,' Tom said.

Clement stepped sideways to see the man's face. Before him was John Connor. Connor's eyes shifted from Archer to Clement, the icy stare was, so Clement believed, intended to intimidate. In a second Clement realised Connor had not been recently recruited to a life in espionage. Clement could see the emotionless gaze of a professional. 'Help Mr Connor into the dinghy would you Tom?'

'It will be a pleasure.' Tom climbed onboard the launch and grasped Connor by the back of his neck. With his other hand, he twisted Connor's right arm up behind his back, then held him firmly while Lowe held a pistol on him.

'Climb over the rail, slowly. Then on your knees. Then lower yourself into the dinghy. You try anything, and you'll regret it,' Archer whispered.

Tom climbed over the side of the launch beside Connor and waited while Connor lowered himself into the dinghy.

As he did, Connor grabbed a concealed knife in his belt and twisting, lunged at Archer. Archer swung back to avoid the slicing blade. Then Connor stopped, motionless. Clement stared at Tom then Connor. The man's eyes were wide, and he stood rigid, as though caught in an imagined vice. A second later, he slumped sideways, falling backwards into the boat below. Lowe caught hold of Connor's shoulders as he fell and lowered him into the dinghy floor.

'Tom?' Clement asked.

'Not me.'

Connor lay curled on the floor of the dinghy, gasping for air, his right arm holding his side. Lowe flicked on a torch. Blood was soaking into Connor's shirt.

'Gunshot wound,' Lowe said.

'Mick doesn't miss. But it's usually not fatal. Unless he wants it to be,' Archer said.

'What was in the briefcase?' Clement asked, but Connor couldn't answer. His raspy breathing made answering questions unlikely. If the briefcase contained secret information sourced from the *Chicago*, it would not be of any use to the Japanese for more than a few hours. Vice-Admiral Leary would be notified, and the plans altered.

Clement climbed back down into the dinghy. With Connor lying curled on the floor of the boat, Tom rowed back to the wharf. Archer and Lowe lifted Connor onto the jetty then Tom and Mick carried him to the waiting police car.

'Clement, you need to let your people know about tonight's events. I'll get Connor to Sydney Hospital, but he'll be under police guard in a private room and no visitors allowed. If he lives, he's not going anywhere. Except to prison. But there isn't room for all of us in the car. Can your team get their own way back?'

'Don't worry about us, Clem. See you back at VB later,' Tom answered.

'Best I take the rifle, Mick. Don't want to alarm the public.'

They put Connor on the back seat with Clement in front and Lowe driving and locked all the doors. With the siren blaring, it took less than fifteen minutes to get Connor to Sydney Hospital. But the hospital was in chaos from the evening's events. People were everywhere. Some with minor injuries, from splintered timber or shattered glass. Others, like the survivors from the explosion, were given priority. Clement watched the stretcher bearers take Connor inside.

Lowe stood on the footpath beside Clement. 'Keep that rifle well hidden, would you Clement. Don't need any more mayhem in the streets. I'd better go with him. Don't want him absconding after all this. And well done tonight. You and your team are a formidable force. I'll need to get back to Central Avenue soon. Paperwork. Endless quantities of the stuff. Well, I suppose we have our killer, although I'll let you know more when I can question him.'

'Thank you, Henry.' Clement watched Lowe walk into the hospital casualty department.

He glanced along Macquarie Street. People was still everywhere. Despite the inclement weather, he wanted to walk for a while. Adrenaline had kept him going but now it was wearing off, he felt exhausted. And, he needed to think. For that, he needed to be alone. Pulling his coat around him, he pushed his hands into his pockets and started to walk along Macquarie Street.

'Have you heard?' a man near Clement said.

'Sorry?'

'They sank the *Kuttabul*? Some of our chaps are dead. Blown to pieces while they slept! Why would the Japs do that?'

Clement's thoughts went immediately to Jim Lockhart. 'Are there any survivors?'

'I think so. Although, they're pretty bad. It was just an old ferry turned navy ship. Of no strategic importance at all.' The man shook his head in disbelief and wandered away.

Clement's thoughts returned to Lockhart. If Lockhart had been aboard the vessel at the time of the explosion, he had most likely not survived. But Clement wanted to know. Walking back into the hospital he approached a nurse.

'Do you know if a James Lockhart has been brought in tonight? He was on the *Kuttabul*.'

'Are you a relative?'

'No.'

'I'm sorry. Until the next of kin have been contacted, I cannot say.'

'Thank you, anyway.'

Clement walked away. He prayed Lockhart had not been aboard or, if he had, that he'd been saved. Lockhart wasn't completely off Clement's list, but if the young man was innocent of any involvement with the conspirators, then Clement felt nothing but sadness for a life so utterly wasted.

The cold night air burrowed into his flesh, and he checked his watch; four o'clock in the morning. He needed to contact Long in Melbourne, but given the early morning hour and the enemy's attack on the harbour, Clement thought it unlikely Commander Long would be a busy man. Another hour wouldn't make much difference to the outcome. With the mayhem on the harbour, the Japanese submarines would be caught. He pondered the courage of such men. Enemy or not, to die under the sea in not much more than a tin was true bravery.

Clement stared at the buildings as he walked along Macquarie Street, Mick's rifle tucked under his arm and beneath his coat. He wanted to ask someone about the message Nave had sent and he knew only one person who could help. Even though it was late, and given the events of the night, he thought it unlikely anyone living in the city could have slept through the booming noise of bombardment. Most people, he surmised would be waiting for news. Only the people who lived around the harbour itself would know the ships had left port. That had been done with as much speed as the various captains could manage. He recalled hearing the bellowed orders coming from aboard the *Chicago* and *Perkins* as they fled the disorder in the harbour.

Catching a late tram, he rode it uptown, alighting near the Metropole Hotel. Swinging the glass door wide, he walked towards the man at the hotel reception desk. He glanced around the foyer, but few people were about. 'Would Miss Evelyn Howard still be in residence at the hotel?'

'Room 27, Sir.'

Clement made his way to the second floor and knocked at the door. A few minutes passed before Evelyn opened it. As she peered into the corridor, she gathered the dressing gown around her. 'Clement?'

'I'm so sorry to disturb you at this hour.'

'It's perfectly alright. Given what's happened tonight, I'm not surprised to see you. What is it?'

'I need to ask you about something.'

She opened the door wide.

'I'd feel better if you came into the corridor.'

'Is it a security issue?'

Clement nodded.

'Inside is best.' Evelyn stood back and Clement walked in, Evelyn closing the door behind him.

'You once said Mrs Pendleton listened to opera almost continuously. And that she had a favourite. Can you recall what that was?'

Evelyn laughed aloud. 'Of all the things I thought you would ask about, Clement, grand opera wasn't one of them. But yes, I remember. It was an aria called *One Fine Day*. It's from Puccini's opera *Madame Butterfly*.'

'Butterfly? You said, Butterfly?'

'Clement! You look like you've seen a ghost. What is it?'

Clement told her about the telephone call he'd received from Eric Nave. *Operation Butterfly, on standby*. And signed *Sorrow*.

'When did he decrypt the message?'

'A few days ago. But it was dismissed as either a mistake or unimportant.'

'You think it's about tonight's event in Athol Bight?'

'It must be. I just can't work out why Veretti, a purple heart recipient, would betray his country by passing intelligence to the enemy. And if he was one of them, why they killed him!'

'We need to know the identity of *Sorrow*.' She paused. 'There must be a clue in the opera. The Conservatorium of Music is a few streets away. Tomorrow, we can get a copy of the operatic score from them. There will be some reference to something or rather, someone being sorrowful.'

'What was the plot?'

'An American sailor married a Japanese girl, referred to as *Butterfly,* and she became pregnant. But he left Japan and returned to his so-called *real* wife, in America. When Butterfly learns this, she kills herself leaving a young child. The key is the identity of *Sorrow.*'

CHAPTER THIRTY-FOUR

Monday 1st June 1942

Clement took the tram to Victoria Barracks. All he could think about was *Sorrow*. He didn't have a name, but he felt he understood. And it explained the motivation for Mrs Pendleton's treachery. Now he just had to wait for the various government departments of open for the day. Going straight to the briefing room, he sat in a chair with his feet on another and waited till nine o'clock then placed a call to Commander Rupert Long.

'I'll inform Leary about the theft of classified documents from the *Chicago,* and he can deal with Captain Bode. As for the identity of these murderers, you could leave it now with Inspector Lowe. Although, knowing you, Clement, you'll want to stay to the end. Just let me know when you're back in Melbourne.'

Thanking Long, Clement sat in the chair, his gaze on the map. With so many knowing about the attack, Clement knew it wouldn't be long before the enemy submarine was caught. He wondered if there was more than one. Regardless, the harbour defence authorities and the many anti-submarine patrol boats in the harbour would locate and apprehend them. But he thought it more likely that the Japanese crews would kill themselves and scuttle the vessel rather than let anything fall into enemy hands. Whatever the outcome, all the stolen documents would be destroyed.

The door opened.

'You look done in, Clem,' Archer said, striding into the room.

'You're right, Tom. Thank you both for last tonight. I owe you my life, both of you. And thank you, Mick, for your calm initiative in Athol Bay.'

'We're a team, Clem. And we're mates. That's what mates do,' Archer said.

Clement smiled. 'Get some rest, both of you. If I need you again later, I'll call. But please don't leave the barracks. We still have a spy to catch. Mick don't forget your rifle,' Clement added, handing the weapon to Savage.

Archer and Savage left him sitting in the briefing room. Leaning back in the chair, his mind and body yearned for rest and sleep. He could sleep now. For a few hours at least. Having chosen to follow the launch in Garden Island to Athol Bay, Clement knew that the two men Connor had left at the naval dockyard would, by now, have vanished. Or *gone bush*, as Lowe would say. And although Long had said to leave it to the police, he'd read Clement correctly. These people still had to be found. He visualised Win Hughes sitting on the windowsill at WESC. Her death perplexed him still.

Strolling back to his quarters, he fell onto the bed, then glanced at his watch. The weak morning sunlight was just coming over the windowsill. Windowsills. Images flashed through his mind as exhaustion took hold. Evelyn had left a shoe on one. Win used to sit on the windowsill at WESC warming her feet. Why had Win gone with Hank Veretti? And who was the woman in the pink shoes? And according to Joan's assessment, Hank wasn't Win's type. Clement sat up, frowning. Overtiredness was clouding his judgement. Why had Joan's assessment of Hank Veretti been so different to Billie's? And where was Joan? If they now had John Connor in custody albeit in hospital, where was Joan? With questions swirling around his mind, he set his alarm for noon and laid back on the pillow.

Clement woke with the alarm. Noon. He took his razor from his cupboard and went to the bathrooms to shower and shave. Standing under the warm running water, he tried to recall everything Joan and Billie had said about Veretti. But whichever way he thought about it, it sounded like they were describing two different people.

Clement held the razor, his arm still, his eyes on his own reflection. He could hear Billie's voice describing Veretti. Billie had called him a gentleman. Joan had described a scoundrel. Were there two men? Did that explain the difference in the belt buckle markings? How well did either woman know Hank Veretti? If neither had met Veretti before, it was possible they could describe him physically, but how well would they know his character, unless they'd been in his company for longer? Billie hardly knew him. She'd left him with Win and Joan in Clarence Street. But Joan had gone with them a few blocks further. And Joan lived at the guest house. She even accompanied Evelyn home. And now Joan had disappeared.

Going to the Mess, he drank a cup of tea, and walked out of the barracks onto Oxford Street then took the tram into the city. He needed to talk with Lowe but first he wanted to see Evelyn. Alighting near the Metropole Hotel, he hurried inside.

From the corner of his eye, he saw her sitting in the chair by the window. She was reading *Smith's Weekly's* report of the previous night's harbour fireworks.

'Clement? What more news?'

'Not here. If you get your coat, we can walk down to the quay.'

Evelyn left him to retrieve her coat, then joined him in the foyer.

'Have you seen Veronica?' Clement asked.

'Yes. We had breakfast together. She's back at WESC. And the reason for asking?'

'There's something more to tell you about last night.' He told her about John Connor and the submarine in Athol Bight.

'My goodness! A Japanese submarine! Dear Eric. I said he was undervalued. Thanks to him putting two and two together, you may find these killers. But now they have passed the information to the enemy, I suspect they'll go to ground. You may never find them if Mrs Pendleton can't be persuaded to tell you what she knows.'

'I need to find out about Mrs Pendleton's financial affairs. Sergeant Preston was looking into it this morning. And another matter. Could you do something for me?'

'Name it.'

'Could you go to the Conservatorium of Music and get a copy of the operatic score for Madame Butterfly?'

'Of course.'

'Can you bring it to Central Avenue?'

'Consider it done. I'll bring it to you there.'

Leaving her, he hailed a cab and went downtown to Central Avenue Police Station. It was congested with people, as usual. Clement asked to see Preston.

'If you'll wait here, Sir,' the constable said.

Fifteen minutes later, Preston took him to the first floor where they could talk without being overheard.

'I suppose Mrs Pendleton hasn't said anything?' Clement asked.

'Not a word.'

'Did you contact the Department of Births, Deaths and Marriages about her?'

'Yes. Spoke to them myself. There is no record of a Muriel Pendleton giving birth to anyone. So I checked the marriage register. No marriage either under that name. Sorry to say, unless she tells us her former name, I have no way of finding out if she was ever married.'

'Is there another register? In Melbourne, perhaps or elsewhere?'

'The Sydney register is for the state, so that's possible. However, she may have had another child or children and never registered them. It happens. This is a big country and if a child is born on a farm or in a remote country town, they may never be registered.' Preston paused. 'Of course, if the child is illegitimate, that would be reason enough for the mother not to register the baby at all.'

'And her financial affairs?'

'Still waiting on the bank records. I'll let you know once I've received something.'

Thanking Preston for his trouble, Clement took the stairs to leave. He could hear Lowe's voice coming from the lower floor and resounding on the hard walls of the stairwell. Clement waited, hoping he'd meet Lowe on the steps.

'Clement? Come to my office,' Lowe said, when he saw Clement. 'Quite a night! With those Jap submarines entering the harbour, it gave every criminal in Sydney the time and cover to do all sorts of misdemeanours. Do you know there was even a shooting in Woolloomooloo!'

'I think I can explain or at least add to that,' Clement said. They walked into Lowe's office and Clement told Lowe what had happened at Garden Island Naval Dockyards.

'Have you told Commander Long about the sub?'

'Yes. He'll contact the Americans.'

'The *Chicago* has gone, as you know,' Lowe added. 'And the *Perkins*. What a shambles! Ships everywhere, channel patrol boats, huge American warships, our own and all wanting to leave at the same time. Do you know that idiot Bode, left in such a hurry, he left a sailor on the mooring in the middle of the harbour? Wretched chap was yelling to them. And to make matters worse, the *Chicago's* second in command had to rejoin the ship by launch because Bode left without him. If the Japs had ships waiting outside Sydney Heads, they'd have been sitting ducks. It's a miracle they got away.'

'While we now know what they were doing, we still don't have all the killers. And if neither Connor nor Mrs Pendleton aren't talking, we may never have them,' Clement said. 'But I have some news about an intercept decrypted message intercepted in Melbourne. Clement told Lowe about *Operation Butterfly.*

'So who is this *Sorrow?*' Lowe asked.

'I don't know, yet. Evelyn is asking for a copy of the opera from the Conservatorium of Music. She said she'd bring it here.'

Lowe leaned back in his chair. 'Bad business all round. Do you have any hunches about *Sorrow's* identity?'

'I thought I did.'

'But not now?'

'They are certainly connected with Mrs Pendleton.' Clement wasn't sure any more about another child. With no records of her having another, earlier baby, he was no closer to identifying *Sorrow* than they had been previously.

Miss Simpson stuck her head around the office door. 'Miss Howard to see you, Inspector.'

Clement and Lowe stood as Evelyn took the vacant chair in Lowe's office.

'Anything?' Clement asked.

'Oh yes. *Sorrow* was male, approximately four years of age, and Madame Butterfly's child.'

'There is no record of Muriel Pendleton having other children, unfortunately Evelyn.'

'That's not to say she didn't have another. And it is, as far as I know, one of the strongest motivations for a woman to remain silent. She's protecting someone and with the threat of the gallows over her head, it could only be for her child. Although, I fear not Nigel. *Sorrow* could only be a favourite child, one born to the love of her life.'

'Henry, do you still have the photograph in the silver frame?'

'Yes. I'll get Preston to bring it up.' Lowe walked out of his office. Clement heard him requesting Miss Simpon to contact Preston. 'He's on to it.' Lowe resumed his seat. 'I have Peggy Seaton's parents coming in today. To officially identify her and for the undertakers to remove her body. If you'd care to stay, you're welcome to.'

Five minutes later, Preston knocked at the door. He handed the silver framed picture to Lowe. Turning it over, Lowe removed the photograph from the frame.

'Anything?' Clement asked.

It says, *Archie, me and Rick.*

Clement thought for a moment. 'Have you ever heard that name in connection with this investigation?'

'No. And Connor isn't talking. The other lad you talked about, Jim Lockhart? Sorry to tell you but he died on the *Kuttabul*. Doesn't rule out any involvement, but at least we don't have to look for him now.'

'That is terrible news. It appears he may have always been an innocent party to all this.' Clement thought briefly about Lockhart and wished he'd not been so suspicious of the young man. 'When are Peggy's parents due to arrive?'

Lowe glanced at the clock on the wall. 'I'm expecting them at two o'clock. Would you like to stay?'

Clement didn't wish to make a sad situation worse for the girl's parents; but he did want to ask them a few questions.

'Thank you. I would like to ask them about Peggy.'

'Anything in particular, Clement?' Lowe asked.

'Firstly, about the van and if they have any theories about its theft. I'd also like to know how Peggy got the job at WESC.'

From the corner of Clement's eye, he saw Sergeant Preston standing in the doorway. 'Excuse me, sir. I have the financial reports Major Wisdom asked about.'

'Come in Preston,' Lowe said.

Preston placed the file on the desk. 'I think it will surprise you.'

Clement reached for the file.

'Read it aloud, would you, Clement.' Lowe said.

Clement's eye scanned the pages. 'Mrs Pendleton isn't the owner of the guest house.'

'Does it say who is?'

Clement looked up at Lowe. 'The owner is listed as Stephen Bretton esq.'

'We didn't expect that,' Evelyn said. 'And it raises more questions than it answers.'

Clement shuffled the pages. 'It does, indeed. It was purchased three years ago. While Bretton is listed as the legal owner, the bank records show it was paid for by a foreign bank transfer.'

'How much do army doctors earn?' Evelyn said.

'I wouldn't have thought enough to buy big houses in affluent suburbs,' Lowe replied.

'Is it possible Muriel Pendleton is married to Bretton?' Clement added.

'I think, from what we've seen at the guest house that Bretton prefers the company of men.'

'Or both,' Evelyn added.

Lowe lifted the telephone receiver on his desk. 'Preston, two more things. I'd like to know which overseas bank transferred the funds to purchase the guest house and if possible the name of the person who arranged it or who actually paid for it. Then I want you to check the marriage register from Muriel Bretton.' Lowe replaced the receiver. 'It could take a day or two to get this information, Clement.'

With every delay and passing day, Clement knew the traitors could slip from their grasp. 'I think we should go to Goulburn. Preston will have the information for us on our return.'

The telephone on Miss Simpson's desk outside buzzed. She knocked and entered Lowe's office. 'Mr and Mrs Seaton are downstairs.'

'I'll go and meet them,' Lowe said, standing. 'You and Miss Howard can wait downstairs. There's a room beside the mortuary for the next of kin to sit and to identify the deceased. I'll meet you there.'

Clement and Evelyn took the lift to the lower ground floor. The room beside the mortuary was dark and had a window with a cream curtain over it on one side. Several chairs lined the other wall.

'Clement. I'm booked to fly back to Melbourne on Friday,' Evelyn said. 'Inspector Lowe says I can leave.'

Clement nodded. 'Oh! I'm sorry to hear…'

The door opened and a middle-aged couple came in. Clement stood.

'Mr and Mrs Seaton, this is…' Lowe began.

'Reverend Wisdom.' Clement reached forward and extended his hand, which Seaton took. 'And this lady is Miss Howard. I knew your daughter briefly. When you're ready, I'd like to ask you about her. If that would be alright?'

Mr Seaton nodded. Then leaving them, Clement and Evelyn left the viewing room and waited outside. From the corridor, he could hear Peggy's mother weeping. A minute later, Lowe stepped into the corridor.

'Inspector, perhaps you could arrange some tea for Peggy's parents while Clement and I chat to them?' Evelyn suggested.

'Good idea. I'll get Roberts to arrange it.' Lowe turned to leave. 'Probably best you talk to them, Clement. As a vicar, you'll have done this sort of thing before. I'm not good at it. Too gruff, I suppose. But I want to know what they tell you.'

Clement and Evelyn went back into the room and sat beside Peggy's distraught parents. 'Firstly, I wish to extend my sincerest condolences. Peggy was a vivacious and a competent young woman.' He paused. 'I know my next question will sound odd, and for that I apologise, but the security of the nation may be at stake and time is important. Could I ask you about your stolen van?'

'What? The van? Why would you want to know about that?' Wilfred Seaton asked.

'It's in Sydney. Did you know that?' Clement said.

'What's it doing here? It's been very inconvenient. And I can't afford to replace it.

If it's here, I'd like it returned.'

'I'm sure Inspector Low can arrange that, in due course. I'm sorry to have to tell you that it was used in connection with a number of crimes. Were you aware of this?'

Wilfred Seaton shook his head. 'What has this to do with Peggy's death?'

'What can you tell us about Peggy?'

Diasy Seaton wiped her nose. 'She was always drawn to the bright lights. Her father and I worried about her coming to Sydney. But then she got the job with Mrs McKenzie. We were so pleased. Mrs McKenzie is a very superior woman, and we thought she'd be a good influence on Peggy. We thought perhaps she'd meet some nice people. Maybe get married. Have a family.'

'She was always headstrong, but she wasn't a bad girl. The inspector said she died from an overdose of drugs. I can't think where she got them. It just wasn't like her,' Wilfred Seaton said.

Mrs Seaton went on. 'She liked pretty clothes and nice things. I suppose she got in with the wrong crowd. It happens to country girls. Too naïve, I expect. Perhaps we should have been firmer.' Mrs Seaton's voice trailed off. 'She wasn't a bad girl.'

'Do you know how she got the job at WESC?' Clement asked.

'She just applied for it. It was advertised in the paper,' Mr Seaton said.

'Did she know anyone there before she started working for them?' Evelyn asked.

'No, but she helped a lass from our town to get a position there learning Morse Code.'

'Really, do you know who?'

'What was her name, Daisy? Muriel's girl?'

'Muriel? Muriel Pendleton?' Clement said.

'I've never heard that name. Muriel Caide. Billie, that was it!'

CHAPTER THIRTY-FIVE

Monday 1st June 1942

Mrs Seaton pursed her lips. 'Muriel was always very free with her favours! The stage, I suppose. As I recall, there were several children born on that farm.'

Making his apologies, Clement left the viewing room and ran upstairs to Lowe's office.

'Ask Sergeant Preston to check the Births, Deaths and Marriages for Muriel Caide as well as Bretton. Anything he can find. And look at the births as well for more children.'

'Muriel Caide? Lowe said. 'Isn't there a girl at WESC by that name?'

'Yes. Billie. She lives in Greens Road. It's beside Victoria Barracks in Paddington. Henry call WESC and ask Mrs McKenzie if Billie is in today.'

Clement waited while Lowe placed the call.

'Mrs McKenzie? This is Inspector Lowe. Would Miss Billie Caide be in class today?'

Clement waited.

Lowe hung up. 'Not in today. Rang on a public phone to say she wouldn't be returning to the course. I'll get the car brought around. And I'll get Constable Roberts to telephone Victoria Barracks to get Archer and Savage to meet us there.'

'With weapons,' Clement added.

'I'm not thrilled about that, but I suppose in this case, it could be necessary.

Lowe drove quickly but didn't use the siren. Greens Road wasn't far. Clement thought back on Billie. She seemed such a guileless lass, always happy and laughing. Was it possible she knew nothing about her mother's traitorous activities?

The car turned into Greens Road and parked a few houses away from John Caide's house. Clement saw Archer and Savage standing on the opposite side of the street. Clement could see the butt of Mick's rifle, half concealed under a coat. He lifted his gaze and stared at the half-finished brown paper blackout window covering. Its checker-board appearance, once a light was on inside the house, would cast a distinctive pattern visible to anyone flying overhead. He thought of the Japanese planes that had flown over Sydney. Had they been guided in by the checkered window display? Turning, he beckoned for Archer and Savage to join him.

'Tom, go around the back. Be careful Tom, you may meet a few coming out that way soon.'

'Constable Roberts, go with Sergeant Archer. And arrest anyone you see coming out,' Lowe added.

'And Mick?' Archer asked.

'I want him here, with his rifle trained on the entry to the house,' Clement said.

Lowe pushed the front gate wide then walked up the short path to the door. He knocked, but no one answered. 'Clement, can you use your special skills here?'

Retrieving his lock-picks, Clement stood beside Lowe and opened the door, pushing it wide with his foot.

'Anyone here?' Lowe called, stepping inside.

The house was cold. Doors were closed. Clement opened the door to the front sitting room. Dust cloths were spread over the furniture as though the inhabitants had gone and were not expected back for some time. He closed the door and joined Lowe in the front hall. All was quiet. But he felt a presence.

'I'll check the upper floor,' Clement said.

Placing his foot on the bottom tread, he reached for the balustrade. He felt an icy breeze and knew a door or window had been opened. He stood still, listening. Then a shot rang out, the bullet lodging in the wall beside him. Falling to his haunches, Clement reached for his Welrod. 'Billie? It's Clement Wisdom. I don't want to hurt you. I want to talk to you. Are you alright?'

No one responded. Then he heard running footsteps upstairs. Carefully, he took another step. The footsteps upstairs pounded along a corridor, then stopped. Clement climbed another step, but he couldn't see anyone. Quietly, he climbed a fourth, then a fifth. Then he saw her. Joan was standing at the top of the stairs. Her eyes wide with terror. Billie was behind her, a pistol at Joan's head.

'Let me pass, or she dies?' Billie screamed.

'We have John Connor in custody, Billie. For your sake, please put the gun down and let Joan go.'

'You haven't got a clue, have you? And I don't believe you about John.'

'What don't I know about?' Clement said.

'My mother hasn't told you anything, has she? Or you would have been here sooner. So you won't learn anything from me either.'

'Is your uncle here, Billie?'

'I'm not answering any more questions. Leave now, or Joan dies?'

'Why did you kill Win?'

'I didn't want that. It was her fault. I had to. She saw him in the van.'

'Who did she see?'

Billie laughed. 'If she'd just stayed asleep, she'd be alive.'

'You drugged her at *The Australia*?'

'It wasn't me! He didn't put enough into her drink. He wanted her. So he didn't use enough. And she woke up and saw him in the back.'

'Did you kill him, Hank Veretti?'

'We hated him!'

'We?'

'My brother.'

'Nigel?'

Billie laughed again. 'That little creep is only useful for killing flies.'

'Who is your brother, Billie?'

Billie didn't answer.

'Do you mean, Rick?'

Billie's eyes widened. He'd played a hunch, and it worked.

'Who is Rick's father, Billie?'

'Well, I'll tell you this much. He's American, and his name is Veretti, Antonio Veretti and he promised he'd marry my mother. Only he was already married. 'My *real* family,' he called them when my mother told him she was pregnant.'

'Is Rick, *Sorrow*?'

'I've told you enough! I'm not saying anything more.'

'Where is Rick now?'

'Where you'll never find him.'

'Your uncle's farm in Goulburn?' Clement saw the confusion on Billie's face. 'Give up, Billie. You can't escape. And please don't commit any more murders.'

Joans whimpered. 'Listen to him, Billie! If you kill me, they'll hang you.'

'Treason in wartime is a hanging offence, anyway,' Billie said, and lifting her arm pressed the tip of the gun into Joan's throat.

Clement gripped his Welrod.

'Put the gun down!' Billie screamed.

Clement bent to place the Welrod on the stair. A burst of air came from behind him. In his head, Clement heard Tom's words; *Mick doesn't miss*. Joan screamed as Billie fell forward onto the stairs. Joan stood rigid with fright, too terrified to move.

'You're safe now Joan,' he said, reaching for her arm.

Joan stared in front of her, the fear still gripping her frame.

'Take a deep breath, Joan,' Clement said, inching forward.

'Thank God you're here. I thought no one would come. Or that you'd forgotten me. Please take me away from here. I've been imprisoned here for days.'

Clement helped Joan to the street. As he walked her to the car, Henry Lowe rushed up the stairs and knelt beside Billie Caide, searching for a pulse.

Clement returned and stood in the doorway. 'Is she alive?'

'She's dead.' Lowe stood. 'If there's a telephone downstairs, I'll call the mortuary and get someone round to collect the body.'

'Do you still intend to go to Goulburn?'

'First thing tomorrow.'

Clement nodded. He wanted to check upstairs before leaving the house. With Lowe attending to Billie, Clement climbed the stairs. Two suitcases were beside one of the bedroom doors. Walking along the hall, he found a narrow staircase to an attic room above. Climbing the stairs, he found a single room with an attic window that overlooked the front of the house. Under the window was a table and chair. Looking around the space, he saw many footprints on the dusty floor. He believed it was from here that the *Operation Butterfly* message had been transmitted. And, it was within three miles of the city. He stared out to the street below. Beyond, he could see over the high stone wall to the buildings and parade ground of Victoria Barracks. He could also see the door to the briefing room.

CHAPTER THIRTY-SIX

Tuesday 2nd June 1942

Clement stood by the front gate to Victoria Barracks.
Lowe had told him to bring warm clothing. As he waited
for Lowe to arrive, his hand played with the balaclava in
the right pocket of his overcoat. He checked his watch.
A few minutes before eight. It was a dull day, but at least
it wasn't raining. Clement paced the pavement, looking
along the street in both directions. At the newsagency
across the road, people stood reading the daily papers.
Clement had seen the graphic pictures of the wreck of
the *Kuttabul* and the raising of a Japanese submarine
found in Taylor's Bay. It was a salient reminder to all that
the war had come to Australia's doorstep and, with no
thanks to Muirhead-Gould or Captain Bode, a disaster
had been averted.

Lowe drove through the main gate and Clement
climbed in.

'Morning, Clement,' Lowe said.

'Good morning, Henry. Remind me just how far away
Goulburn is?'

'A good four to five hours' drive.'

'Should we stay overnight there? It will be a long drive for you.'

'Perhaps. Have you ever been out of the city?'

Clement thought back on all the places he'd seen in the vast country. Darwin, Exmouth in Western Australia, Perth, even Adelaide and Melbourne, although he'd only seen the airports in Perth and Adelaide. 'No,' he said. He liked Lowe, but all his missions to date were secret and couldn't be discussed outside the Secret Intelligence Bureau.

For some time, Lowe drove through suburban neighbourhoods heading south and west. An hour later, the suburbs gave way to rolling verdant hills where sheep grazed.

'I understand that Miss Veronica Evans has taken Joan in. I hear she's offered Miss Olivant a position at the college,' Lowe said.

'Really. That's very decent of her.'

'I'm also pleased that Mrs McKenzie's school will continue despite recent events.'

'Pleased to hear it, Henry. I see no reason whatever to prevent women from performing whatever task the country needs. And Mrs McKenzie has a talent for teaching Morse Code and Kana Morse. Her school will be a great asset to the war effort in the Pacific especially.'

'How do you know Miss Howard?'

'I met her a little while ago. But what she does and with whom, I'm sorry I cannot say.'

'And you, Clement, will you go back to England?'

'Yes. If that's where they want me.' Clement stared at the passing green fields and grazing sheep. 'Do you know where Caide's farm is?'

'Not really. But the local lads do. They tell me it's on the Taralga Road. A dirt track, apparently, that leads back into the mountains. Quite isolated.'

'What are you expecting to find there?'

'I'm hoping we find John Caide and his nephew Rick. And anyone else caught up in this mess.'

'Morphine is made from poppies, isn't it?'

Lowe glanced sideways at him. 'Yes. There are different types of poppies, but all poppies require bare ground, no weeds, well-drained soils and a cool climate.'

'But didn't you say this Taralga Road leads into the hills?'

'There is plenty of room for cultivated cropping. It's winter now, of course. They may have sown already, but there won't be a crop to harvest till November. They'd need a remote place to grow it. Hard to disguise all those bobbing poppy heads in the spring sunshine.'

Lowe drove over the crest of a hill, then commenced the steep descent into the township of Goulburn. To his right, Clement could see a prison with its high walls and festooned barbed wire fences. Driving into the town centre, they crossed a river, then turned left into the main street. Lowe drove straight to the police station and parking outside, switched off the engine.

'Thank you, Henry. A long drive. But very enjoyable.'

Clement opened the door and stretched his legs then followed Lowe into the police station. Lowe presented his warrant card to the constable on duty.

'Good afternoon, Sir. There is a message for you from Sergeant Preston,' the constable said. He handed Lowe a folded note.

Lowe unfolded the note and read aloud. 'It's from Preston. It says the price paid for the property was thirty thousand pounds! In cash!'

'Would an army doctor make that sort of money?'

'Unlikely. Unless he had another illegal income.'

Clement gazed out the door of the police station to the street beyond. Goulburn was not a sophisticated place. Lowe, so Clement believed, presumed Bretton had acquired the funds for dealing in opium, but Clement already knew from his time in Cambridge in '41 that enemy spies were given huge amounts of money to recruit foreign nationals and gather valuable information on a regular basis. But it always came at a cost. If the Japanese government had paid for the house, something would be required in return. And Clement guessed that something was information sourced from the *Chicago*.

'Does he mention anything about other births or a marriage between Muriel and Stephen Bretton?' Clement asked.

'No record of any births for Muriel Pendleton, not even Nigel. It is possible that she was married outside Australia. And no record of a marriage in the names of Pendleton, Bretton or Caide.' Lowe sighed. 'No further advanced there then.' Lowe turned to the young constable. 'Do you have a police wagon, Constable?'

'We have a van, sir.'

Lowe and Clement exchanged looks. 'Capable of carrying prisoners?'

'Yes, Sir.'

'Does it have any police markings on it?'

'A light at the top, Sir.'

'Take it off or paint it black, constable. And hurry about it.'

'Would you like me to come with you, Sir?'

'Yes. And bring several sets of hand cuffs with you. You drive the wagon and follow me. But stay well back. And no sirens, Constable, I don't want the police wagon seen. Once we get to the farm, stay with the vehicle until I call for you. Understand?'

'Sir.'

'Do you have a map of the area?' Lowe asked.

'Yes, Sir.' The constable took a large map from a drawer in the office and unrolled it on the front counter. Clement and Lowe stared at the discoloured map. Only a few tracks crisscrossed the country. The Taralga Road weaved its way north-west and into steep ravines and mountainous country. 'Do you know Caide's Farm, Constable?'

'I know where it is, Sir. It's here,' the constable pointed to an area adjacent to a creek. 'It's pretty remote.'

'Yes, I imagine it is. How long to get there?' Lowe asked.

'It's a dirt road, so about forty minutes, I suppose.'

Lowe folded the map and handed it to Clement. 'Remember, Constable, don't be seen. Do you have a whistle I can use to summon you when I need you?'

'You can use mine, Sir.'

Lowe put the whistle in his coat pocket, and they left the station. Clement and Lowe drove out of the police yard, the police wagon about thirty feet behind them. Leaving Goulburn, they drove onto the Taralga Road. It was unsealed and had more potholes than any road Clement had ever experienced. Instantly, he was reminded of the first time he met Tom Archer. Archer had collected him from Darwin airport during the wet season in an army lorry with uneven tyres, the result of which was a bone-rattling trip in muddy terrain.

Descending a steep hill, Clement could see in the distance, the corrugated iron roof of a house. A thin trail of smoke was issuing from the only chimney. Lowe pulled off the road and parked it behind some high bushes. Taking some binoculars from the glove box, Clement alighted and walked to where he could see the farmhouse clearly. He focused the binoculars on the house. Parked to one side was a dark green van. Clement recognised it immediately.

Lowe joined him by the fence. 'Well, we know they're here. Now it's just a case of who and how many.'

Clement passed the binoculars to Lowe.

'I don't see a dog,' Lowe whispered. 'But we need to get closer. Hopefully, they aren't looking out the window as we approach.'

They drove more slowly now, descending the hill and crossing an old wooden bridge over a shallow creek. 'There's the farm gate,' Lowe said. He pulled the car up on the side of the road. Clement wound down the window and using the binoculars, checked again for any dogs.

'There could be one at the rear,' Lowe said.

'If they had one, surely by now it would have heard us and barked,' Clement said.

'Perhaps. Or it could be inside. Just be aware that if they have a cattle dog, they usually bite.'

'I'll remember that. What do they look like?'

'Small, stocky and brindle or light brown in colour.'

'Right.' Clement panned the binoculars around the farm. 'I don't see a soul, animal or human. I should go in first, Henry. I'll edge around the northern side of the house and see what's behind it. Can you imitate any bird calls?'

'Ever heard a kookaburra's call?'

'I have. Quite raucous.'

'That's the one. If I see any movement at the front, I'll do my best impression.'

Clement left Lowe by the fence and walked along the dusty road towards the wire gate into the property. He's preferred method of approach would be to knock at the door and feign being a stranger asking direction but as he'd met both Caide and Rick, although at the time purporting to be Hank Veretti, it wasn't an option available to him. Once through the gate, he climbed over the wire fence into a field to the northern side of the homestead.

The house was a single storey dwelling made of wood with a corrugated iron roof. It had a front veranda with roughly hewn poles. To one side was a wide, level field. No one was about. Clement found the silence eerie.

Using a line of trees, he crept near to an empty chicken coup, then squatted in some long grass and using the binoculars, checked for activity. Still, he saw none. Slowly he panned the binoculars around the yard.

Given the hour, it was possible both men were in the house eating a meal. And, so Clement reminded himself, Mick had shot one of them in the leg. While it may prevent the man from running, it didn't stop him using a gun.

Hunching low, Clement dashed across the yard to the house. Running along the side, he paused at the back corner. Washing was on a line out the back. But none were clothes. Hessian sacks swung on the wind. Further away was an outbuilding of some size. He could hear machinery. Sprinting to the corner of the shed, he peered through a side window. Rick was standing by a grinding wheel. But there was no sign of John Caide. Clement ran back to the passageway at the side of the house. Staying low, he returned to the front corner then hoping the fence into the next field, returned to the road.

'I think Caide must be inside alone. Rick is out the back in a shed working a machine. He shouldn't hear us. But we need to hurry. I propose I kick down the door and rush in. Frontal attack always causes confusion.'

'Right. I'm guessing you've done this before so let's go.'

Hunching, they ran across the field to the house then crept onto the front veranda. Clement withdrew his Welrod and kicked in the flimsy front door. Caide was sitting in a chair with his leg on a stool. The noise of the timbers shattering woke him. Lowe rushed in, his pistol tight in his grip and pointing it at Caide. 'Not a sound!'

Caide's eyes went wide.

'You are under arrest, John Caide.'

'Now for Rick,' Clement said.

Clement walked through the house to the kitchen at the rear. From the window, he could see Rick walking towards the house. From his unhurried gait, Clement knew he didn't know they were there. Waiting behind the kitchen door with his Welrod raised, he waited for Rick to enter.

CHAPTER THIRTY-SEVEN

Tuesday 2nd June 1942

'*Sorrow*, I'm guessing,' Clement said, staring into a killer's eyes.

Rick spun around. Gone was the swagger and the chewing gum, but the thick dark hair and the air of arrogance were still there.

'Your uncle is now in custody. As is your mother and younger brother. Your sister is dead.'

'I don't believe you.'

'Unless you have someone else here to shoot me and the police outside, you are outnumbered. You may as well give up now.'

'You think you're smart, don't you, Clement Wisdom.'

Clement waited. 'You'll have plenty of time to reflect on that in prison. And I didn't mention that we also have John Connor. Now for the record, Rick, I think Connor is the real spy in all this. He is a true professional, isn't he?'

'You tell me. You seem to have it all worked out.'

'Alright, I'll play your game. How's this. Connor met Bretton in Japan twenty years ago. Bretton was the perfect recruit informant for a spy: itinerant, foreign and poor. Bretton knew Muriel had had a relationship with a wealthy American because he looked after her and the child. When war broke out, Bretton told Connor about Muriel's baby and who the father was. Connor would know just which strings to pull to get Muriel involved. Manipulate resentment and you'll get revenge. What is the going rate for treachery? A house in a fashionable suburb?'

Clement saw the eyes flare. 'Why would I tell you anything?'

'Doesn't matter now. We already know the legal owner of the guest house is Stephen Bretton. And we know, Clement bluffed, it was the Japanese Government who paid for the house. Although, I doubt it cost thirty thousand. Bretton's lived a comfortable life on the proceeds of espionage. And possibly also the drug trade.'

Clement heard Lowe blow the police whistle. Rick shot a glance at the door. But Clement didn't move. Then he heard the police wagon drive in. 'Shall we?' Clement indicated the door. Outside, Clement saw Lowe and the young constable put Caide into the police wagon.

Lowe walked back into the house and stared at Rick. 'I suppose you know espionage in wartime is a hanging offence.'

'Hang! All I did was impersonate a radioman.'

'And you passed classified information to the enemy,' Clement said.

'Connor did that.'

'Why did you put Win Hughes's body in the park?'

'A warning.'

'To Peggy?'

'Yes, to Peggy. Little brat was getting greedy.'

'Does the Japanese pistol belong to you?'

'Bretton. He wanted it out of the house.'

'With one bullet missing?'

A grin spread across Rick's face. 'We thought that would confuse you. And, evidently, it did.'

'Take him away, Henry.'

'You are under arrest,' Lowe said. The young constable pulled Rick's arms behind his back and cuffed his wrists.

'You may be interested to know that the information Connor gave to the Japanese was destroyed along with the submarine,' Clement said.

'I was never interested in that. The only thing I wanted was Hank Veretti dead.'

'Why such hatred?'

'Look around you. A run-down farm, miles from nowhere, is my inheritance. My half-brother would have got a fortune. What better way to upset daddy than to kill his *real* son.'

'You won't inherit it now! You killed four people!' Clement said aghast.

'Death and war. Can't have one without the other.'

'How did you know Hank Veretti was on the *Chicago*?' Clement asked Connor.

Rick turned to face Clement. 'Connor told me. Hank was a radioman. They transmit all sorts of stuff, including personal messages to dear old mum and dad. It's not only the Allies who have code breakers, you know, Major Wisdom.'

'That's enough from you,' Lowe said and grasping Connor's cuffed hands, pushed him outside where the police wagon stood waiting.

Lowe drove into the main gate of Victoria Barracks just after midnight.

'Thank you, Henry. Quite a day.'

'Do you have all your questions answered, Clement?'

'I think so. I'll hold a debriefing meeting tomorrow at ten here, if you'd like to come.'

'Perhaps I will. I'll bring McCowage's report on Miss Caide. Perhaps Miss Howard would like to join.'

'Why not. Will you arrange it?'

'On second thought, Clement, why not meet at the police station instead? I'll get Miss Simpson to officially record the meeting for the files. Bring Archer and Savage. You may think of some questions for the Muriel Pendleton or Bretton.'

'Good idea. Thank you, Henry. See you then.' Clement closed the car door and wandered towards the officers' quarters. He felt so tired, he was beyond sleep. He stared up at the sky. He could see stars. They seemed so remote. Sheading their pale light on those below and sitting like a panel of judges on a troubled Earth. He rubbed his day-old beard. Or perhaps it was several day's growth. He just couldn't remember. Wandering out onto the veranda, he stared at the night sky reflecting on how close the Japanese had come to sinking every ship in Sydney. He thought on young Jim Lockhart and others who'd died on the *Kuttabul* and prayed for the survivors. He hadn't seen Joe, but Clement hoped Joe was out celebrating somewhere. Sometime later, he wandered to his room. Throwing off his coat, he fell onto the bed.

Clement tossed and turned. Images of Win Hughes flashed through his mind all night; juxtaposed with Billie and Joan. He felt caught, as though someone was holding him down. He woke. Startled. He took several deep breaths and lay staring at the ceiling. Too many thoughts filled his mind. They'd caught Rick and Bretton. And the real spy, John Connor. So why was he still troubled?

Clement wondered how Muriel had learned about Hank Veretti being at WESC. He breathed out a long sigh as he realised. Peggy had passed on the names of the new attendees. All Connor had to do was befriend Veretti then kill him before he joined WESC and send Rick instead. Rick, who looked similar enough to his half-brother had most likely stolen the classified documents by going onboard the *Chicago* and pretending to be Veretti. He visualised the young man standing on the footpath outside WESC that first day, chewing his gum. Win had innocently gone with him. And Billie and Joan had left them. Billie though, instead of going home, and met them at *The Australia* dressed in a pink dress with pink satin shoes. And she'd drugged Win just as Muriel had drugged Peggy.

Clement reached for his watch. It was still only seven o'clock, although he could hear men outside on the parade ground. He rose and stared through the window to the ground below. The sergeant was accounting for all soldiers and issuing orders for the day. Clement needed to wash and shave. And some clean clothes would be welcome. He had no reason to hurry. Standing under the warm water, it cascaded over his head. But he felt uneasy. 'What is it?' he said aloud to the wall.

CHAPTER THIRTY-EIGHT

Wednesday 3rd June.

At nine o'clock, Clement went to the briefing room. He's sent instructions for Archer and Savage to meet him there at a quarter past nine. Folding the map of Sydney Harbour, he placed it in his pocket. Perhaps someone in authority would one day call on it as documented proof of where all the shipping had been on the night of Sunday 31st of May 1942.

A minute later, Archer and Savage walked in.

'We don't need weapons today. Please leave the Welrods with the armourer.'

'And the Fairbairn Sykes knives?' Tom asked.

'Keep those with you for now.'

Archer grinned. 'Does that mean what I hope it does?'

'I have put in a request to Commander Long, but that decision is for others loftier than me.'

Walking out to Oxford Street, they saw the approaching city tram. Stepping onboard, Clement recognised the ticket collector. It was the same young woman he'd met days earlier.

'Morning, dearie. Do you want a hand with your coat again?'

'What did you say?' Clement asked, the woman's words echoing in his head.

'I thought you might like a hand to take your coat off again. Like the other day?'

'Sorry, we have to get off.' Clement stood then running to the door, jumped from the moving tram. Archer and Savage followed him a few seconds later.

'You'll get yourselves killed that way, dearies,' she called after them.

'What is it, Clem?' Archer shouted as they ran along the footpath.

Clement didn't answer. Standing at the side of the road, he hailed the first taxi he saw. The woman's words were ringing alarm bells in his head. 'Central Police Station, please. And hurry!' he said, opening the rear door for Archer and Savage to get in beside him. He knew Tom and Mick were watching him, but in true manner, Archer and Savage remained silent, waiting.

The cab slowed near the Court House. The traffic and people congested the street. 'We'll walk from here, thanks,' Clement said, handing over the fare. Getting out, they ran into the police station and climbed the stairs two at a time. 'Wait here,' he said to Archer and Savage. Clement turned to Lowe's secretary his voice breathless, 'Is he in?'

'Yes, Major.'

Rushing in, he saw Lowe sitting at his desk and mountain of paperwork in front of him.

'Henry. Where is Joan Olivant?'

'She's with Veronica Evans. Didn't want to go back to that guest house.'

'Get your car. We need to get to Veronica's place. Now! And bring the pink shoes. I'll tell you on the way.'

Lowe grabbed his car keys. Together, they ran to the parking area behind the police station. Archer and Savage following.

With Preston driving and the siren blaring, they raced west over Pyrmont Bridge towards Glebe. 'What are you suspicious about, Clement,' Lowe asked.

'When I spoke to both Billie and Joan the night Win died, I asked each of them their thoughts about Veretti, or rather Rick as we now know him. Billie called him a gentleman. But we also now know she was lying. Joan's assessment was the complete reverse. But she said something odd. Remember, Joan walked with Win and Rick as far as Pitt Street then, according to her, left them. I was on the footpath after class and saw Win talking with Rick and Billie. Joan then joined them. She was carrying a satchel. She told me at the guest house that Rick helped Win with her coat. But Win was already wearing her coat when Joan joined them. And wouldn't have taken it off in Pitt Street, which is like a wind tunnel. How did Joan know Rick helped her with her coat, if she wasn't there?'

'It's slim evidence, Clement. Won't get a conviction on that alone.' A minute later, they drove up Bridge Road. 'Cut the siren, Sergeant,' Lowe called. 'And we'll park the car in Marlborough Street. Take this, Preston, and go around the back.' Lowe handed a pistol to his sergeant. 'I'm assuming you all have your Welrods on you?'

'No. Only me,' Clement said.

'Right. So Major Wisdom and I will knock on the front door. If she's guilty, my guess is she'll do a runner for the back door.'

'Mick and I will go with Sergeant Preston. She won't get away. And maybe Mick should have the pistol. No offence Preston, but you may have to use it without hesitation,' Tom said.

Clement cut in. 'She's cunning, Henry. She had us all fooled into believing she'd been kidnapped. I think it may be better if Mick has the pistol, just in case he has to use it.'

Lowe nodded.

Preston passed the pistol to Mick. 'Thanks, not sure I could kill a woman who is staring at me.'

Waiting only a few minutes for Preston, Archer and Savage to get into position, Lowe knocked.

A minute later, Joan opened the door.

CHAPTER THIRTY-NINE

Wednesday 3rd June.

'Would Veronica be in, Joan?'

'No. She's at work.'

Upstairs, Clement heard the thumping. He looked into Joan's eyes and saw the cunning. Moving his hand slowly, he withdrew his Welrod. 'Henry, get the shoes would you?'

'Mr Wisdom? What are you doing?' Joan protested.

'You be right with her on your own?' Lowe asked.

'Perfectly!' Clement said.

Lowe was gone only minutes. He entered the house and pointed to a chair. 'Sit down, Miss Olivant.'

'I don't know what you're talking about,' Joan protested.

But Clement could see her head twisting back and forth. From where she sat, he knew she could see both the front and rear doors. Clement moved where he too could see the back of the house. Archer was standing in the doorway at the rear.

'There is no escape this time, Joan,' Clement said. He saw her shoulders droop. Lowe walked in carrying the pink satin shoes then dropped them onto the floor beside Joan.

'Put them on!' Lowe barked.

'Why should I?'

'No need,' Clement said, his gaze fixed on Joan. 'We both know they'll fit.' In that moment, he felt nothing but contempt. 'Why?'

Joan looked up at him. 'You have no idea how much money they pay.'

'Thirty thousand pounds is a lot of money. But it's always been about something else, hasn't it. Revenge. That's what it's about.'

The thumping continued. 'Is that Veronica upstairs?'

'I'll go, Clement,' Lowe said, climbing the stairs to the upper floor.

Less than five minutes later, Lowe returned with Veronica.

'Are you alright, Veronica?' Clement asked.

'Yes. A bit bruised. Could have knocked me down with a feather. I never suspected Joan. I found this in her suitcase,' Veronica said and handed a photograph to Clement. It showed Joan in a bridal gown. Connor was beside her.

He stared at Joan, then handed the photograph to Lowe.

'For Muriel and Rick, it was about revenge first and money second. But for you and Connor, it was always and only ever about money,' Lowe said.

Clement stared at Joan. 'Not just money, Henry. For Joan, it was about power. That's why she did it.'

'You have no idea how addictive spying is. I'd have done it for nothing. I felt alive and important.'

'And the people you killed or were killed because of you?'

'They just got in the way, really. Win should have just gone along with it. Many women have. If it means a better life. She may even have been recruited. Peggy, though, was always a risk. But we needed her to supply the names. Once we knew about Veretti's attendance, she was of no use to us.'

'And Billie? How did you get her to hold you at gunpoint?'

'She idolised Rick. If Rick told her to jump off North Head, she'd have done it. It was how we worked out our escape. If Muriel told you about Billie, which we suspected she would, Billie would pretend to kill me. That way, you'd let her go, then I could escape to meet up with John. And we'd keep the network going. And it almost worked.'

'Actually, it was you who told me, Joan.'

'What?'

Clement repeated what she'd said about Win's coat. 'So in the end, you and Connor are responsible for all the deaths.'

'Sacrifice. That's not murder. Besides, everyone dies, sooner or later.'

Clement walked with Lowe from the cells to his office. 'Thank you, Clement for your part in all this. We make quite a team. When the war is over, why not come back to Sydney. There's a job for you here, if you want it.'

'That's very kind of you, Henry. I'll think about it. Right now, however, we have a war to win. And I may not survive to take up your offer.'

'I think you will. You're a smart man. And that Miss Howard is a very smart woman!' Lowe said. Laughing, he shook hands with Clement and returned to his office.

Clement took the stairs to the ground floor. He smiled and nodded to Sergeant Preston. 'I wish you well, Sergeant. One day, I'm sure you will be the Chief of Police.'

'That would require me to be married to the job, Sir.'

Clement smiled. 'Perhaps that is your calling, Will.'

Clement sat in the airport lounge Evelyn beside him. 'I think I'm getting too old for all this, Evelyn.'

'Nonsense. You're just tired. I seem to recall telling you about the plot of Madame Butterfly. Life really is sometimes stranger than fiction.' She smiled at him. 'I have to return Clement. But perhaps when you get home, would you like to come for tea? I'd like you to meet my father. He's a lot like you. Quiet, decent. And nobody's fool. But he doesn't know what I do.'

'I'd like that.'

Joe walked into the terminal and, seeing them walked towards them, his suitcase in his grip.

'Joe!' Clement called.

'Clement? I wondered what happened to you. I finished at the school. But I've been recalled to Melbourne. I'm thinking of asking for a transfer to Commander Nave's section. I don't think Rudy Fabain was too happy with how I handled things. But Bode's not the most popular captain the US Navy right now. He'll be lucky to get away with his handling of the *Chicago* and its part in the raid on Sydney Harbour. Apparently his second had it worked out, but Bode countermanded the orders.'

'I heard something about that. Thank you, Joe for your part in all this.'

'I'm not too sure I did much or what it was all about.'

'I can fill you in, Joe,' Evelyn said. 'It's a long enough flight back to Melbourne.'

'You on that flight, too?'

'I am,' Evelyn said.

'Good to work with you again, Sir.' Joe glanced at Clement and Evelyn. 'I'll get my pack checked in.'

Clement stood and shook Joe's hand in farewell. 'God be with you, Joe.'

'Hope to see you again, Clem.' Smiling, Joe left them.

They watched Joe join the queue at the airline counter.

'Why do you think Veronica wasn't killed?' Evelyn asked.

'Insurance would be my guess. But I don't imagine she'd continue to live, if her usefulness no longer existed.'

342

Their conversation paused for a few minutes. Outside, Clement could see the aircraft preparing to embark the passengers.

'Did you know I've asked Long if Archer and Savage can be assigned to me? I don't know if it can be arranged or if Long or others in England will allow it. But both of them have saved my life and if I have any influence, I owe it to them to make it happen, if that's still what they want.'

'You're a decent sort, Clement Wisdom.' She stood as a voice over the loudspeakers announced the final boarding call for the Melbourne flight. 'I may tell you about my training with,' she leaned forward and whispered into his ear, 'SOE. But then, of course, I'd either have to kill you or you'd have to marry me.' Evelyn winked, and turning suddenly on her heel, hurried towards the departure gate. Clement stared after her. He watched her walk across the tarmac and board the waiting aeroplane. A broad grin spread across his face.

Acknowledgements

My thanks as always to my beloved husband Peter who has had a difficult year and to my dear extended family. Thanks too to Deborrah Myashita for her kind assistance with the Japanese language.

Thanks also to the folk at The Australian War Memorial Museum, and to the wonderful Peter Grose whose book, *A Very Rude Awakening* provided so much food for thought.

My thanks as always to Ian Hooper, my friend and publisher.

Author's Note

Like all my books in the Clement Wisdom series, they are, to some extent, based on actual historical events. Where possible, I like to include real historical figures. In *Code Name Sorrow*, I have included the following real people.

Commander Rupert Long –

Head of Naval Intelligence in Australia and Head of the Combined Operational Intelligence Centre.

Long was a fascinating Australian character. He had the vision to see the need for an overall Intelligence Bureau and strived for its creation well before war broke out. He was an outstanding and charismatic leader and was indeed Head of Naval Intelligence in Australia and the Combined Operational Intelligence Bureau. He was instrumental along with another, Commander Eric Feldt, in the creation and success of the Coastwatcher's networks throughout the South Pacific. These were a genuine success and contributed greatly to Allied Intelligence gathering in the Pacific.

Commander Eric Nave –

Code Breaker and Head of the Special Intelligence Bureau Melbourne.

Nave was an extraordinary man of immense intellect and ability with code breaking. He was born in Australia, joined the Royal Australian Navy, but was then transferred permanently to the (British) Royal Navy. Before the war, he spent time in Japan learning the language and was employed by the British in China then Singapore. He developed a tropical illness that saw him transferred back to Australia. Bletchley Park was keen to have him in Britain but with the help of an Australian Admiral, Commander Long was able to keep Nave in Australia. Nave decoded the Winds Message on 19 November 1941.

Mrs Violet McKenzie –

Founder and Principal of the Women's Emergency Signalling Corps.

Mrs Mac, as she was known, was the first female Electrical Engineer in Australia and was founder of the Women's Emergency Signalling Corps. She saw many of her female graduates taken into the all-male Royal Australian Navy thereby instigating the establishment of the Women's Royal Australian Navy. Thereafter, approximately 12,000 servicemen were taught Morse code and visual signalling at her school in Clarence Street, Sydney.

Lieutenant Rudy Fabian –

Head of US Signals Intelligence and Fleet Radio Unit Melbourne (FRUMEL) - formerly of CAST Corregidor, Philippines.

Fabian was a controversial character who rarely shared information and was suspicious of anyone outside the US Navy. His fractious relationship with Commander Eric Nave was well known.

And I have mentioned in the book the following real-life people:

Rear-Admiral Muirhead-Gould of the Royal Navy in charge of Sydney Harbour.

Rear-Admiral Leary, US Commander of Allied Naval Forces in the South-West Pacific

Captain Howard Bode, Captain of the USS Chicago

Commander Jank Newman, Director of Signals Communications, Melbourne.

John Tiltman, Code Breaker, Bletchley Park.

Also By V M Knox
The Clement Wisdom Series

In Spite of All Terror

In Spite of All Terror is the first in a series of WWII crime / espionage thrillers. Set in September 1940, when Britain stood alone against an imminent Nazi invasion, Reverend Clement Wisdom and other men from the restricted occupations, join the covert Auxiliary Units. Based in East Sussex, these ordinary men by day must become saboteurs and assassins by night. Following the murders of several of Clement's team, he becomes embroiled in the murky world of espionage where things are never what they seem.

If Necessary Alone

If Necessary Alone is the second thriller in this World War II series. Clement Wisdom, now a Major in Special Duties Branch, Secret Intelligence Service, is sent to remote Caithness to investigate illicit encrypted radio transmissions. As soon as he arrives here, an out-station operator is found brutally murdered and Clement becomes entangled in a web of death and silence. Alone, and in the bitter Scottish winter, Clement must stay one step ahead of a killer if he is to remain alive.

The Clement Wisdom Series

Where Death and Danger Go

Where Death and Danger Go is set in the dark days of 1941. Britain fights on alone. Invasion and fear hang in the air. On a winter's night, a German spy parachutes into Cambridgeshire as another man is murdered nearby. Is he another enemy spy or has he been sent to his death? Either way, a killer lurks. Major Clement Wisdom of the SIS is sent to investigate and discovers a web of conspiracy where kidnap, murder and revenge threaten his life and the safety of the nation.

West Wind Clear

By late 1941, the Pacific is a very different place and Japan threatens the security of the region. As Clement is preparing to return to Britain from Australia, he is seconded to lead a small guerrilla force to Singapore, where he is to rescue an important man who is carrying a vital secret. After the apparent suicide of one of his team, Clement becomes suspicious that an enemy spy is among them; one who will kill to safeguard his identity.

The Neither Despise Nor Fear Series

Neither Despise Nor Fear

A Cold War Espionage Thriller

1965 and Alistair Quinn is sixteen. Making a sudden and life-changing decision, he runs away from his prestigious North London school and heads for the bright lights of Soho.

In a brothel there, he meets a prominent politician and a Soviet KGB officer; one MI6 and the CIA hope to turn double agent. Recruited into MI5, he becomes embroiled in a high stakes mission of deception, treachery and death where no one is who they seem. But as one enemy is uncovered, another remains hidden...

Milton Keynes UK
Ingram Content Group UK Ltd.
UKHW010120011223
433552UK00004B/192